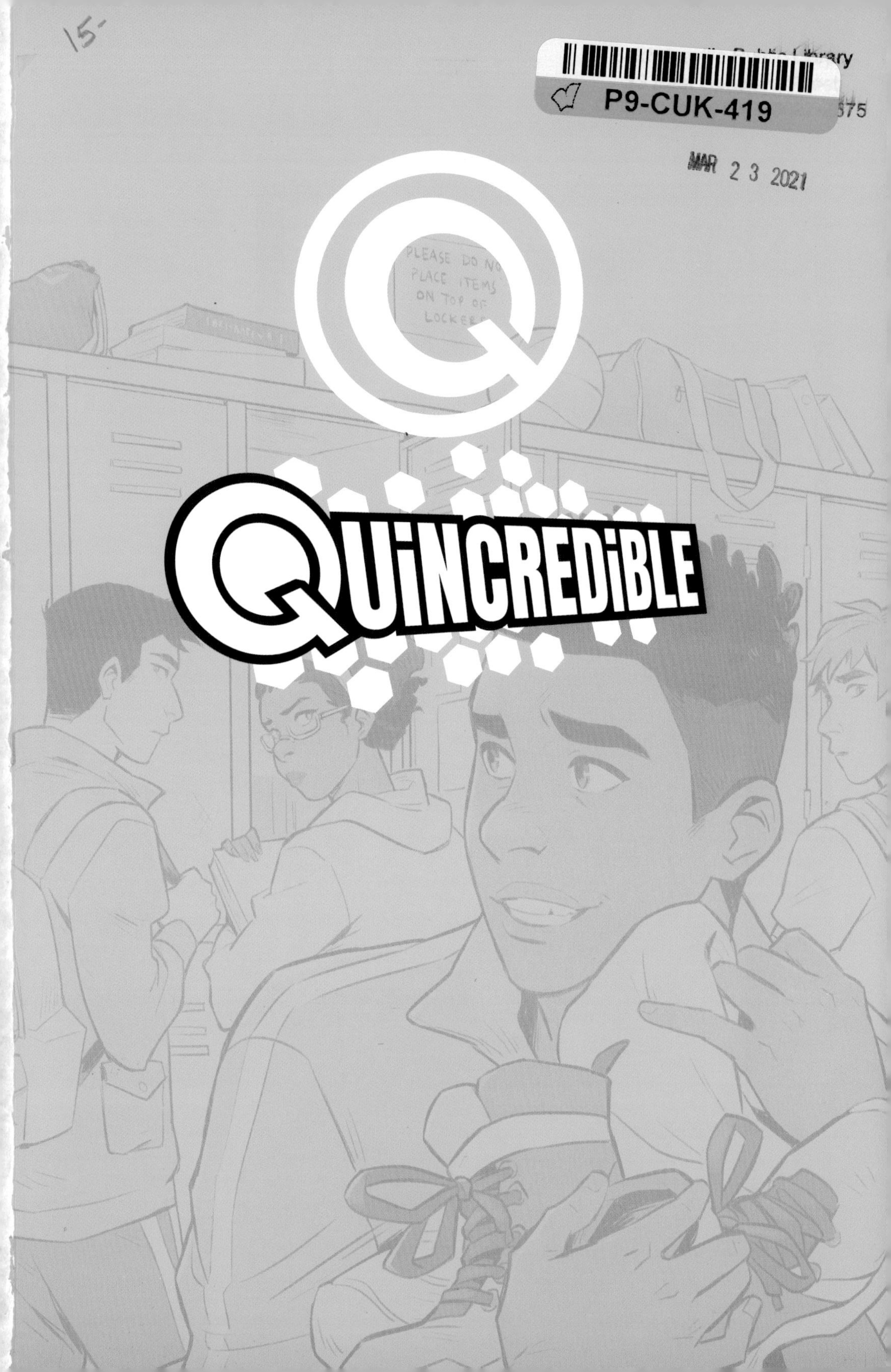
QUINCREDIBLE
PLEASE DO NOT PLACE ITEMS ON TOP OF LOCKERS

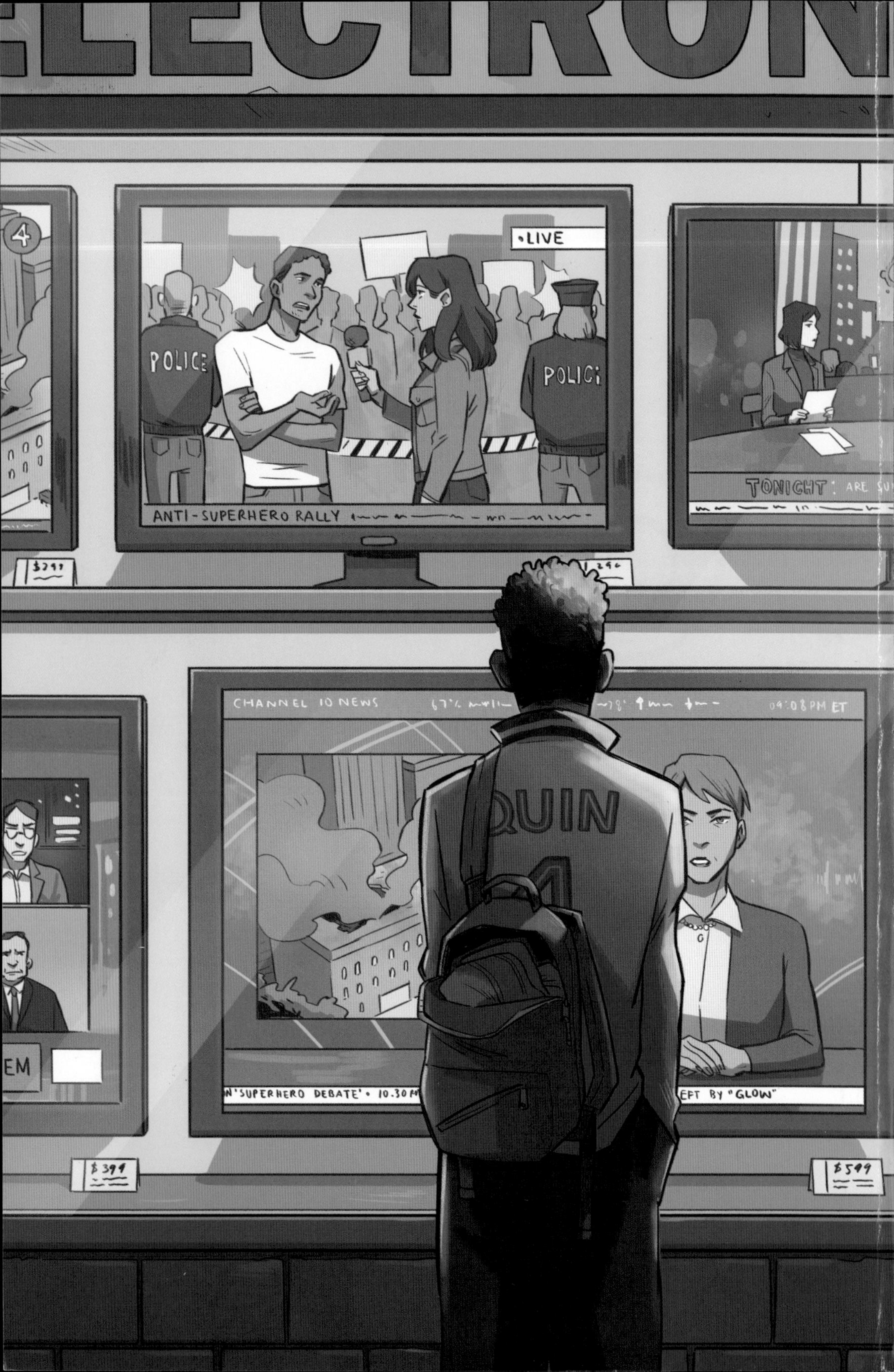
ELECTRON
LIVE
POLICE
POLICE
ANTI-SUPERHERO RALLY
TONIGHT: ARE SU
CHANNEL 10 NEWS
04:08 PM ET
QUIN
'SUPERHERO DEBATE' • 10:30 PM
EFT BY "GLOW"
EM
$399
$599

QUINCREDIBLE

QUEST TO BE THE BEST!

created by **ISSAC REED**
written by **RODNEY BARNES**
illustrated by **SELINA ESPIRITU**
colored by **KELLY FITZPATRICK**
lettered by **AW'S TOM NAPOLITANO**
cover by **SELINA ESPIRITU**

JASMINE AMIRI AND STEENZ · editors
ZOE MAFFITT AND KAT VENDETTI · assistant editors

LION™ FORGE

ISBN 978-1-62010-878-9

Library of Congress Control Number: 2020938075

QUINCREDIBLE Vol. 1, released February, 2021. Published by Oni-Lion Forge Publishing Group, LLC, 1319 SE Martin Luther King Jr. Blvd., Suite 240, Portland, OR 97214. Portions of this book were previously published in Quincredible™ Vol. 1, Issues 1-5 © 2018 and 2019 Illustrated Syndicate, LLC. QUINCREDIBLE™, CATALYST PRIME™, and their associated distinctive designs, as well as all characters featured in this book and the distinctive names and likenesses thereof, and all related indicia, are trademarks of Illustrated Syndicate, LLC. All Rights Reserved. Oni Press logo and icon artwork created by Keith A. Wood. The events, institutions, and characters presented in this book are fictional. No similarity between any of the names, characters, persons, or institutions in this issue with those of any living or dead person or institution is intended, and any such similarity which may exist is purely coincidental. No portion of this publication may be reproduced, by any means, without the express written permission of the copyright holders. Printed in China.

CHAPTER ONE

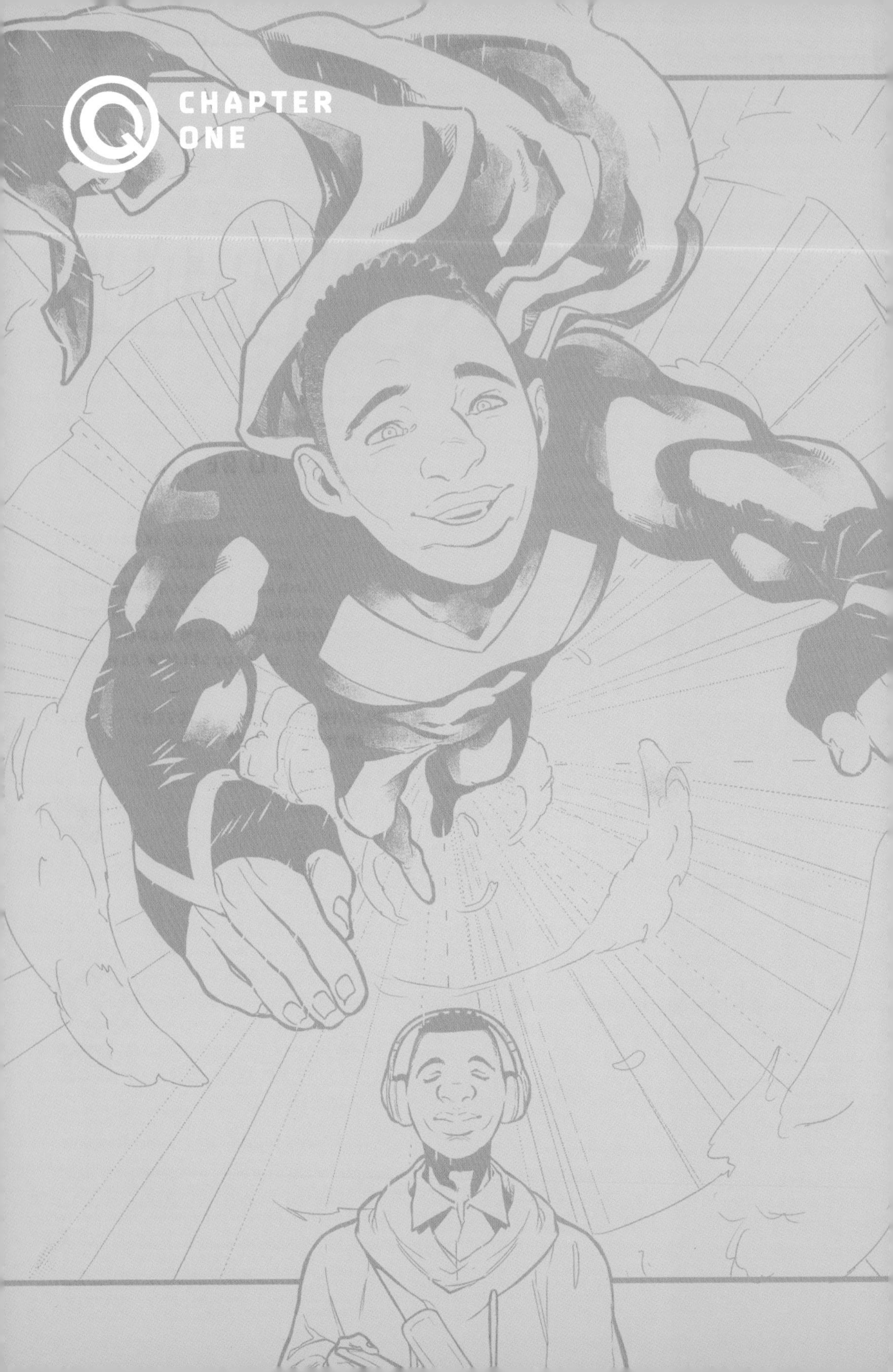

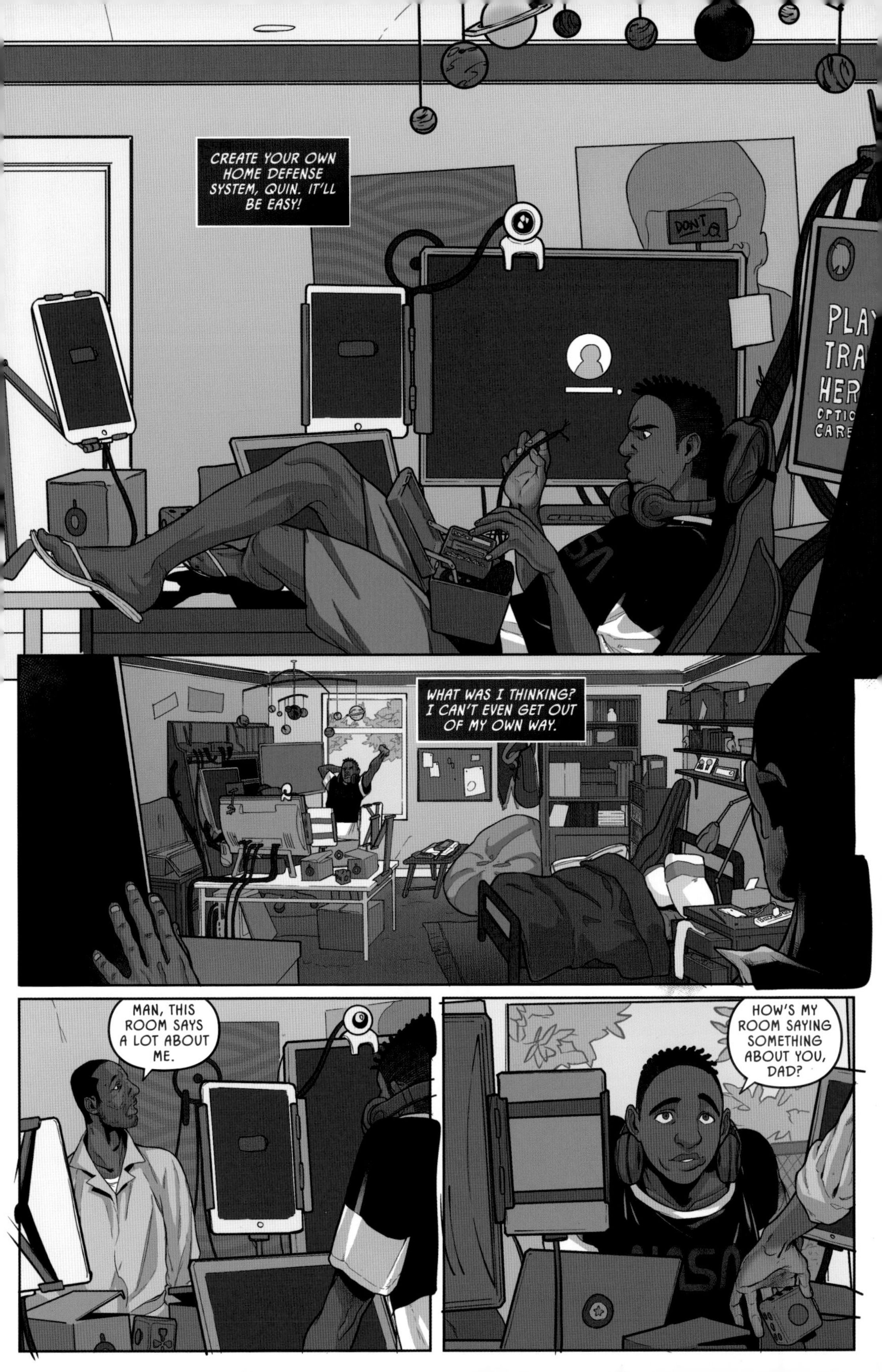
CREATE YOUR OWN HOME DEFENSE SYSTEM, QUIN. IT'LL BE EASY!
WHAT WAS I THINKING? I CAN'T EVEN GET OUT OF MY OWN WAY.
MAN, THIS ROOM SAYS A LOT ABOUT ME.
HOW'S MY ROOM SAYING SOMETHING ABOUT YOU, DAD?

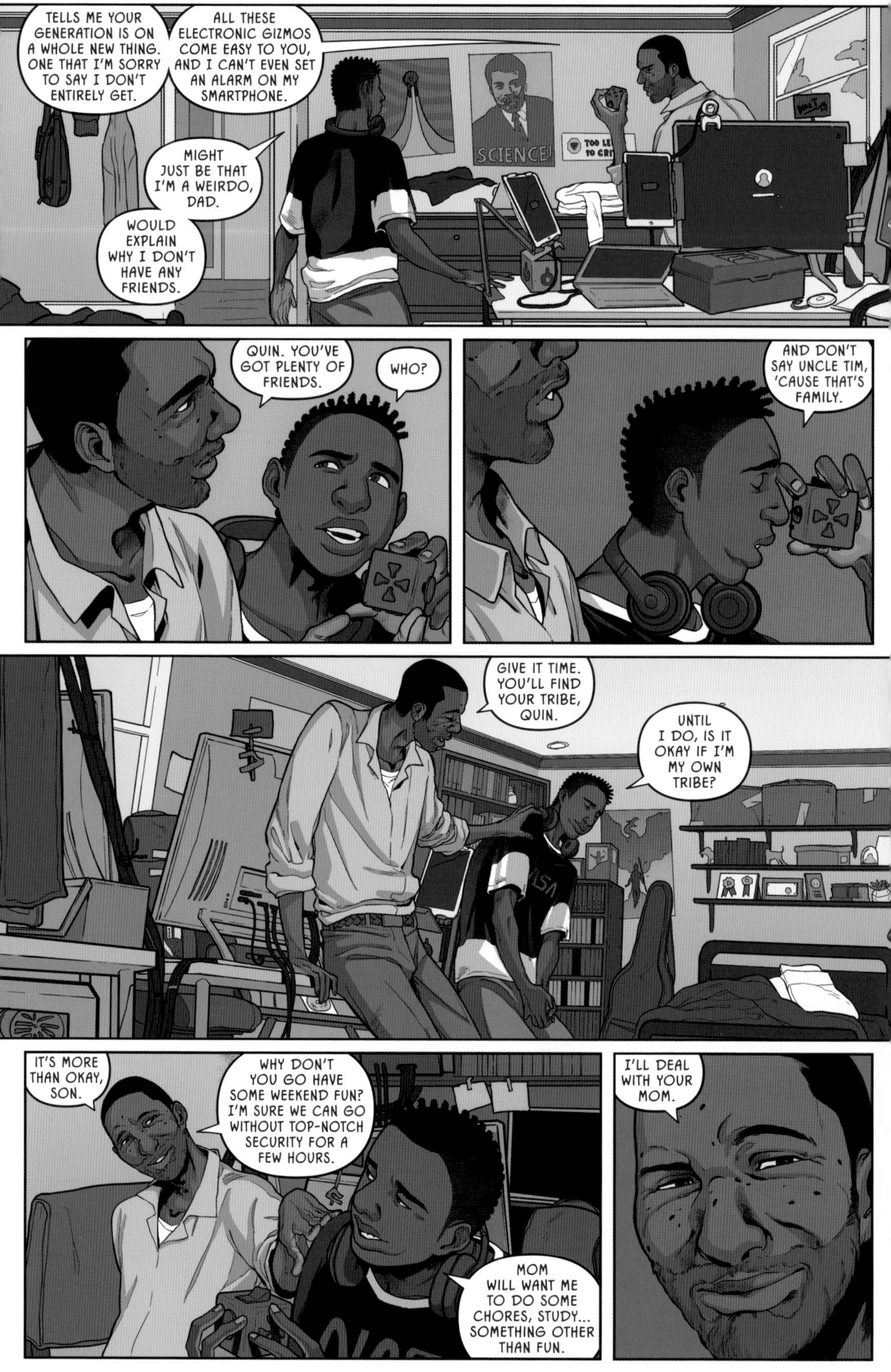
TELLS ME YOUR GENERATION IS ON A WHOLE NEW THING. ONE THAT I'M SORRY TO SAY I DON'T ENTIRELY GET.
ALL THESE ELECTRONIC GIZMOS COME EASY TO YOU, AND I CAN'T EVEN SET AN ALARM ON MY SMARTPHONE.
SCIENCE!
MIGHT JUST BE THAT I'M A WEIRDO, DAD.
WOULD EXPLAIN WHY I DON'T HAVE ANY FRIENDS.
QUIN. YOU'VE GOT PLENTY OF FRIENDS.
WHO?
AND DON'T SAY UNCLE TIM, 'CAUSE THAT'S FAMILY.
GIVE IT TIME. YOU'LL FIND YOUR TRIBE, QUIN.
UNTIL I DO, IS IT OKAY IF I'M MY OWN TRIBE?
IT'S MORE THAN OKAY, SON.
WHY DON'T YOU GO HAVE SOME WEEKEND FUN? I'M SURE WE CAN GO WITHOUT TOP-NOTCH SECURITY FOR A FEW HOURS.
MOM WILL WANT ME TO DO SOME CHORES, STUDY... SOMETHING OTHER THAN FUN.
I'LL DEAL WITH YOUR MOM.

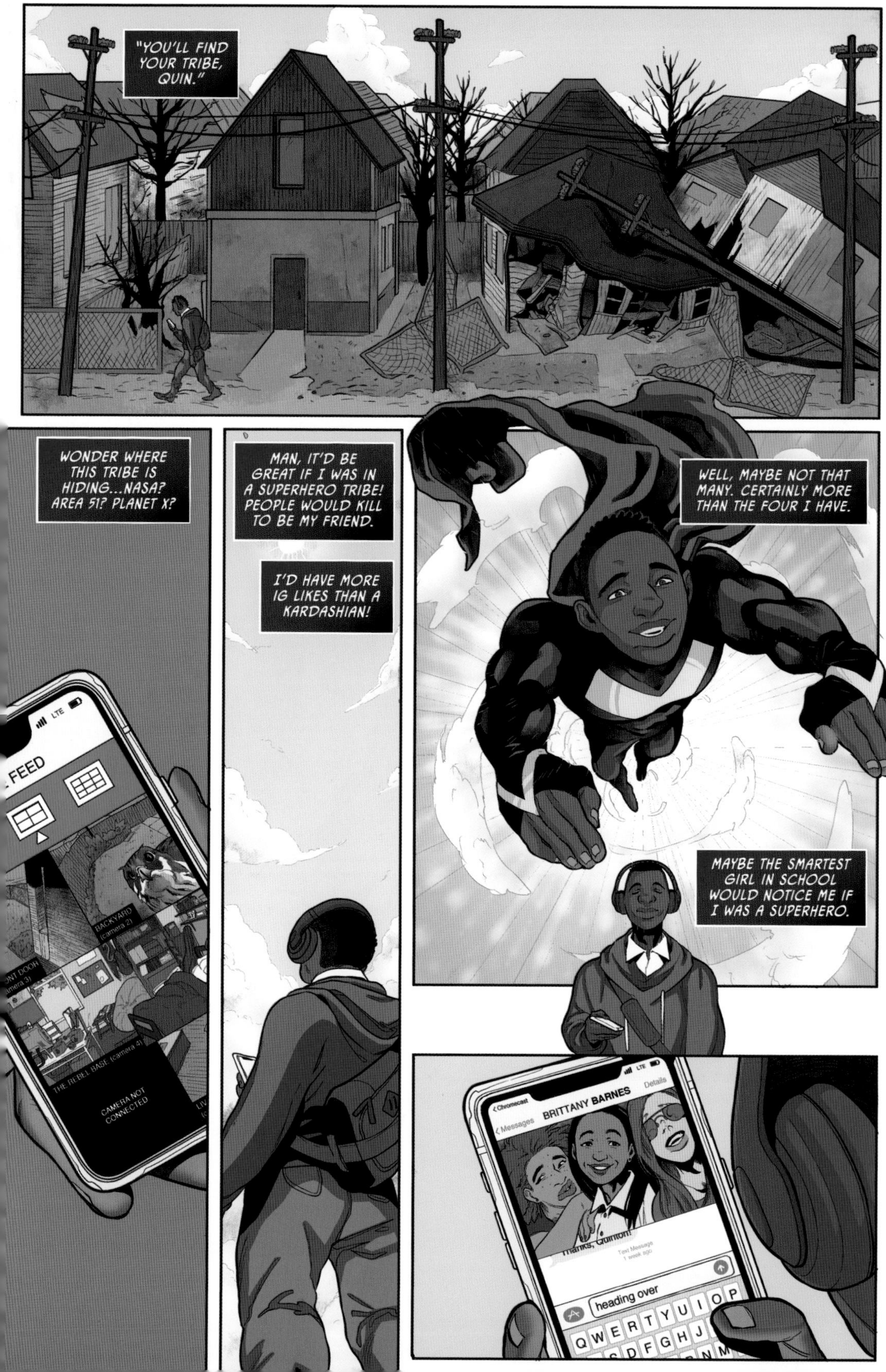

"YOU'LL FIND YOUR TRIBE, QUIN."
WONDER WHERE THIS TRIBE IS HIDING...NASA? AREA 51? PLANET X?
FEED
BACKYARD (camera 2)
THE REBEL BASE (camera 4)
CAMERA NOT CONNECTED
MAN, IT'D BE GREAT IF I WAS IN A SUPERHERO TRIBE! PEOPLE WOULD KILL TO BE MY FRIEND.
I'D HAVE MORE IG LIKES THAN A KARDASHIAN!
WELL, MAYBE NOT THAT MANY. CERTAINLY MORE THAN THE FOUR I HAVE.
MAYBE THE SMARTEST GIRL IN SCHOOL WOULD NOTICE ME IF I WAS A SUPERHERO.
Chromecast
Messages
BRITTANY BARNES
Details
Thanks, Quinton!
Text Message
1 week ago
heading over

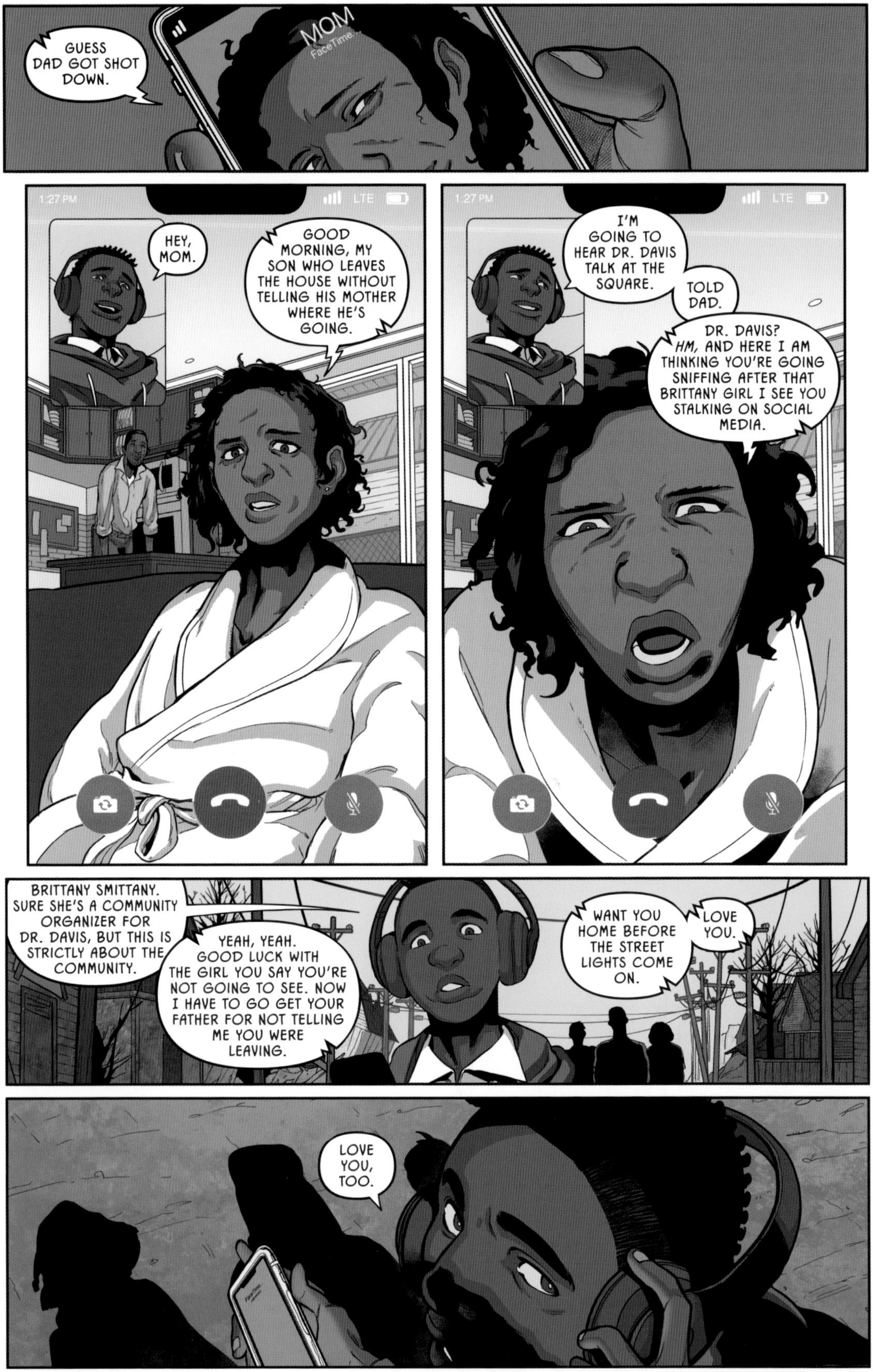
GUESS DAD GOT SHOT DOWN.
MOM
FaceTime...
1:27 PM
LTE
HEY, MOM.
GOOD MORNING, MY SON WHO LEAVES THE HOUSE WITHOUT TELLING HIS MOTHER WHERE HE'S GOING.
1:27 PM
LTE
I'M GOING TO HEAR DR. DAVIS TALK AT THE SQUARE.
TOLD DAD.
DR. DAVIS? *HM,* AND HERE I AM THINKING YOU'RE GOING SNIFFING AFTER THAT BRITTANY GIRL I SEE YOU STALKING ON SOCIAL MEDIA.
BRITTANY SMITTANY. SURE SHE'S A COMMUNITY ORGANIZER FOR DR. DAVIS, BUT THIS IS STRICTLY ABOUT THE COMMUNITY.
YEAH, YEAH. GOOD LUCK WITH THE GIRL YOU SAY YOU'RE NOT GOING TO SEE. NOW I HAVE TO GO GET YOUR FATHER FOR NOT TELLING ME YOU WERE LEAVING.
WANT YOU HOME BEFORE THE STREET LIGHTS COME ON.
LOVE YOU.
LOVE YOU, TOO.

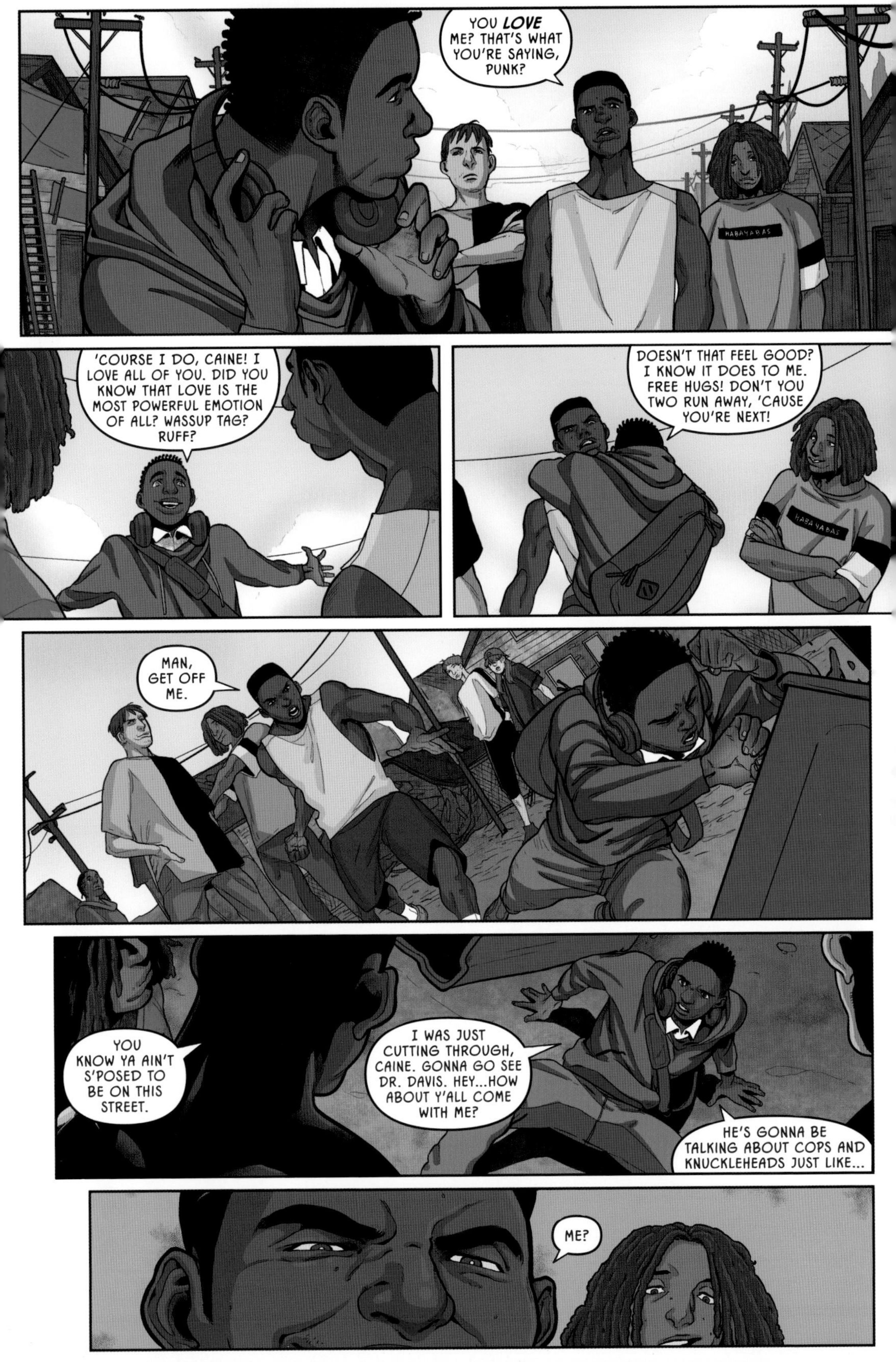
YOU LOVE ME? THAT'S WHAT YOU'RE SAYING, PUNK?
HABAYABAS
'COURSE I DO, CAINE! I LOVE ALL OF YOU. DID YOU KNOW THAT LOVE IS THE MOST POWERFUL EMOTION OF ALL? WASSUP TAG? RUFF?
DOESN'T THAT FEEL GOOD? I KNOW IT DOES TO ME. FREE HUGS! DON'T YOU TWO RUN AWAY, 'CAUSE YOU'RE NEXT!
HABAYABAS
MAN, GET OFF ME.
YOU KNOW YA AIN'T S'POSED TO BE ON THIS STREET.
I WAS JUST CUTTING THROUGH, CAINE. GONNA GO SEE DR. DAVIS. HEY...HOW ABOUT Y'ALL COME WITH ME?
HE'S GONNA BE TALKING ABOUT COPS AND KNUCKLEHEADS JUST LIKE...
ME?

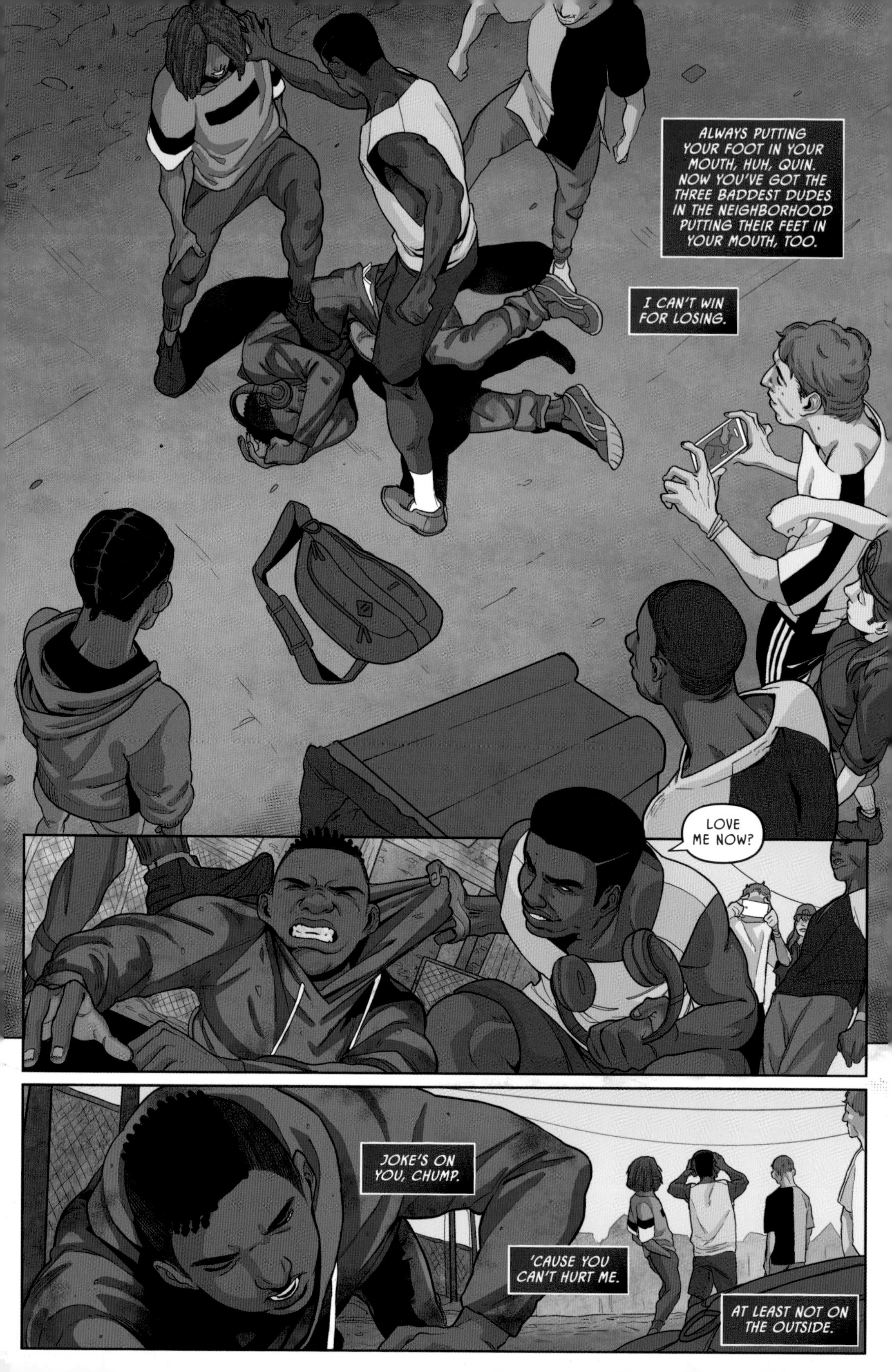
ALWAYS PUTTING YOUR FOOT IN YOUR MOUTH, HUH, QUIN. NOW YOU'VE GOT THE THREE BADDEST DUDES IN THE NEIGHBORHOOD PUTTING THEIR FEET IN YOUR MOUTH, TOO.
I CAN'T WIN FOR LOSING.
LOVE ME NOW?
JOKE'S ON YOU, CHUMP.
'CAUSE YOU CAN'T HURT ME.
AT LEAST NOT ON THE OUTSIDE.

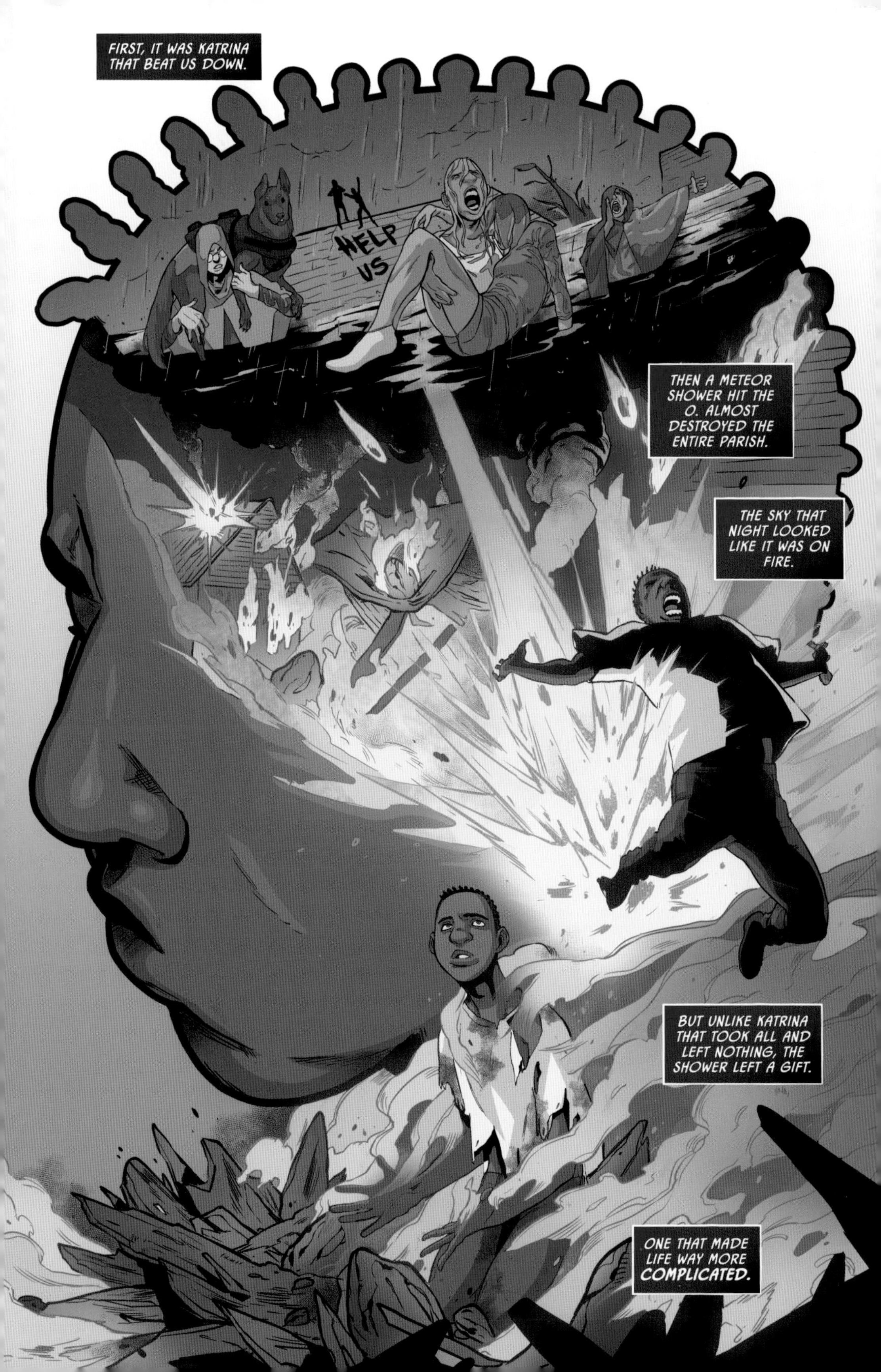
FIRST, IT WAS KATRINA THAT BEAT US DOWN.
HELP US
THEN A METEOR SHOWER HIT THE O. ALMOST DESTROYED THE ENTIRE PARISH.
THE SKY THAT NIGHT LOOKED LIKE IT WAS ON FIRE.
BUT UNLIKE KATRINA THAT TOOK ALL AND LEFT NOTHING, THE SHOWER LEFT A GIFT.
ONE THAT MADE LIFE WAY MORE COMPLICATED.

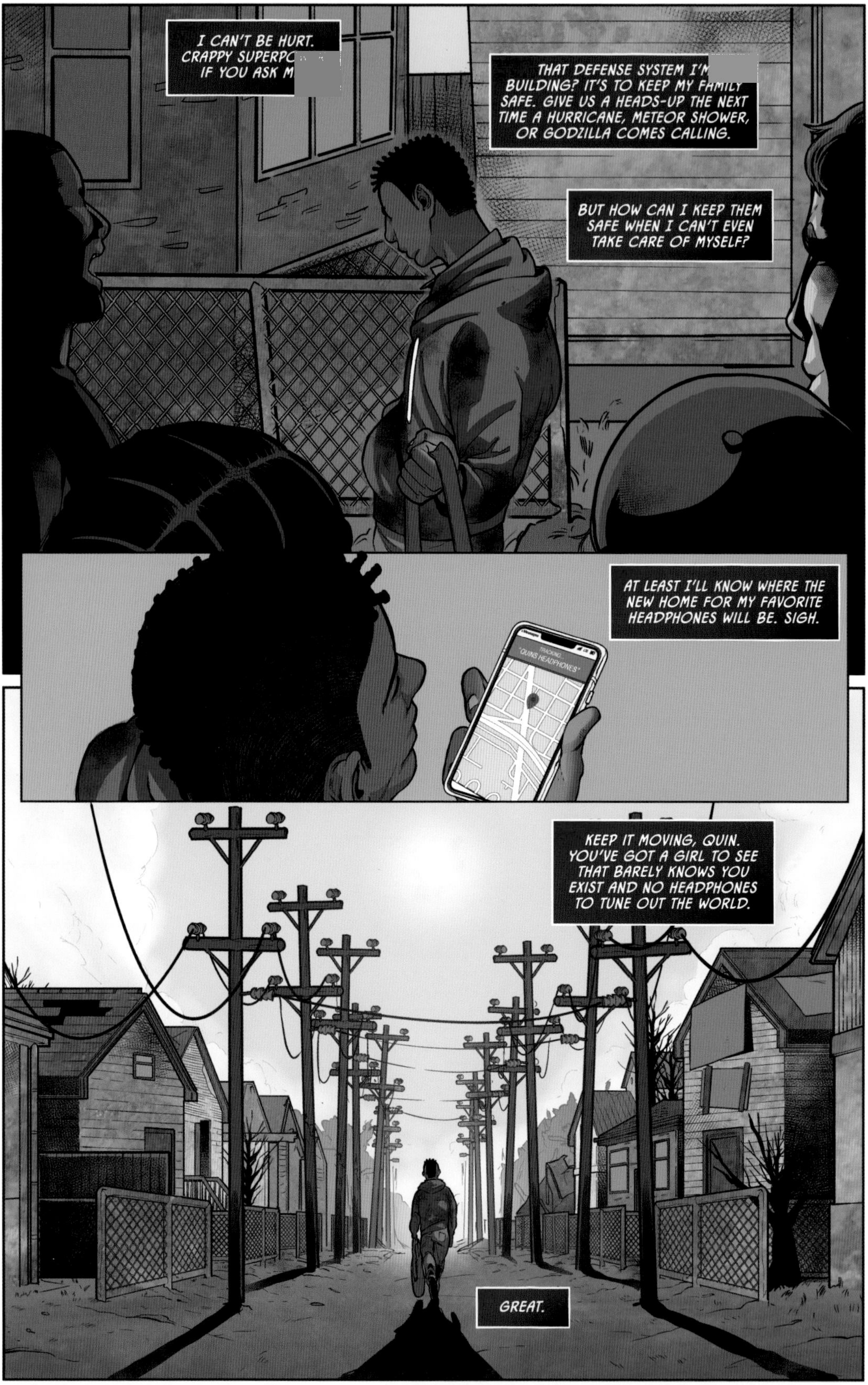
I CAN'T BE HURT. CRAPPY SUPERPO IF YOU ASK M
THAT DEFENSE SYSTEM I'M BUILDING? IT'S TO KEEP MY FAMILY SAFE. GIVE US A HEADS-UP THE NEXT TIME A HURRICANE, METEOR SHOWER, OR GODZILLA COMES CALLING.
BUT HOW CAN I KEEP THEM SAFE WHEN I CAN'T EVEN TAKE CARE OF MYSELF?
AT LEAST I'LL KNOW WHERE THE NEW HOME FOR MY FAVORITE HEADPHONES WILL BE. SIGH.
TRACKING...
"QUINS HEADPHONES"
KEEP IT MOVING, QUIN. YOU'VE GOT A GIRL TO SEE THAT BARELY KNOWS YOU EXIST AND NO HEADPHONES TO TUNE OUT THE WORLD.
GREAT.

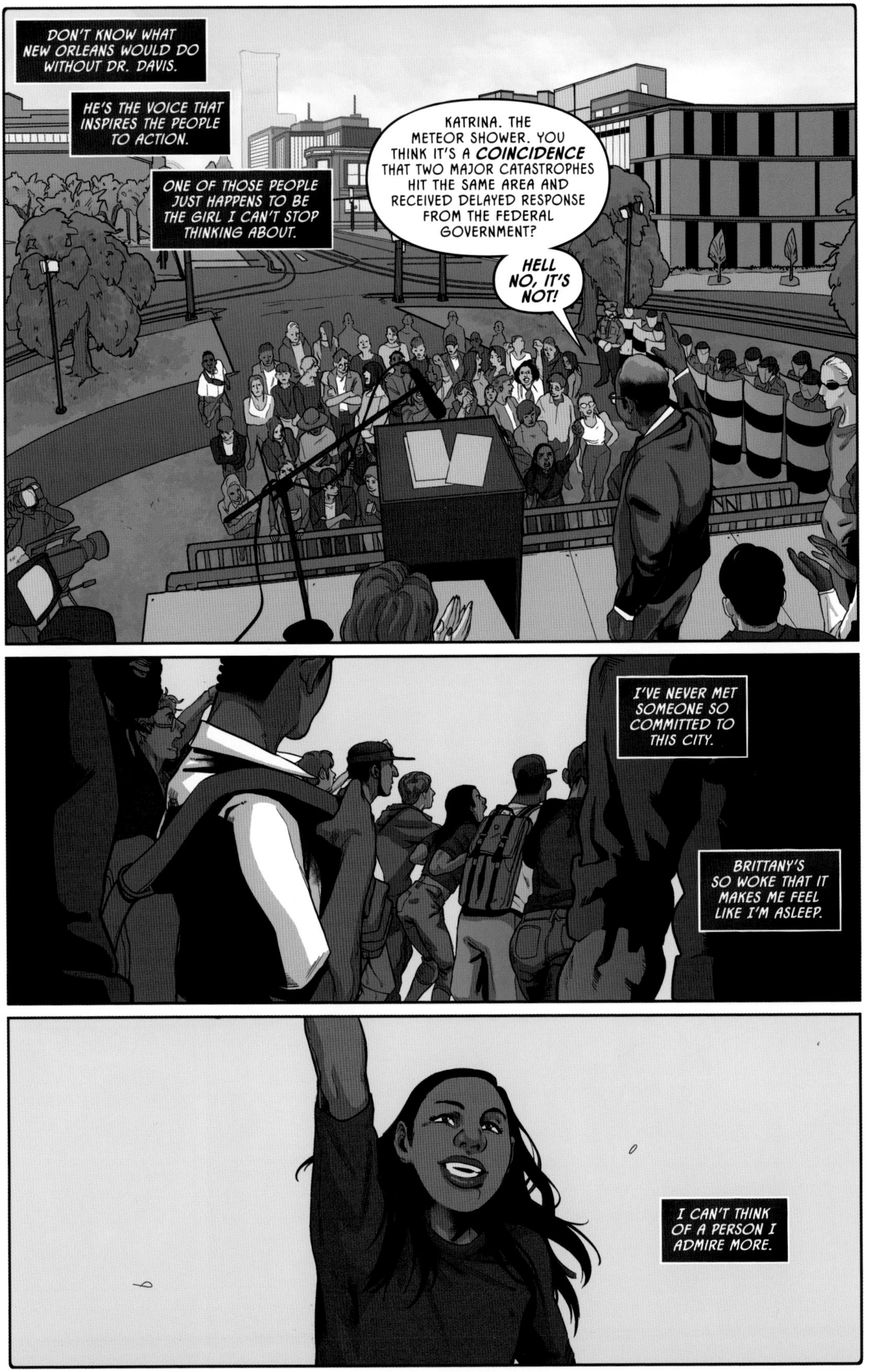
DON'T KNOW WHAT NEW ORLEANS WOULD DO WITHOUT DR. DAVIS.
HE'S THE VOICE THAT INSPIRES THE PEOPLE TO ACTION.
ONE OF THOSE PEOPLE JUST HAPPENS TO BE THE GIRL I CAN'T STOP THINKING ABOUT.
KATRINA. THE METEOR SHOWER. YOU THINK IT'S A COINCIDENCE THAT TWO MAJOR CATASTROPHES HIT THE SAME AREA AND RECEIVED DELAYED RESPONSE FROM THE FEDERAL GOVERNMENT?
HELL NO, IT'S NOT!
I'VE NEVER MET SOMEONE SO COMMITTED TO THIS CITY.
BRITTANY'S SO WOKE THAT IT MAKES ME FEEL LIKE I'M ASLEEP.
I CAN'T THINK OF A PERSON I ADMIRE MORE.

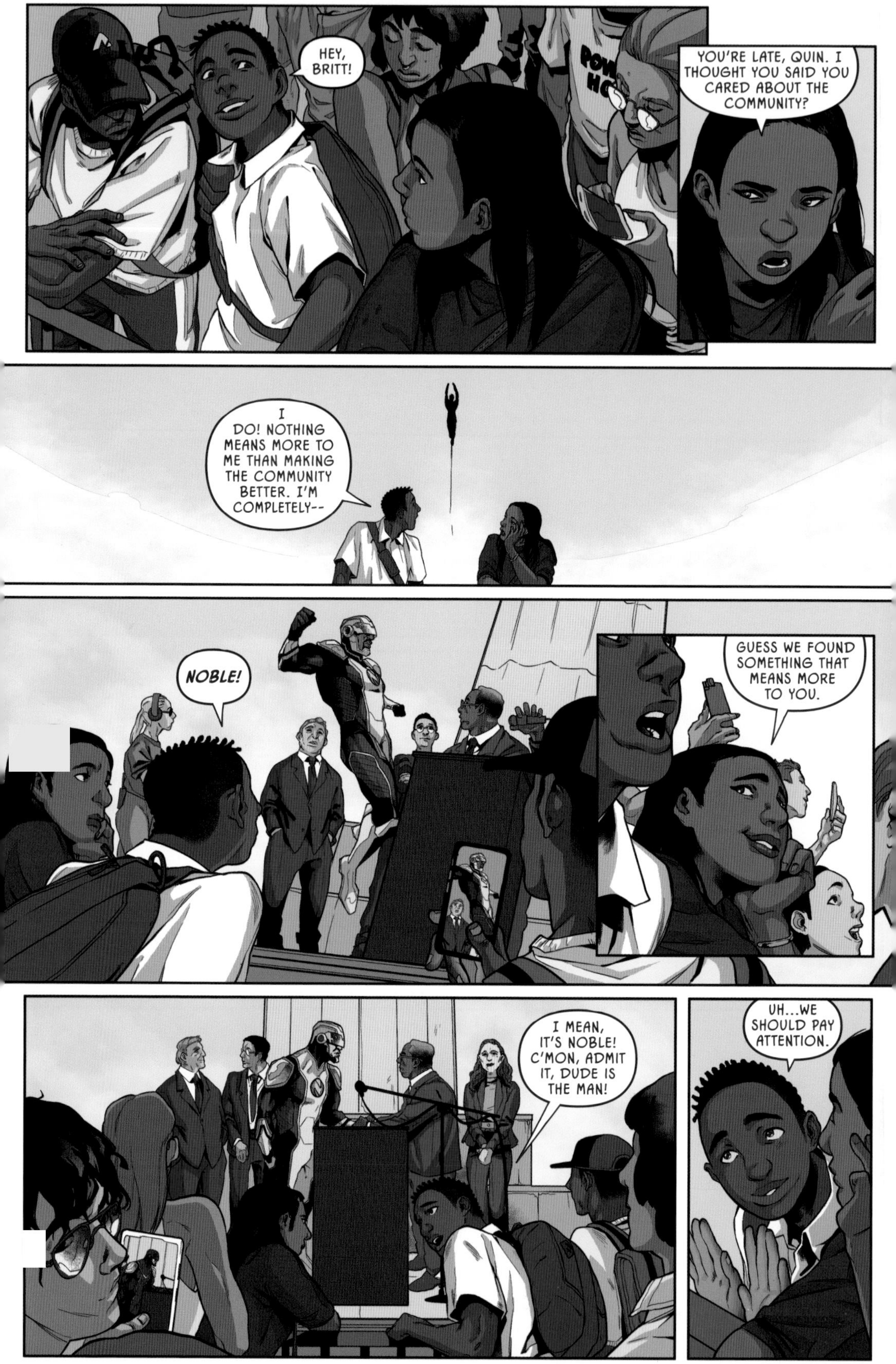
HEY, BRITT!
YOU'RE LATE, QUIN. I THOUGHT YOU SAID YOU CARED ABOUT THE COMMUNITY?
I DO! NOTHING MEANS MORE TO ME THAN MAKING THE COMMUNITY BETTER. I'M COMPLETELY--
NOBLE!
GUESS WE FOUND SOMETHING THAT MEANS MORE TO YOU.
I MEAN, IT'S NOBLE! C'MON, ADMIT IT, DUDE IS THE MAN!
UH...WE SHOULD PAY ATTENTION.

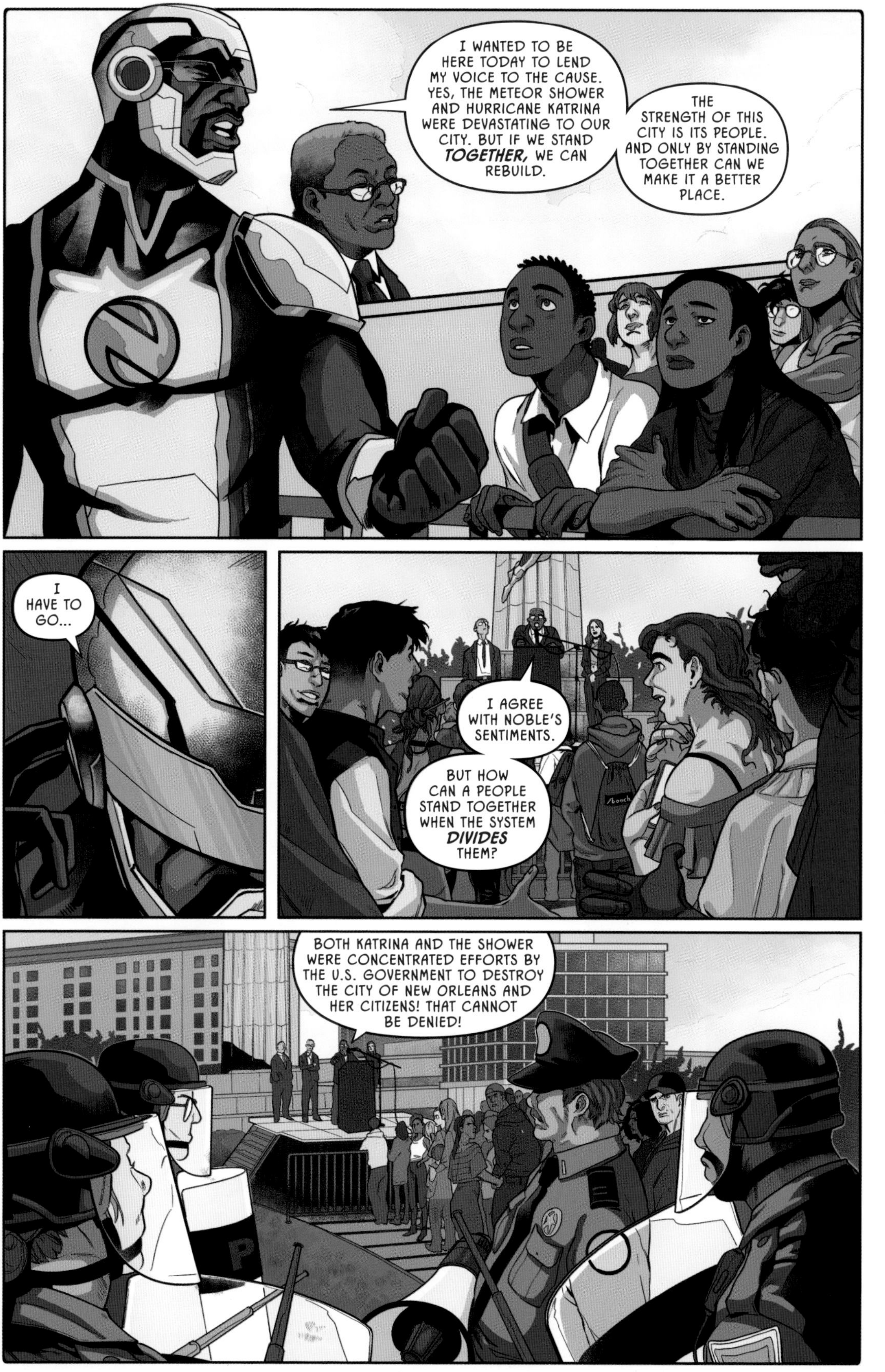
I WANTED TO BE HERE TODAY TO LEND MY VOICE TO THE CAUSE. YES, THE METEOR SHOWER AND HURRICANE KATRINA WERE DEVASTATING TO OUR CITY. BUT IF WE STAND *TOGETHER,* WE CAN REBUILD.
THE STRENGTH OF THIS CITY IS ITS PEOPLE. AND ONLY BY STANDING TOGETHER CAN WE MAKE IT A BETTER PLACE.
I HAVE TO GO...
I AGREE WITH NOBLE'S SENTIMENTS.
BUT HOW CAN A PEOPLE STAND TOGETHER WHEN THE SYSTEM *DIVIDES* THEM?
BOTH KATRINA AND THE SHOWER WERE CONCENTRATED EFFORTS BY THE U.S. GOVERNMENT TO DESTROY THE CITY OF NEW ORLEANS AND HER CITIZENS! THAT CANNOT BE DENIED!

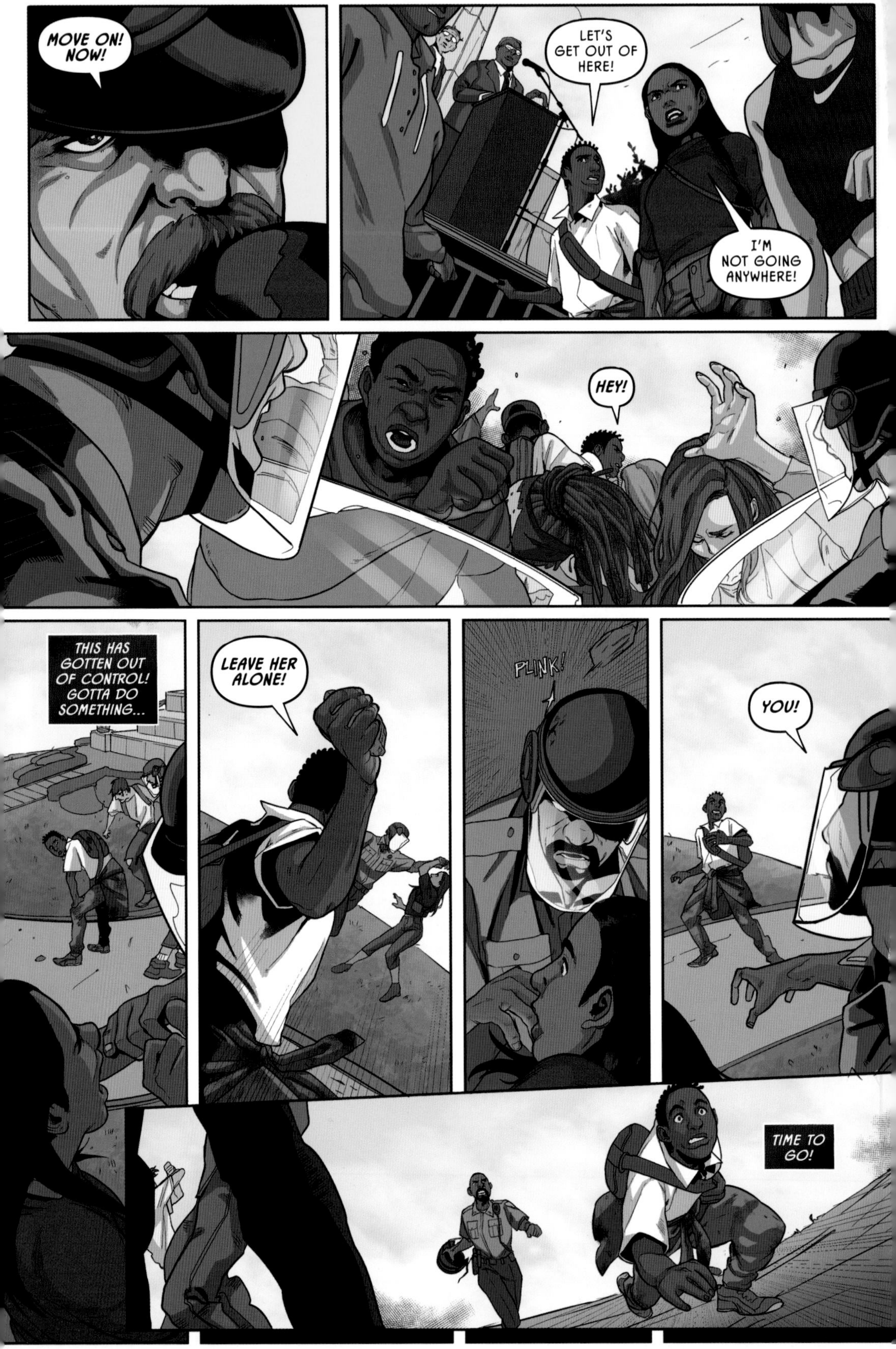
MOVE ON! NOW!
LET'S GET OUT OF HERE!
I'M NOT GOING ANYWHERE!
HEY!
THIS HAS GOTTEN OUT OF CONTROL! GOTTA DO SOMETHING...
LEAVE HER ALONE!
PLINK!
YOU!
TIME TO GO!

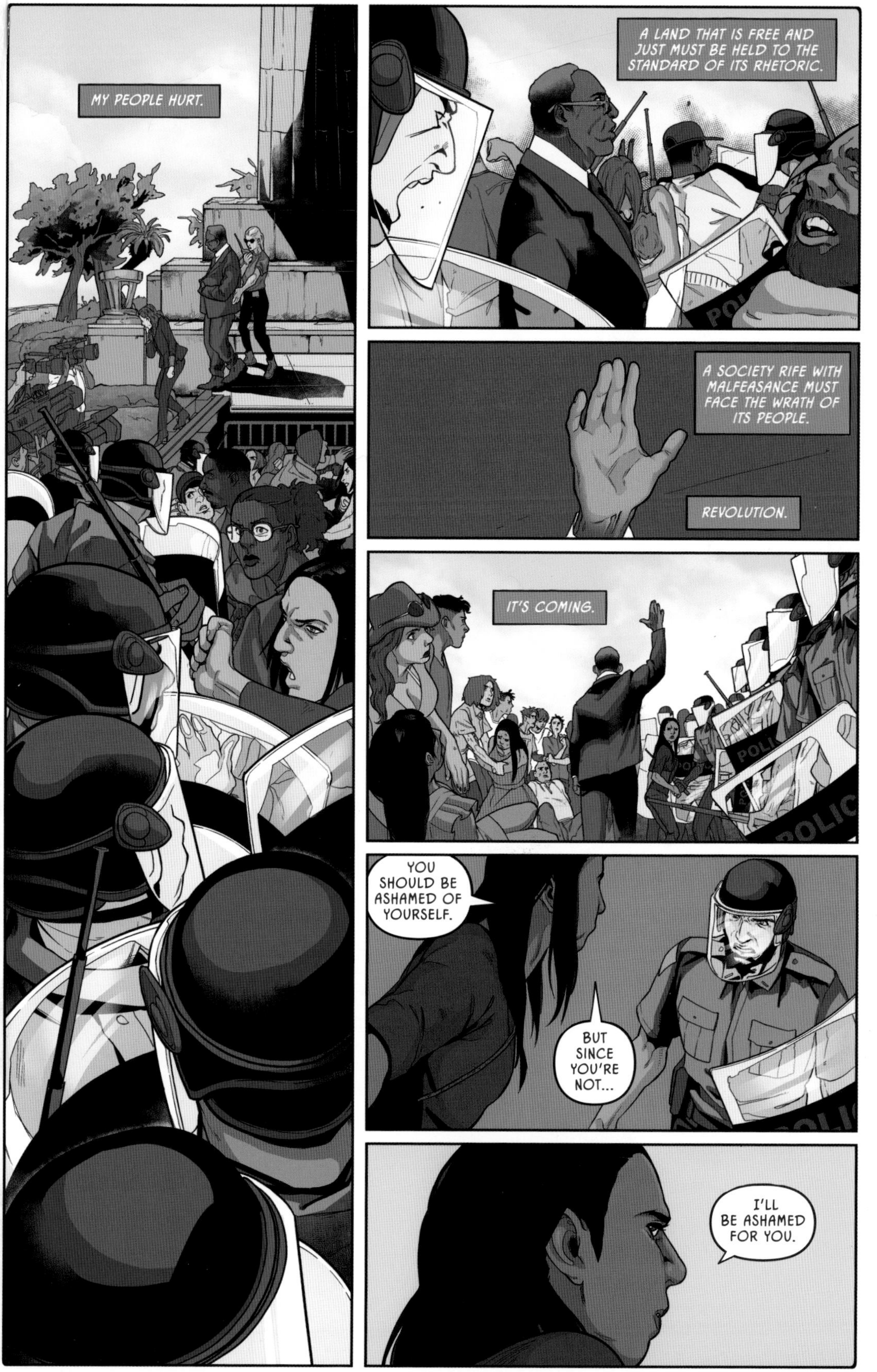
MY PEOPLE HURT.
A LAND THAT IS FREE AND JUST MUST BE HELD TO THE STANDARD OF ITS RHETORIC.
A SOCIETY RIFE WITH MALFEASANCE MUST FACE THE WRATH OF ITS PEOPLE.
REVOLUTION.
IT'S COMING.
YOU SHOULD BE ASHAMED OF YOURSELF.
BUT SINCE YOU'RE NOT...
I'LL BE ASHAMED FOR YOU.

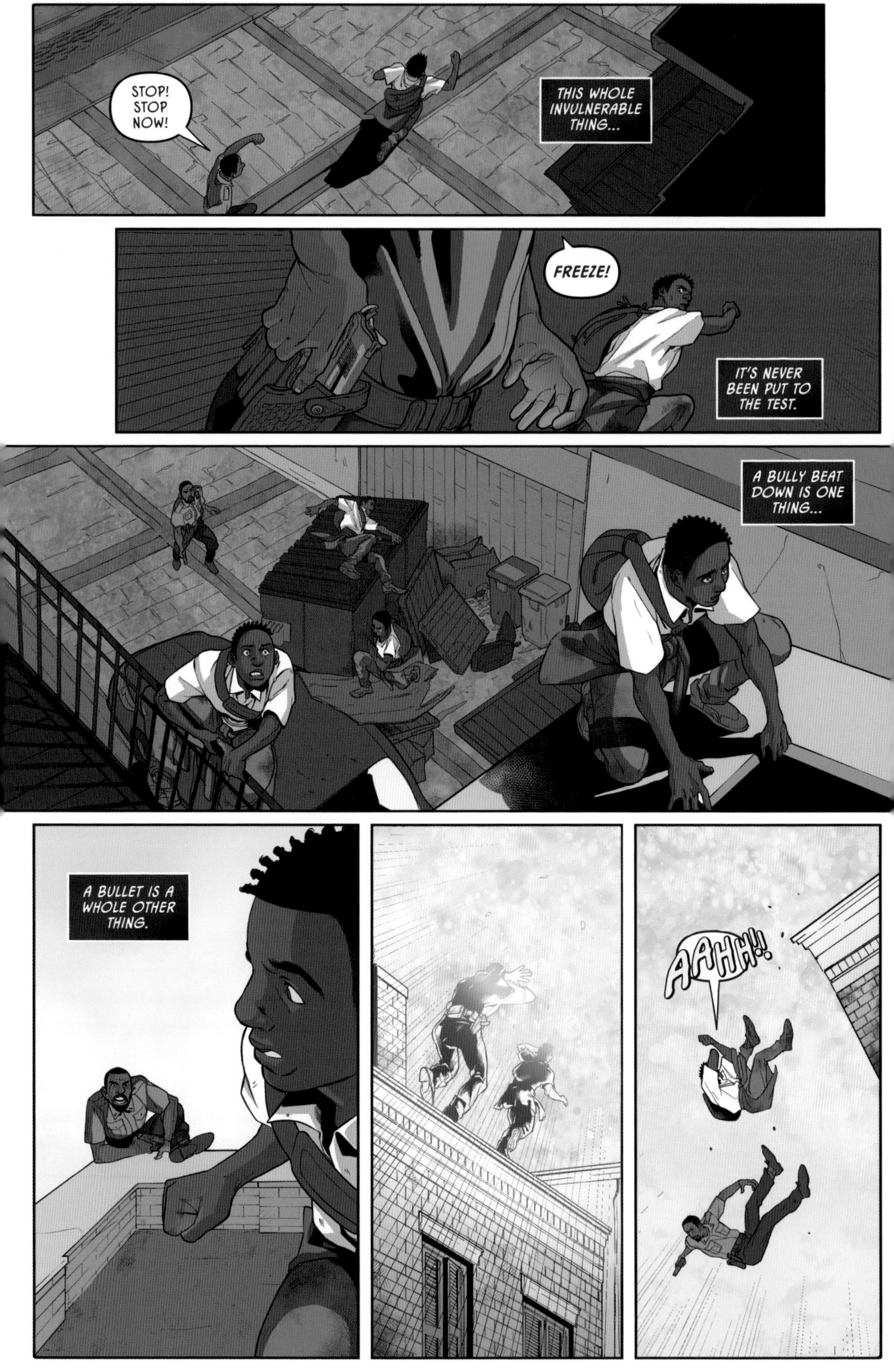
STOP! STOP NOW!
THIS WHOLE INVULNERABLE THING...
FREEZE!
IT'S NEVER BEEN PUT TO THE TEST.
A BULLY BEAT DOWN IS ONE THING...
A BULLET IS A WHOLE OTHER THING.
AAHH!!

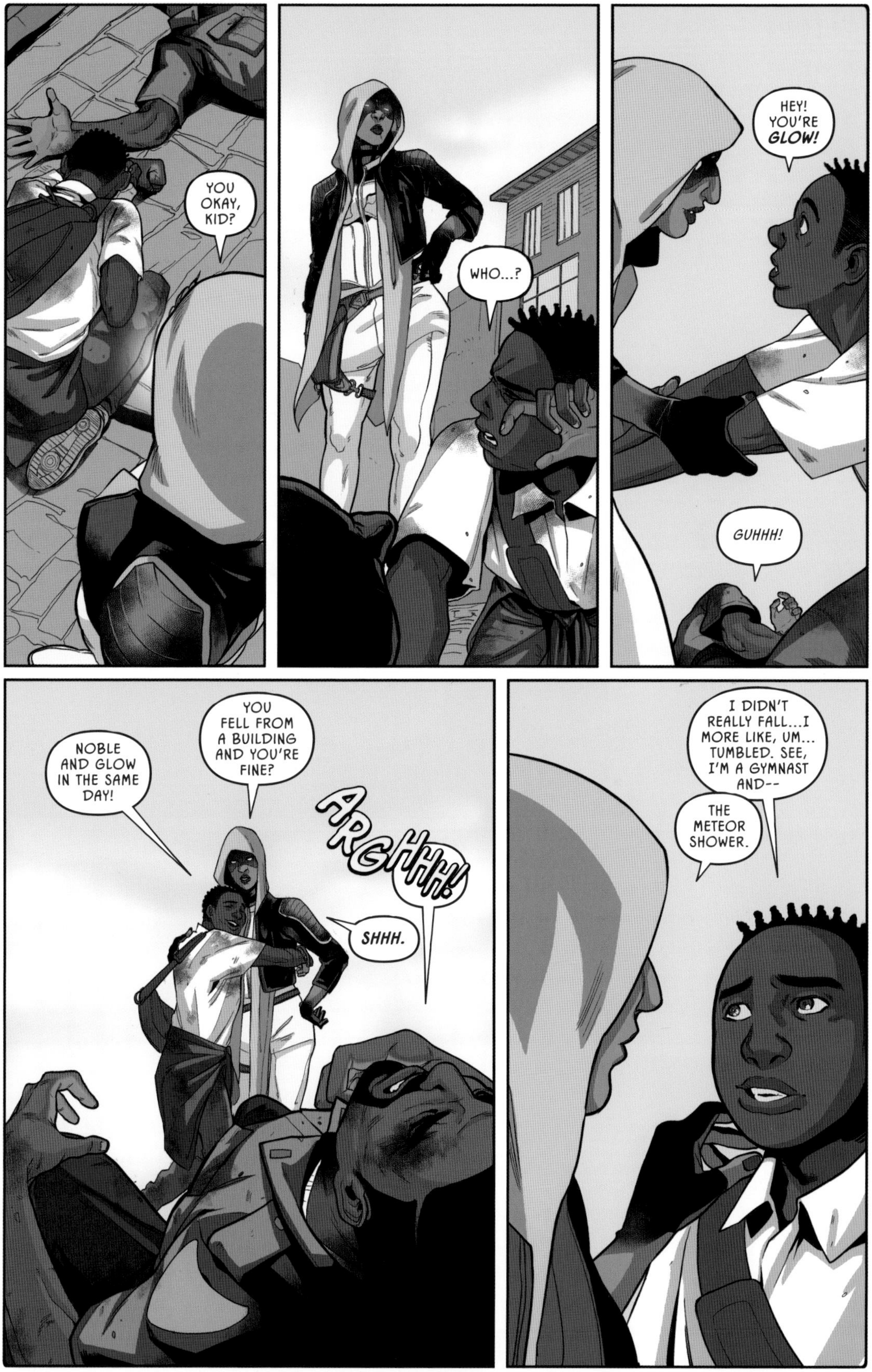
YOU OKAY, KID?
WHO...?
HEY! YOU'RE GLOW!
GUHHH!
NOBLE AND GLOW IN THE SAME DAY!
YOU FELL FROM A BUILDING AND YOU'RE FINE?
ARGHHH!
SHHH.
I DIDN'T REALLY FALL...I MORE LIKE, UM... TUMBLED. SEE, I'M A GYMNAST AND--
THE METEOR SHOWER.

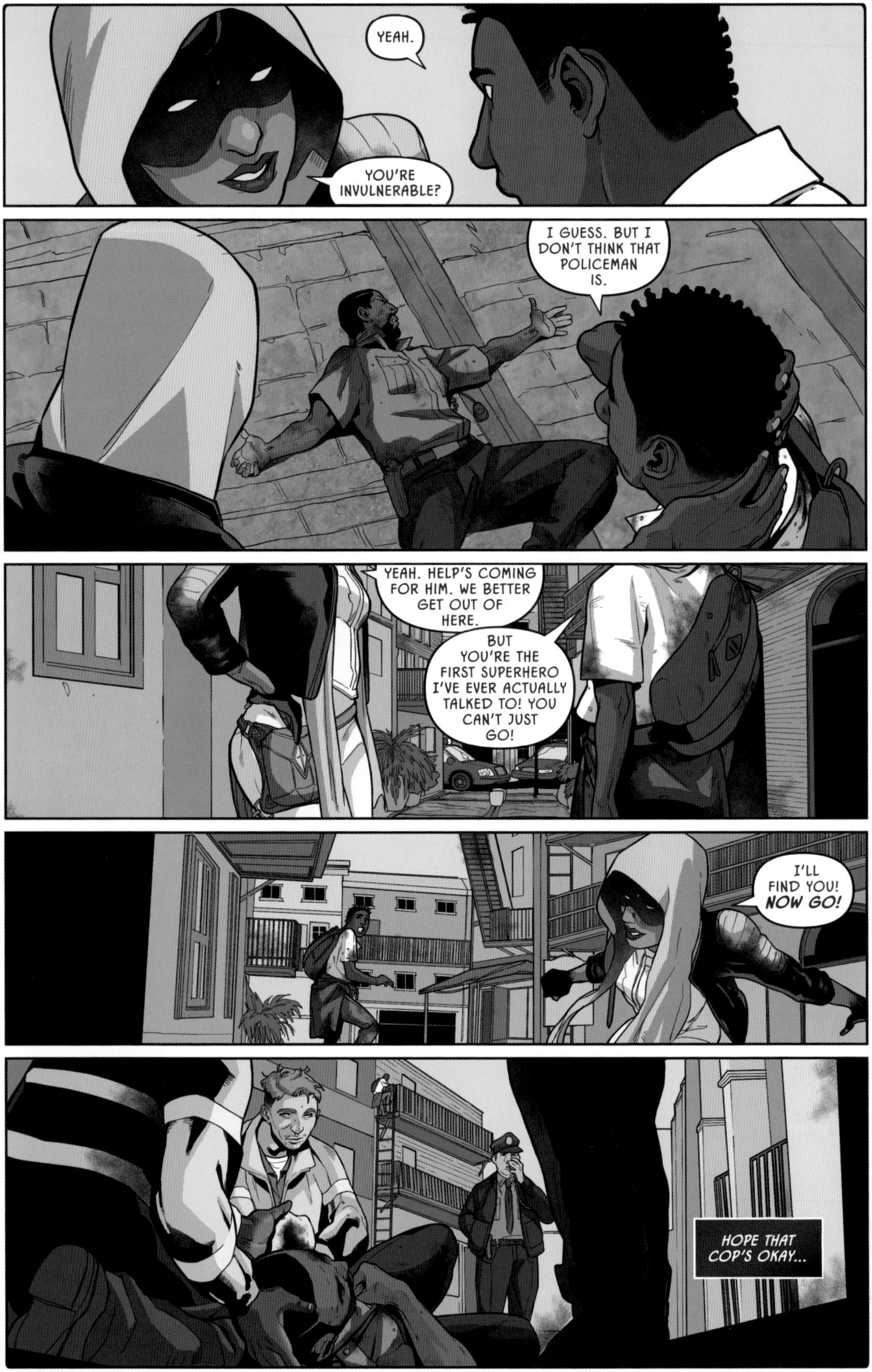

YEAH.
YOU'RE INVULNERABLE?
I GUESS. BUT I DON'T THINK THAT POLICEMAN IS.
YEAH. HELP'S COMING FOR HIM. WE BETTER GET OUT OF HERE.
BUT YOU'RE THE FIRST SUPERHERO I'VE EVER ACTUALLY TALKED TO! YOU CAN'T JUST GO!
I'LL FIND YOU! NOW GO!
HOPE THAT COP'S OKAY...

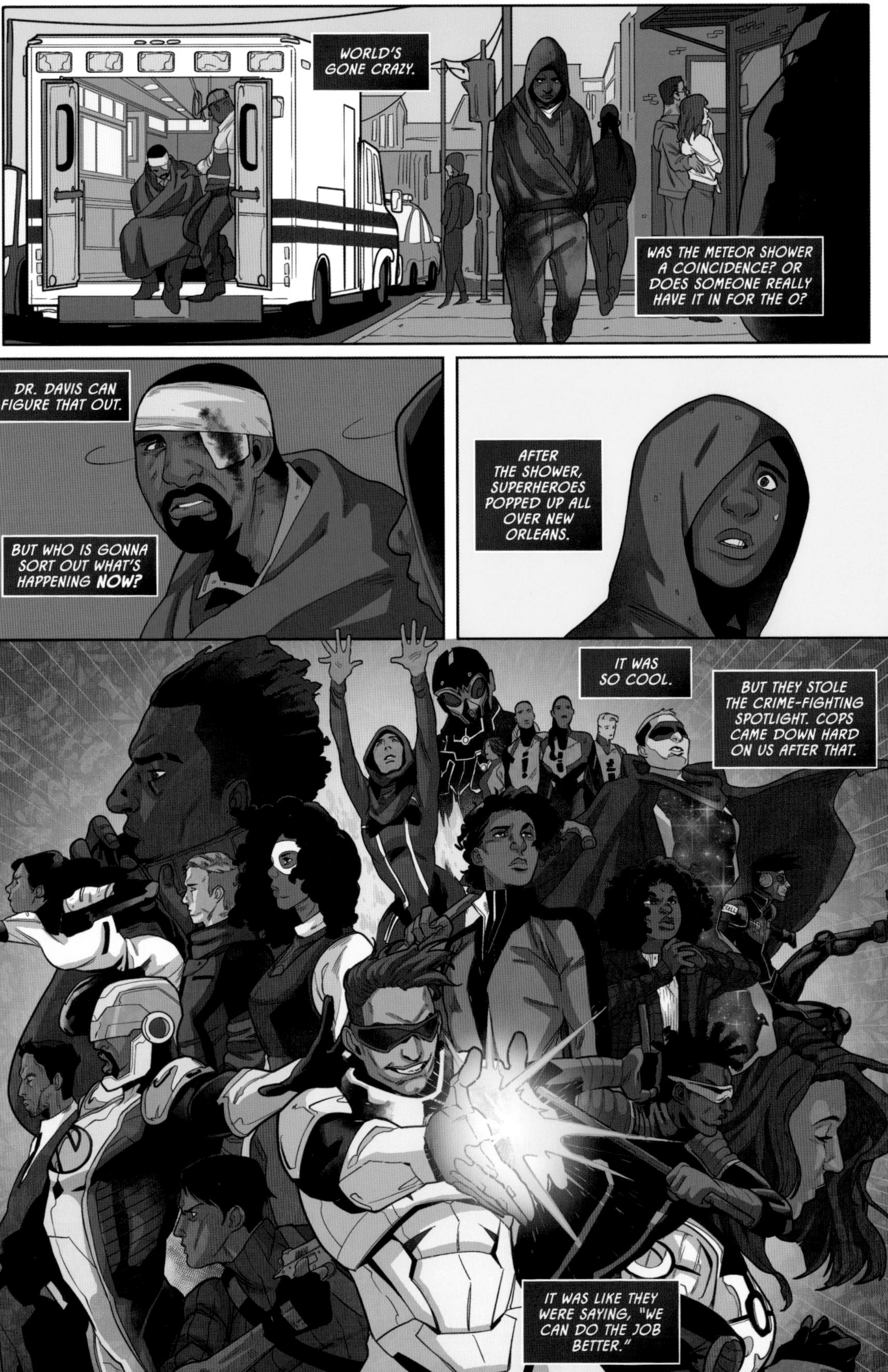
WORLD'S GONE CRAZY.
WAS THE METEOR SHOWER A COINCIDENCE? OR DOES SOMEONE REALLY HAVE IT IN FOR THE O?
DR. DAVIS CAN FIGURE THAT OUT.
BUT WHO IS GONNA SORT OUT WHAT'S HAPPENING NOW?
AFTER THE SHOWER, SUPERHEROES POPPED UP ALL OVER NEW ORLEANS.
IT WAS SO COOL.
BUT THEY STOLE THE CRIME-FIGHTING SPOTLIGHT. COPS CAME DOWN HARD ON US AFTER THAT.
IT WAS LIKE THEY WERE SAYING, "WE CAN DO THE JOB BETTER."

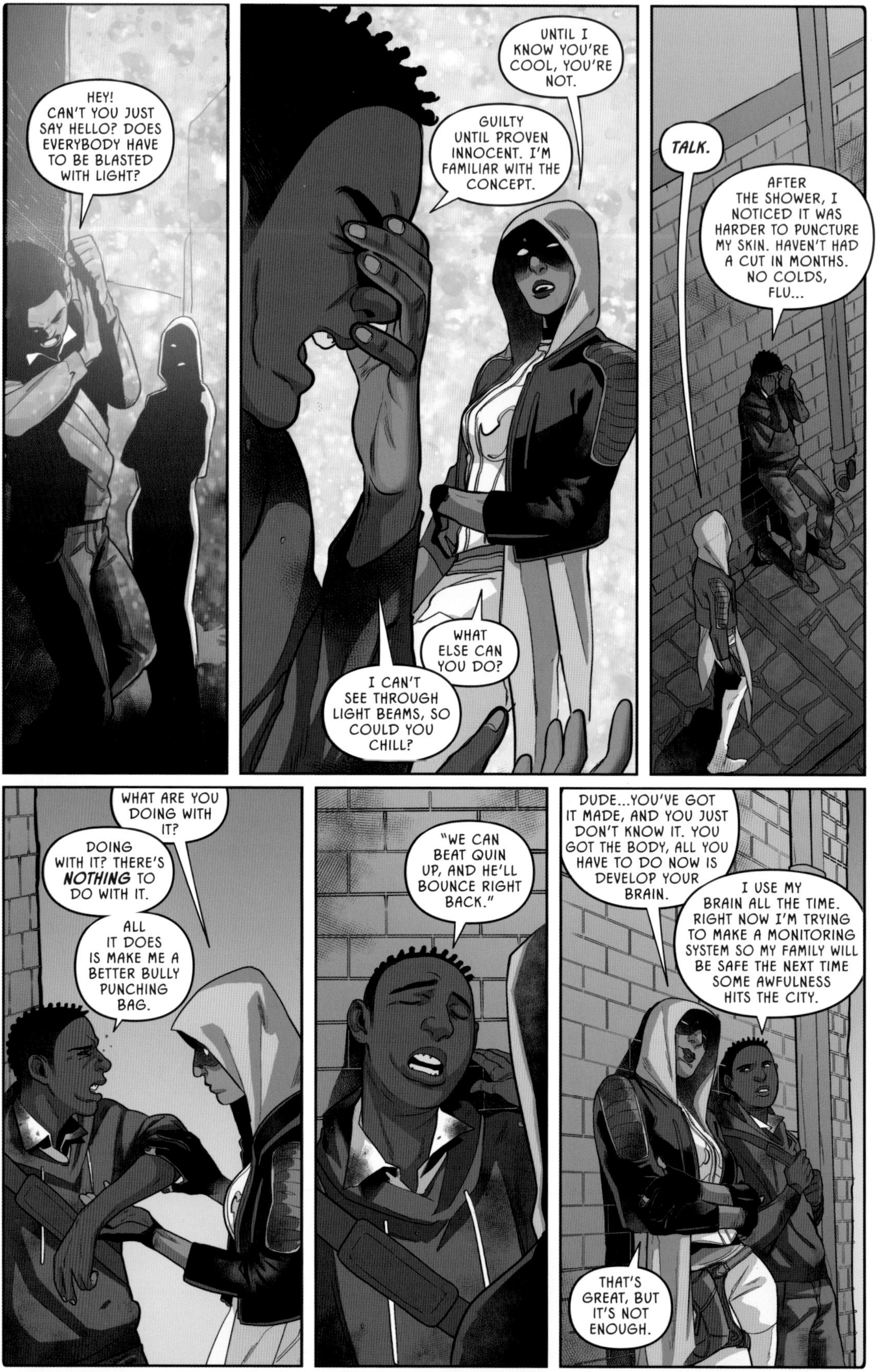
HEY! CAN'T YOU JUST SAY HELLO? DOES EVERYBODY HAVE TO BE BLASTED WITH LIGHT?
UNTIL I KNOW YOU'RE COOL, YOU'RE NOT.
GUILTY UNTIL PROVEN INNOCENT. I'M FAMILIAR WITH THE CONCEPT.
WHAT ELSE CAN YOU DO?
I CAN'T SEE THROUGH LIGHT BEAMS, SO COULD YOU CHILL?
TALK.
AFTER THE SHOWER, I NOTICED IT WAS HARDER TO PUNCTURE MY SKIN. HAVEN'T HAD A CUT IN MONTHS. NO COLDS, FLU...
WHAT ARE YOU DOING WITH IT?
DOING WITH IT? THERE'S NOTHING TO DO WITH IT.
ALL IT DOES IS MAKE ME A BETTER BULLY PUNCHING BAG.
"WE CAN BEAT QUIN UP, AND HE'LL BOUNCE RIGHT BACK."
DUDE...YOU'VE GOT IT MADE, AND YOU JUST DON'T KNOW IT. YOU GOT THE BODY, ALL YOU HAVE TO DO NOW IS DEVELOP YOUR BRAIN.
I USE MY BRAIN ALL THE TIME. RIGHT NOW I'M TRYING TO MAKE A MONITORING SYSTEM SO MY FAMILY WILL BE SAFE THE NEXT TIME SOME AWFULNESS HITS THE CITY.
THAT'S GREAT, BUT IT'S NOT ENOUGH.

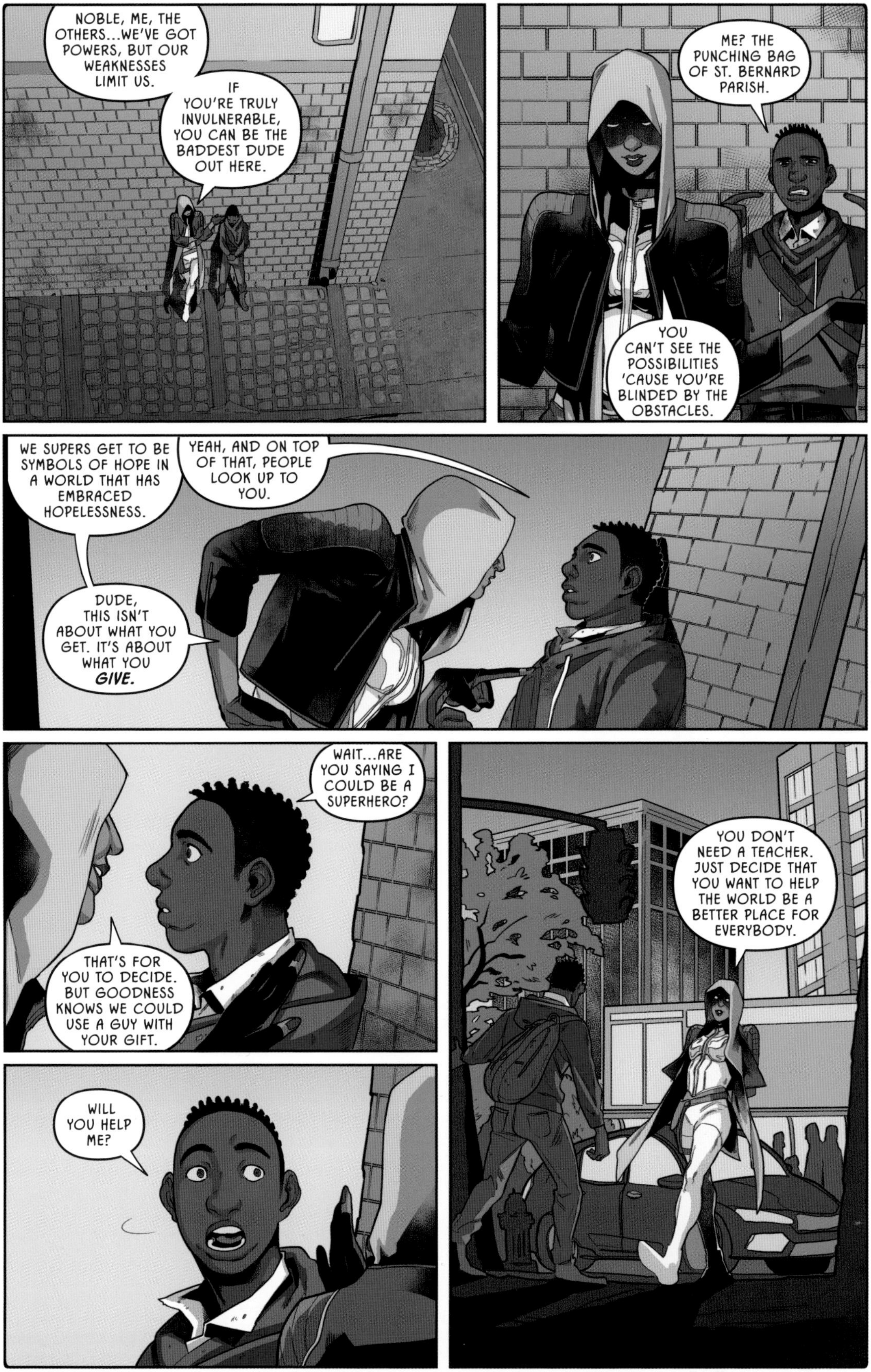
NOBLE, ME, THE OTHERS...WE'VE GOT POWERS, BUT OUR WEAKNESSES LIMIT US.
IF YOU'RE TRULY INVULNERABLE, YOU CAN BE THE BADDEST DUDE OUT HERE.
ME? THE PUNCHING BAG OF ST. BERNARD PARISH.
YOU CAN'T SEE THE POSSIBILITIES 'CAUSE YOU'RE BLINDED BY THE OBSTACLES.
WE SUPERS GET TO BE SYMBOLS OF HOPE IN A WORLD THAT HAS EMBRACED HOPELESSNESS.
YEAH, AND ON TOP OF THAT, PEOPLE LOOK UP TO YOU.
DUDE, THIS ISN'T ABOUT WHAT YOU GET. IT'S ABOUT WHAT YOU GIVE.
WAIT...ARE YOU SAYING I COULD BE A SUPERHERO?
THAT'S FOR YOU TO DECIDE. BUT GOODNESS KNOWS WE COULD USE A GUY WITH YOUR GIFT.
WILL YOU HELP ME?
YOU DON'T NEED A TEACHER. JUST DECIDE THAT YOU WANT TO HELP THE WORLD BE A BETTER PLACE FOR EVERYBODY.

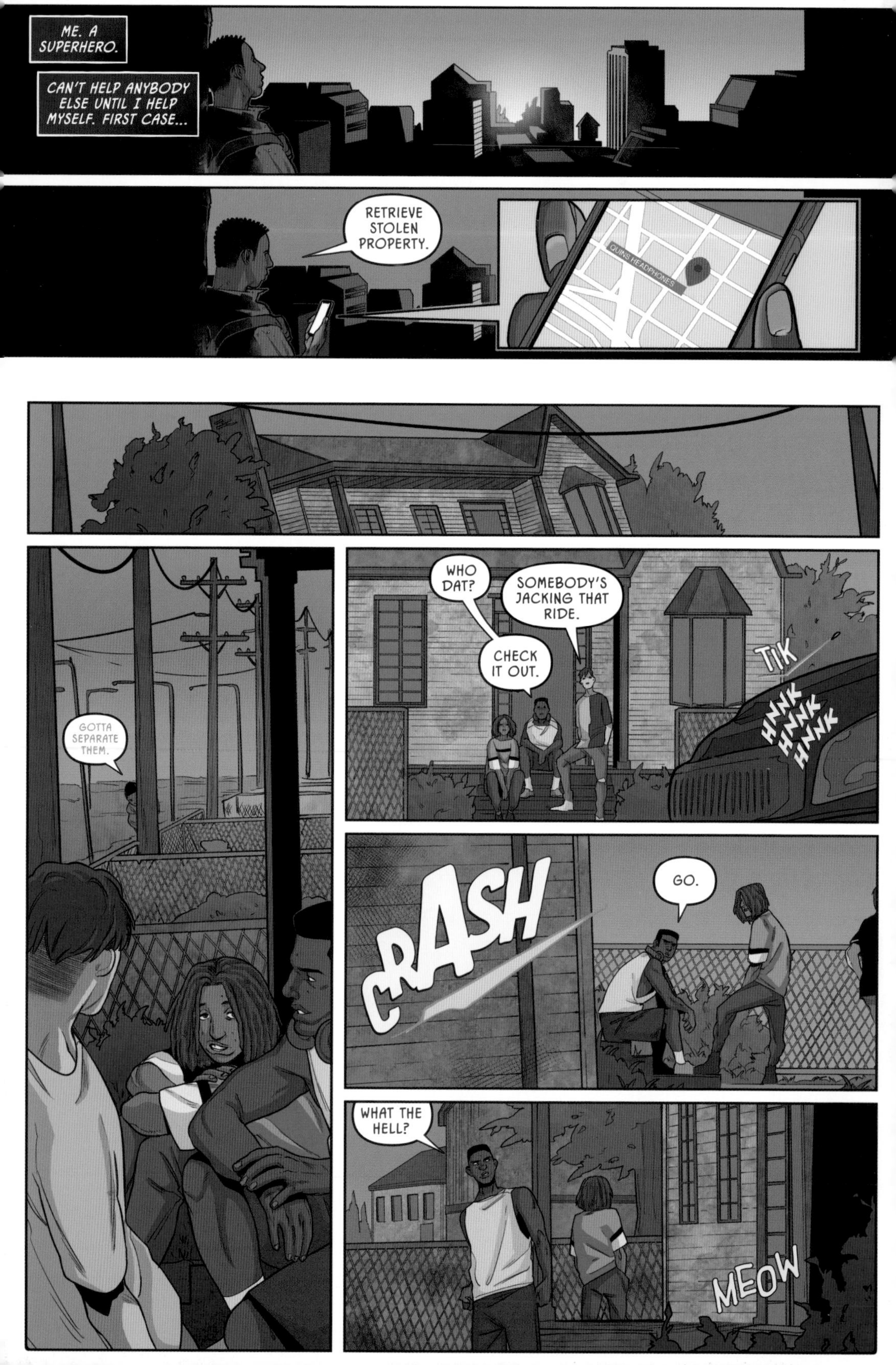
ME. A SUPERHERO.
CAN'T HELP ANYBODY ELSE UNTIL I HELP MYSELF. FIRST CASE...
RETRIEVE STOLEN PROPERTY.
QUINS HEADPHONES
GOTTA SEPARATE THEM.
WHO DAT?
SOMEBODY'S JACKING THAT RIDE.
CHECK IT OUT.
TIK
HNNK HNNK HNNK
CRASH
GO.
WHAT THE HELL?
MEOW

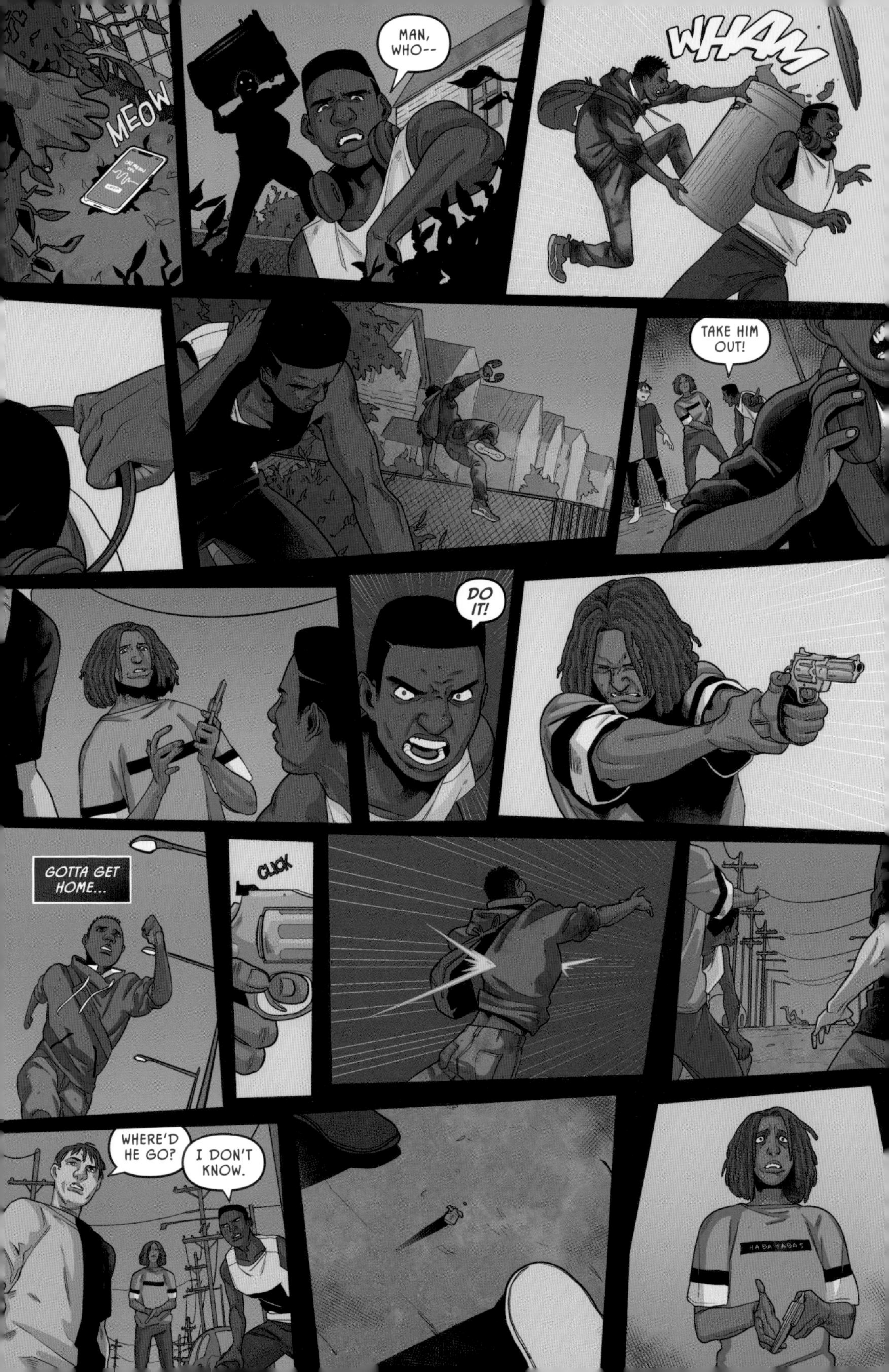
MEOW
MAN, WHO--
WHAM
TAKE HIM OUT!
DO IT!
GOTTA GET HOME...
CLICK
WHERE'D HE GO?
I DON'T KNOW.

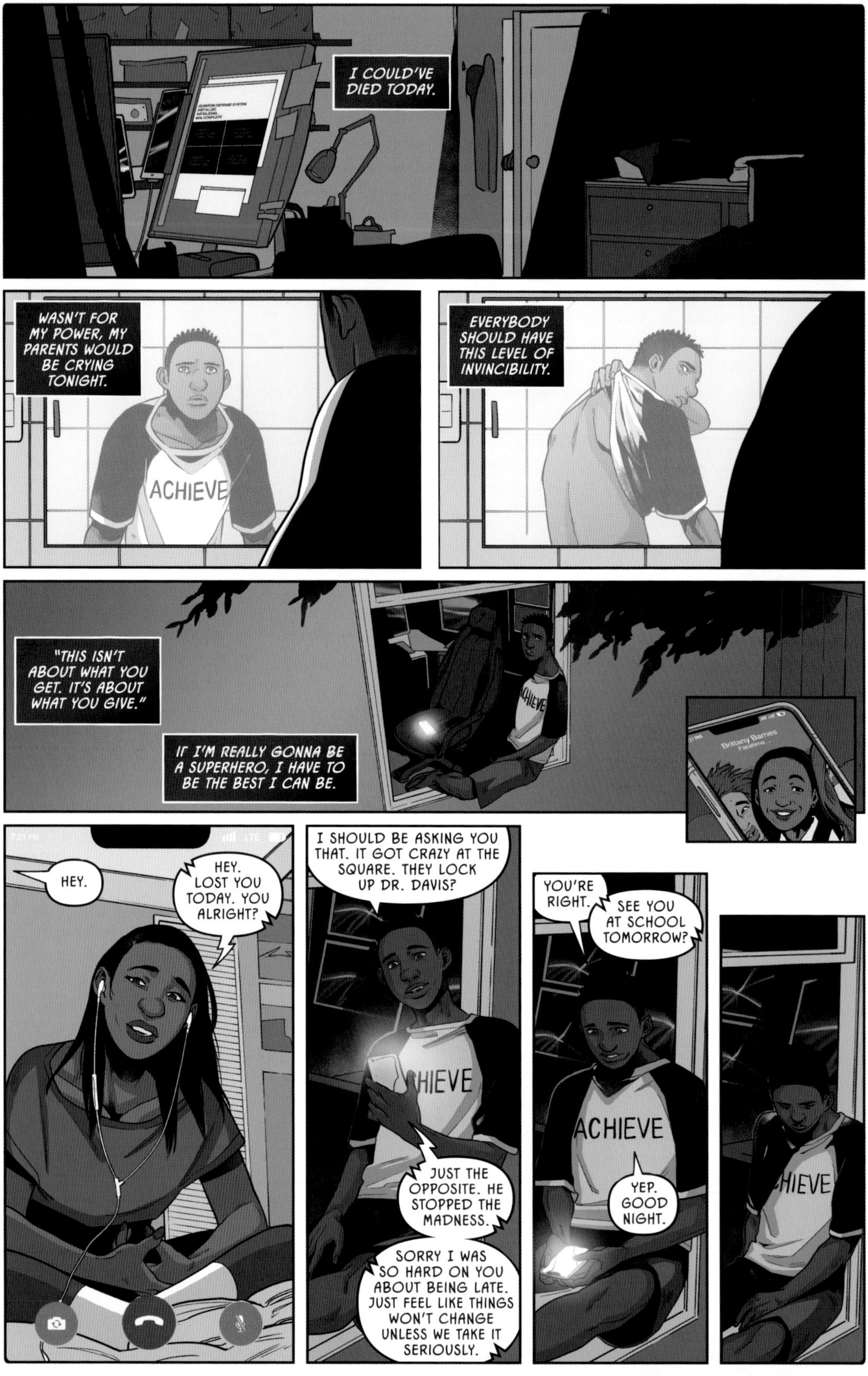
I COULD'VE DIED TODAY.
WASN'T FOR MY POWER, MY PARENTS WOULD BE CRYING TONIGHT.
ACHIEVE
EVERYBODY SHOULD HAVE THIS LEVEL OF INVINCIBILITY.
"THIS ISN'T ABOUT WHAT YOU GET. IT'S ABOUT WHAT YOU GIVE."
IF I'M REALLY GONNA BE A SUPERHERO, I HAVE TO BE THE BEST I CAN BE.
ACHIEVE
Brittany Barnes
HEY.
HEY. LOST YOU TODAY. YOU ALRIGHT?
I SHOULD BE ASKING YOU THAT. IT GOT CRAZY AT THE SQUARE. THEY LOCK UP DR. DAVIS?
JUST THE OPPOSITE. HE STOPPED THE MADNESS.
SORRY I WAS SO HARD ON YOU ABOUT BEING LATE. JUST FEEL LIKE THINGS WON'T CHANGE UNLESS WE TAKE IT SERIOUSLY.
YOU'RE RIGHT.
SEE YOU AT SCHOOL TOMORROW?
YEP. GOOD NIGHT.

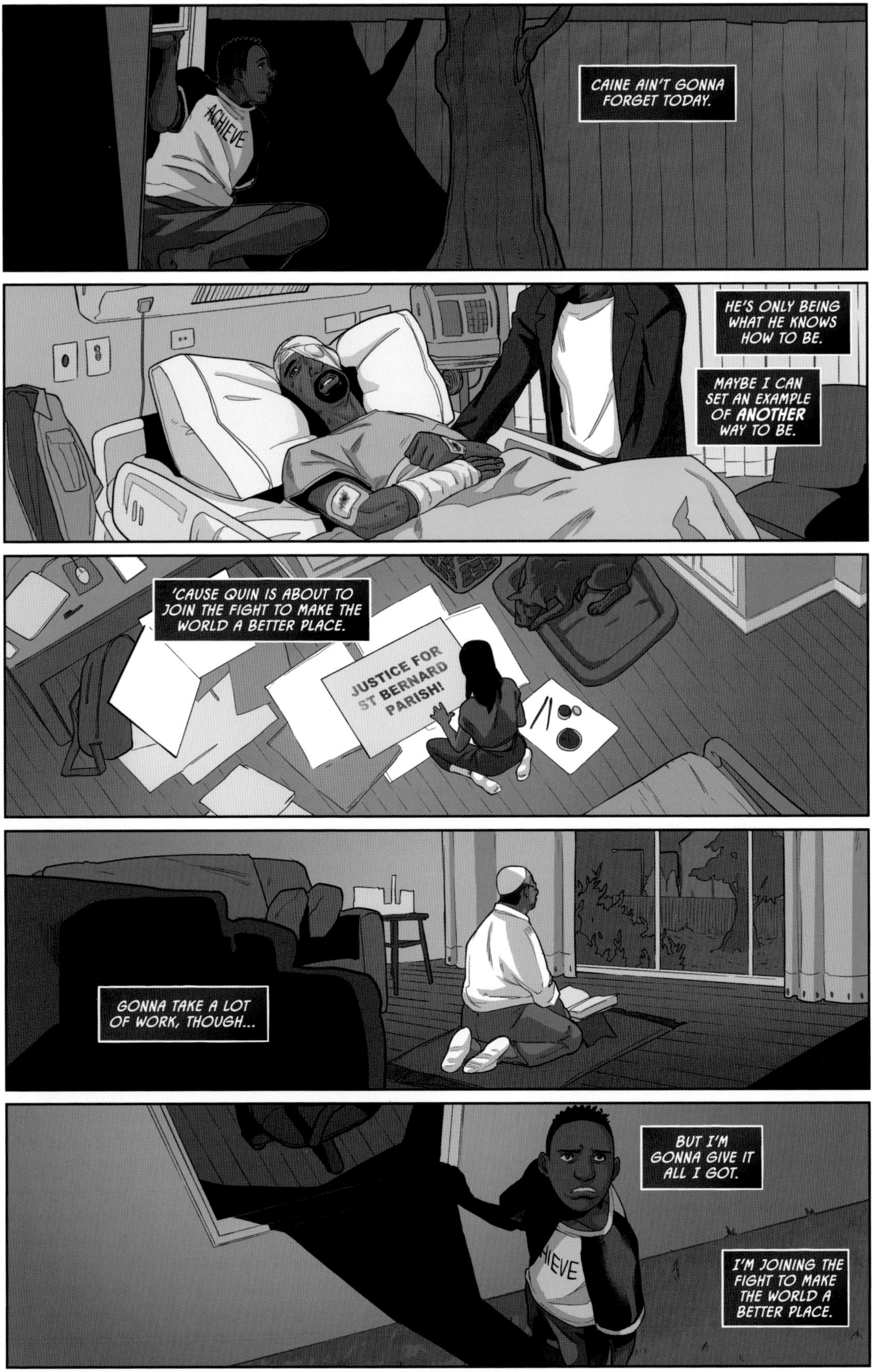
ACHIEVE
CAINE AIN'T GONNA FORGET TODAY.
HE'S ONLY BEING WHAT HE KNOWS HOW TO BE.
MAYBE I CAN SET AN EXAMPLE OF **ANOTHER** WAY TO BE.
'CAUSE QUIN IS ABOUT TO JOIN THE FIGHT TO MAKE THE WORLD A BETTER PLACE.
JUSTICE FOR ST BERNARD PARISH!
GONNA TAKE A LOT OF WORK, THOUGH...
BUT I'M GONNA GIVE IT ALL I GOT.
HIEVE
I'M JOINING THE FIGHT TO MAKE THE WORLD A BETTER PLACE.

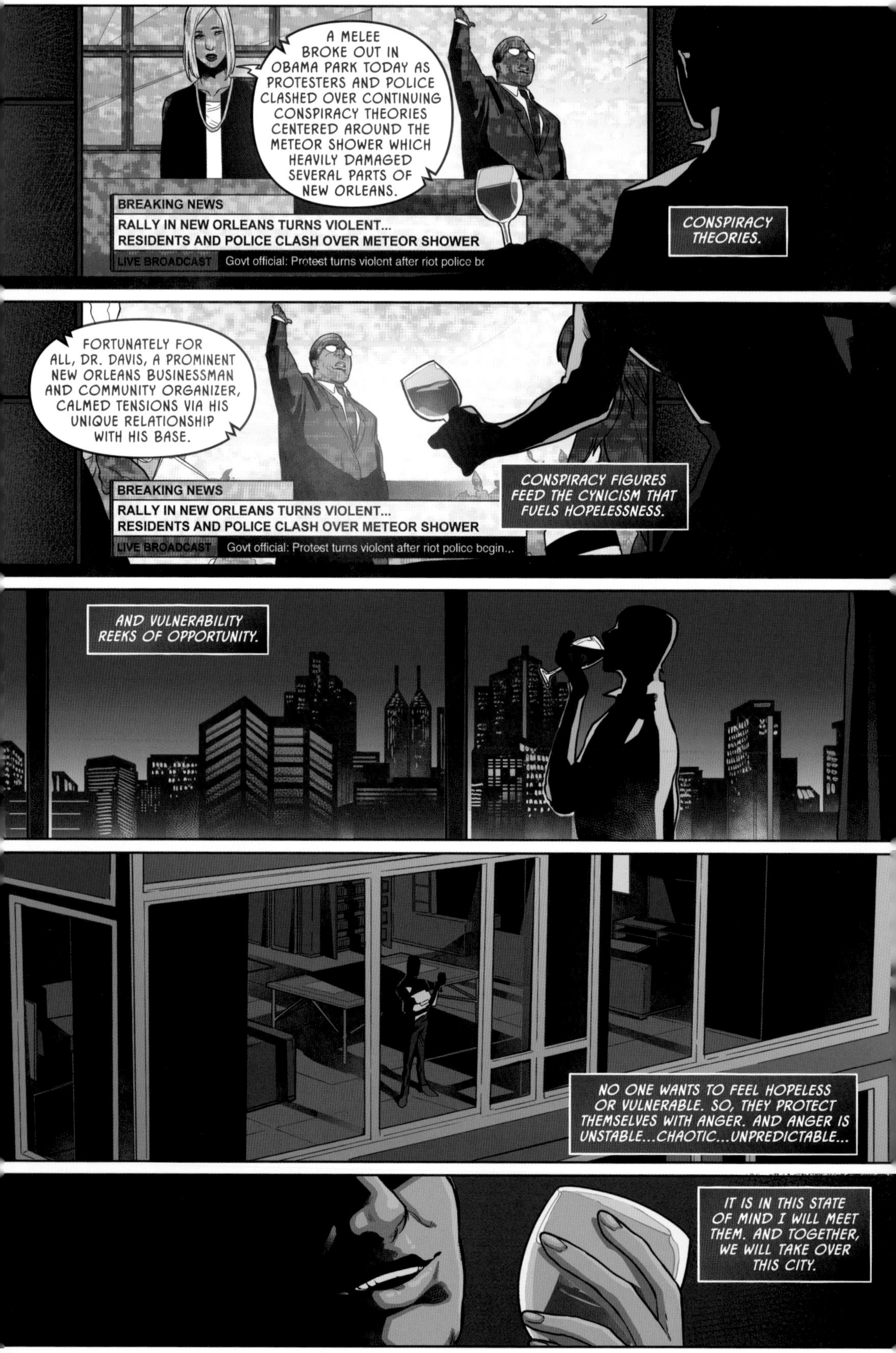
A MELEE BROKE OUT IN OBAMA PARK TODAY AS PROTESTERS AND POLICE CLASHED OVER CONTINUING CONSPIRACY THEORIES CENTERED AROUND THE METEOR SHOWER WHICH HEAVILY DAMAGED SEVERAL PARTS OF NEW ORLEANS.
BREAKING NEWS
RALLY IN NEW ORLEANS TURNS VIOLENT...
RESIDENTS AND POLICE CLASH OVER METEOR SHOWER
LIVE BROADCAST
Govt official: Protest turns violent after riot police be
CONSPIRACY THEORIES.
FORTUNATELY FOR ALL, DR. DAVIS, A PROMINENT NEW ORLEANS BUSINESSMAN AND COMMUNITY ORGANIZER, CALMED TENSIONS VIA HIS UNIQUE RELATIONSHIP WITH HIS BASE.
BREAKING NEWS
RALLY IN NEW ORLEANS TURNS VIOLENT...
RESIDENTS AND POLICE CLASH OVER METEOR SHOWER
LIVE BROADCAST
Govt official: Protest turns violent after riot police begin...
CONSPIRACY FIGURES FEED THE CYNICISM THAT FUELS HOPELESSNESS.
AND VULNERABILITY REEKS OF OPPORTUNITY.
NO ONE WANTS TO FEEL HOPELESS OR VULNERABLE. SO, THEY PROTECT THEMSELVES WITH ANGER. AND ANGER IS UNSTABLE...CHAOTIC...UNPREDICTABLE...
IT IS IN THIS STATE OF MIND I WILL MEET THEM. AND TOGETHER, WE WILL TAKE OVER THIS CITY.

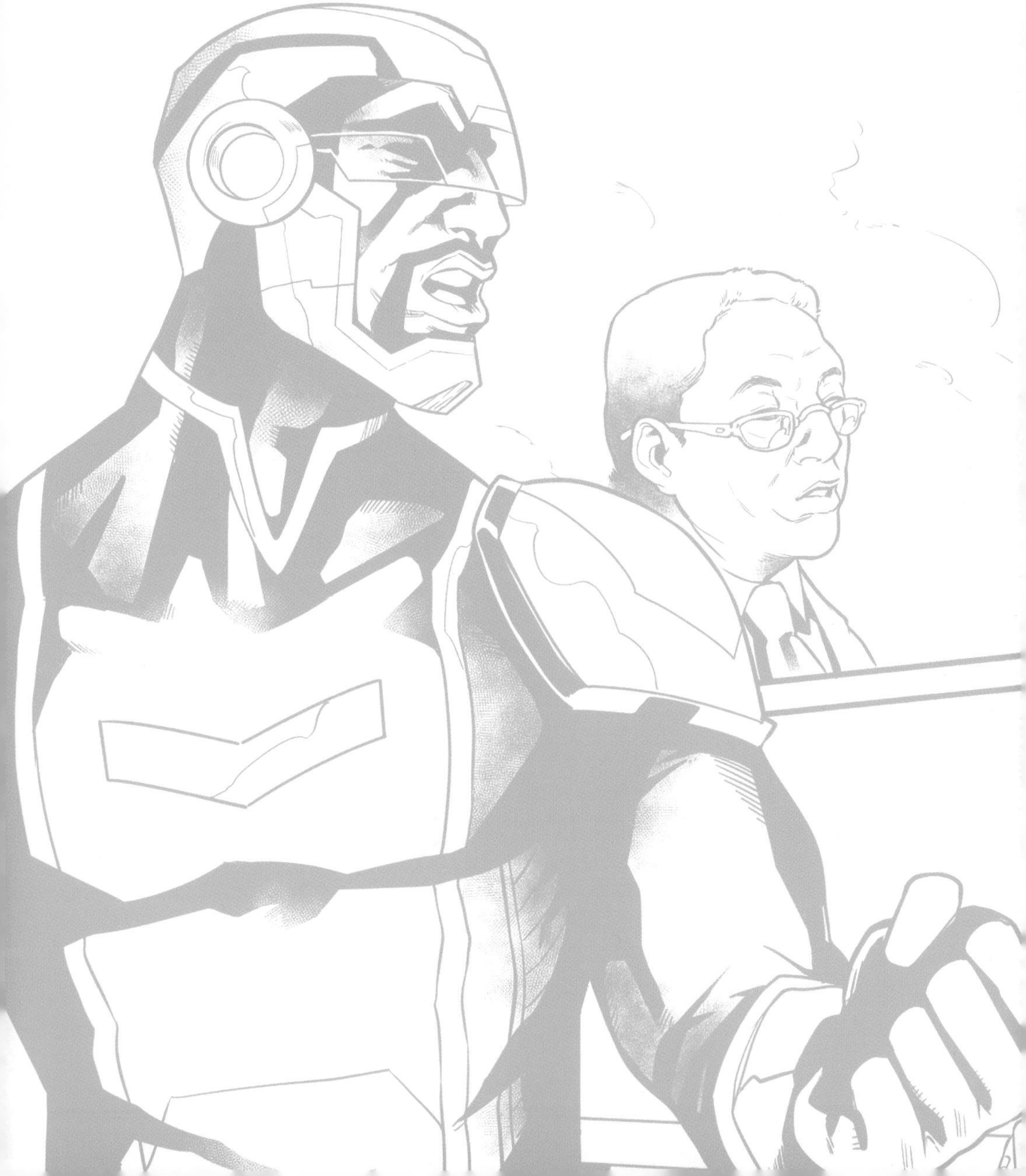

CHAPTER TWO

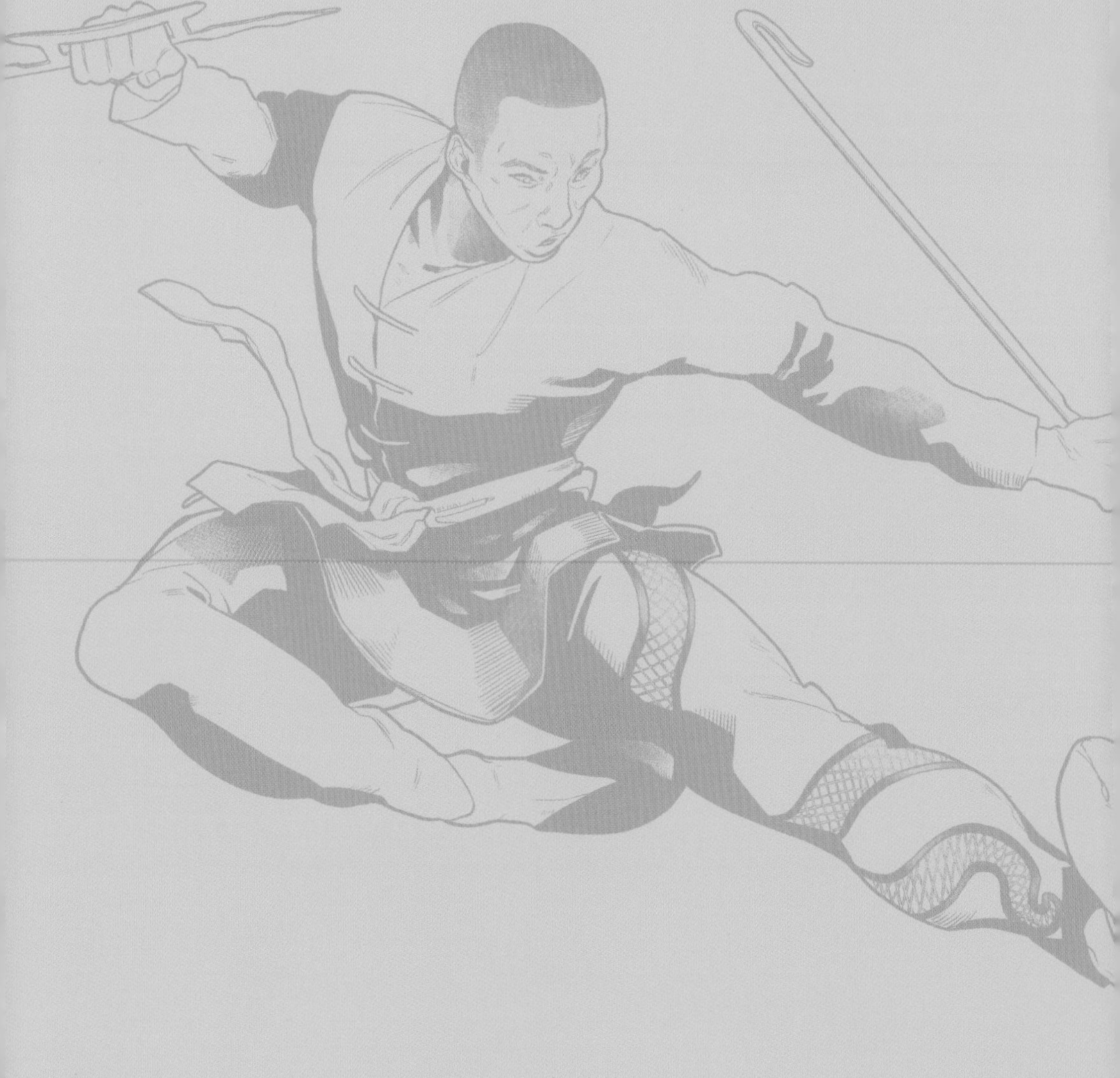

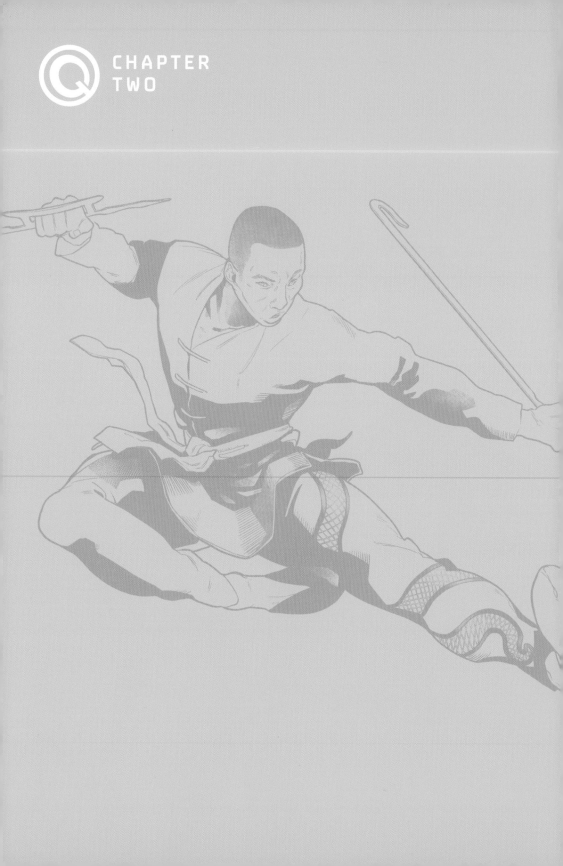

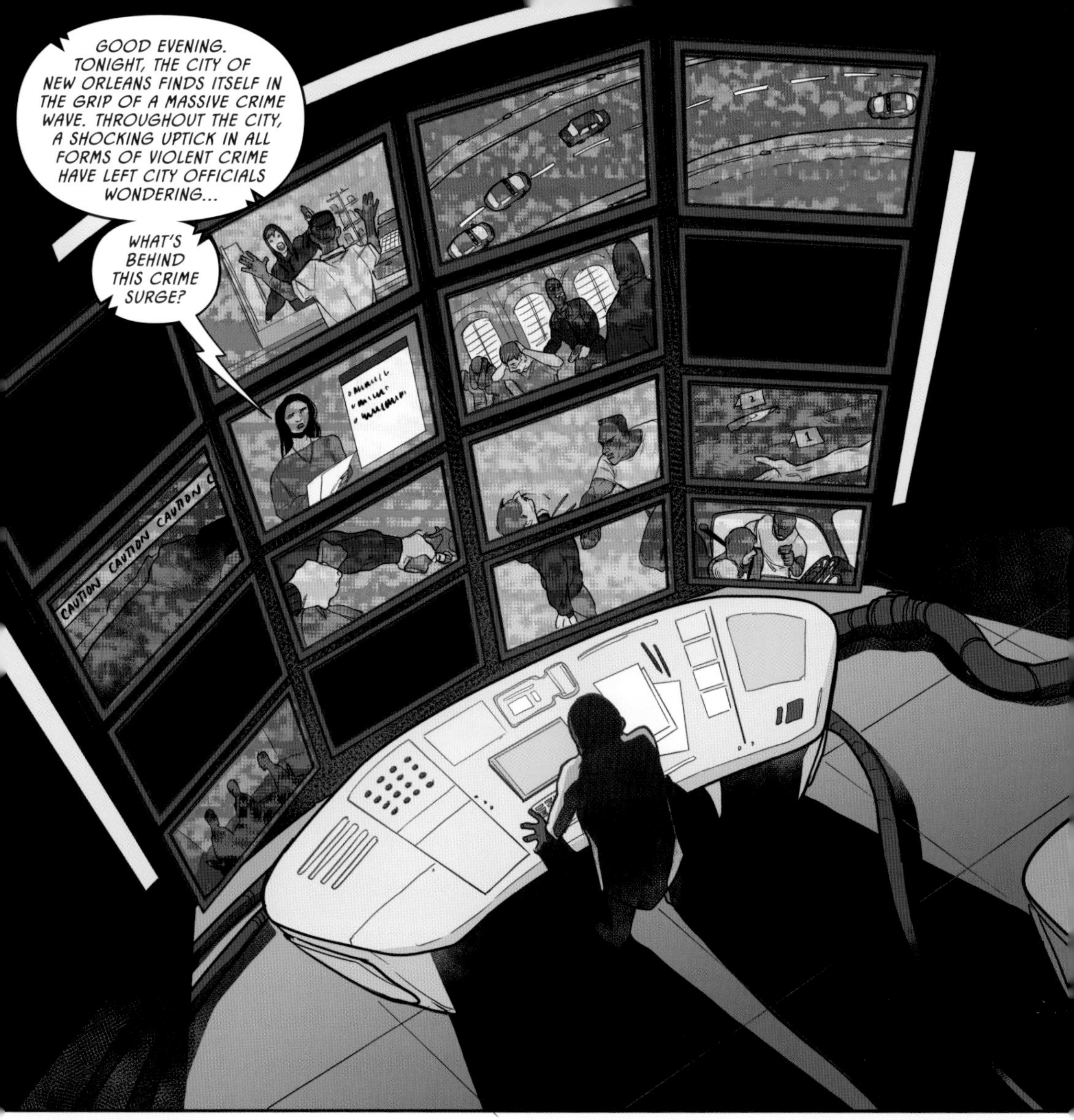
GOOD EVENING. TONIGHT, THE CITY OF NEW ORLEANS FINDS ITSELF IN THE GRIP OF A MASSIVE CRIME WAVE. THROUGHOUT THE CITY, A SHOCKING UPTICK IN ALL FORMS OF VIOLENT CRIME HAVE LEFT CITY OFFICIALS WONDERING...
WHAT'S BEHIND THIS CRIME SURGE?
CAUTION CAUTION CAUTION

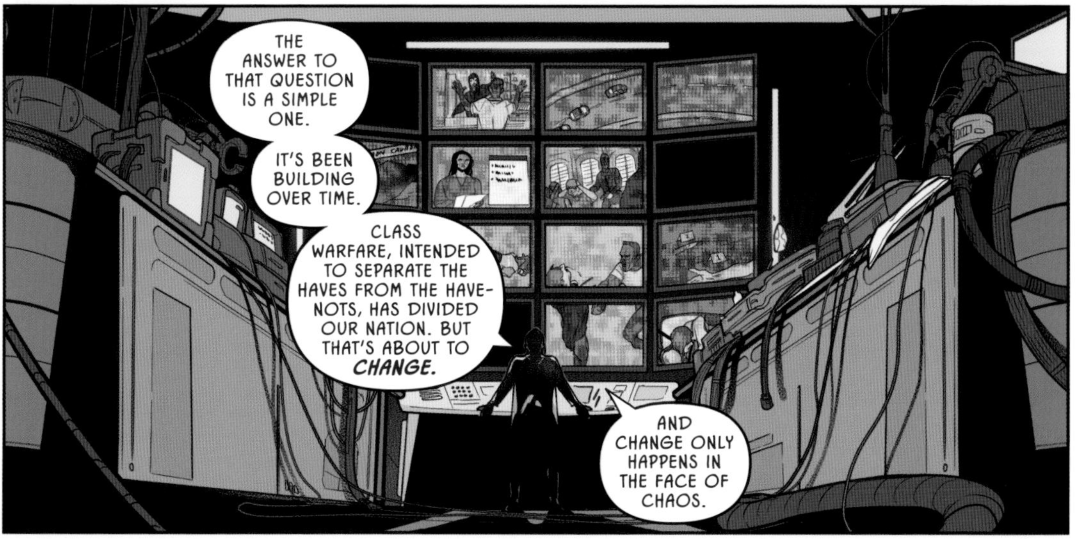
THE ANSWER TO THAT QUESTION IS A SIMPLE ONE.
IT'S BEEN BUILDING OVER TIME.
CLASS WARFARE, INTENDED TO SEPARATE THE HAVES FROM THE HAVE-NOTS, HAS DIVIDED OUR NATION. BUT THAT'S ABOUT TO **CHANGE.**
AND CHANGE ONLY HAPPENS IN THE FACE OF CHAOS.

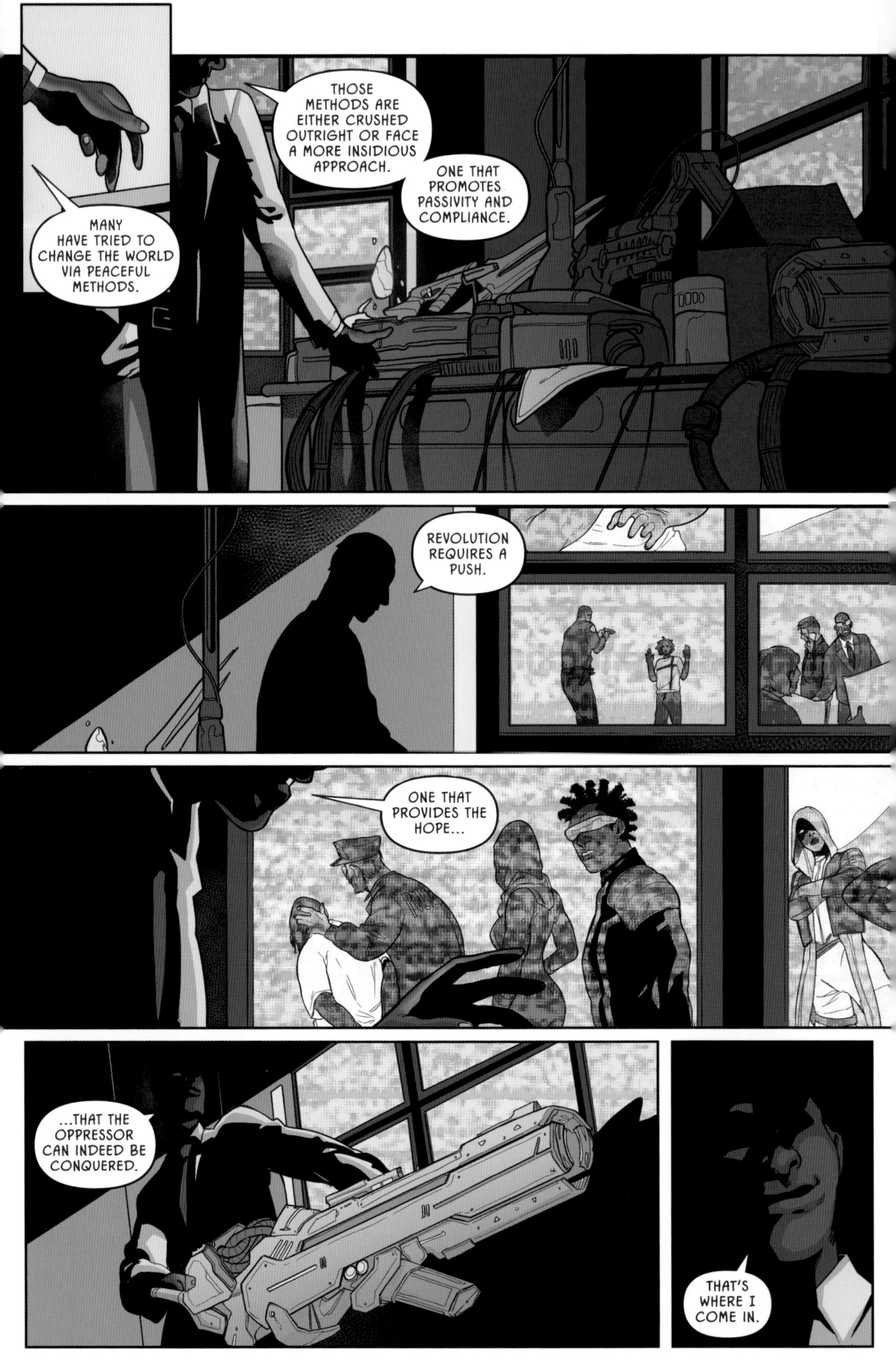
MANY HAVE TRIED TO CHANGE THE WORLD VIA PEACEFUL METHODS.
THOSE METHODS ARE EITHER CRUSHED OUTRIGHT OR FACE A MORE INSIDIOUS APPROACH.
ONE THAT PROMOTES PASSIVITY AND COMPLIANCE.
REVOLUTION REQUIRES A PUSH.
ONE THAT PROVIDES THE HOPE...
...THAT THE OPPRESSOR CAN INDEED BE CONQUERED.
THAT'S WHERE I COME IN.

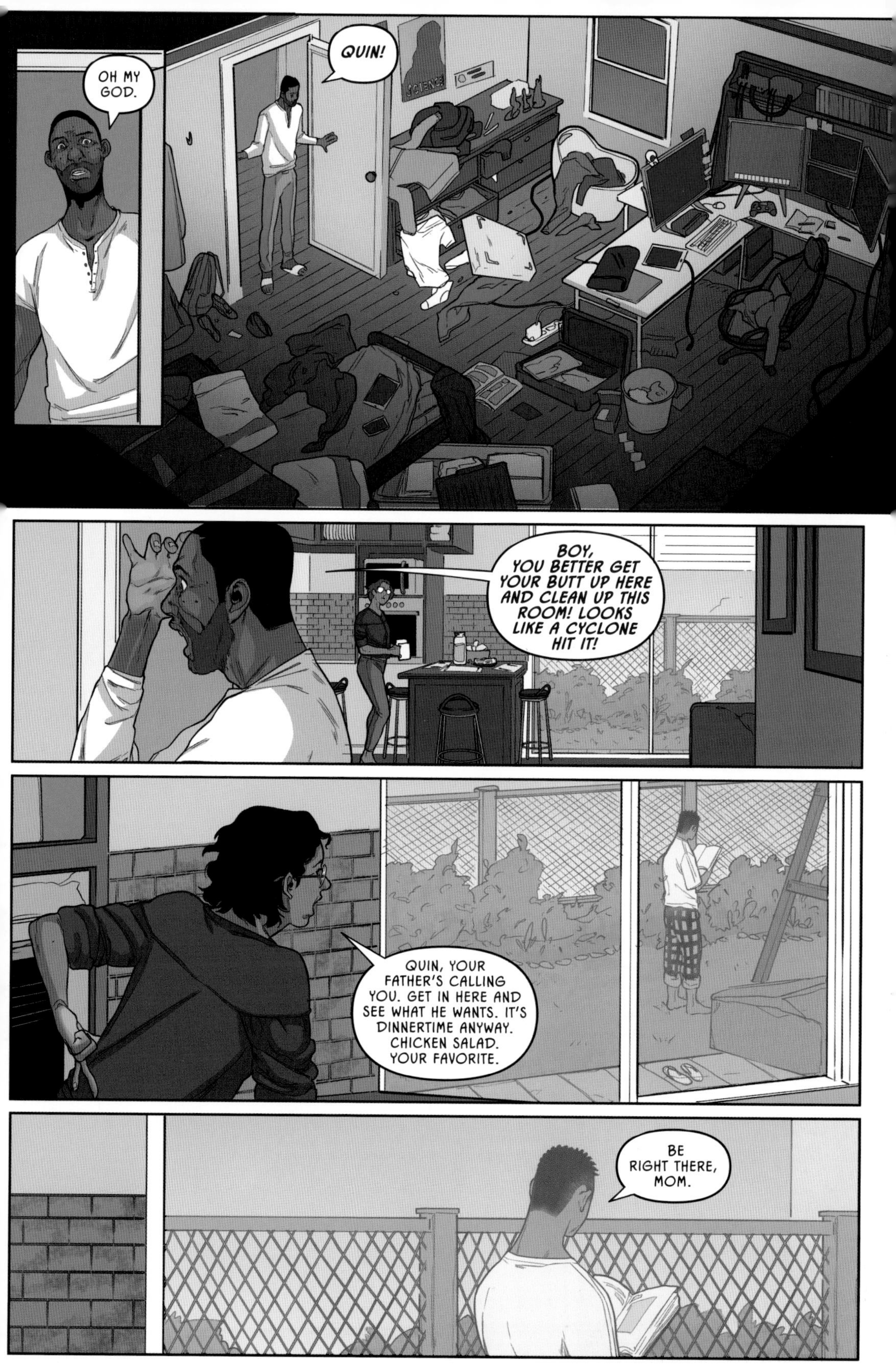
QUIN!
OH MY GOD.
BOY, YOU BETTER GET YOUR BUTT UP HERE AND CLEAN UP THIS ROOM! LOOKS LIKE A CYCLONE HIT IT!
QUIN, YOUR FATHER'S CALLING YOU. GET IN HERE AND SEE WHAT HE WANTS. IT'S DINNERTIME ANYWAY. CHICKEN SALAD. YOUR FAVORITE.
BE RIGHT THERE, MOM.

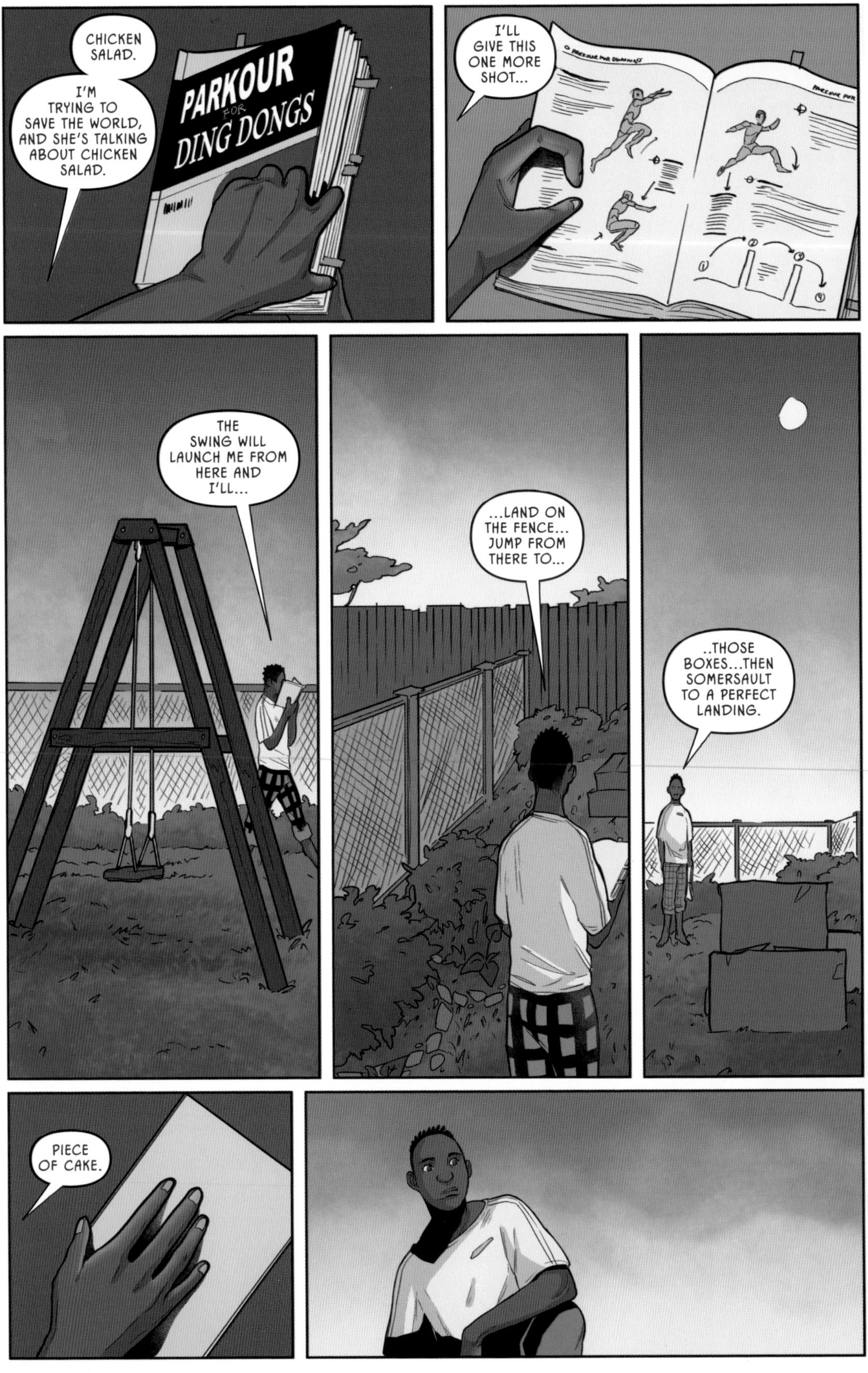
CHICKEN SALAD.
I'M TRYING TO SAVE THE WORLD, AND SHE'S TALKING ABOUT CHICKEN SALAD.
PARKOUR FOR DING DONGS
I'LL GIVE THIS ONE MORE SHOT...
THE SWING WILL LAUNCH ME FROM HERE AND I'LL...
...LAND ON THE FENCE... JUMP FROM THERE TO...
..THOSE BOXES...THEN SOMERSAULT TO A PERFECT LANDING.
PIECE OF CAKE.

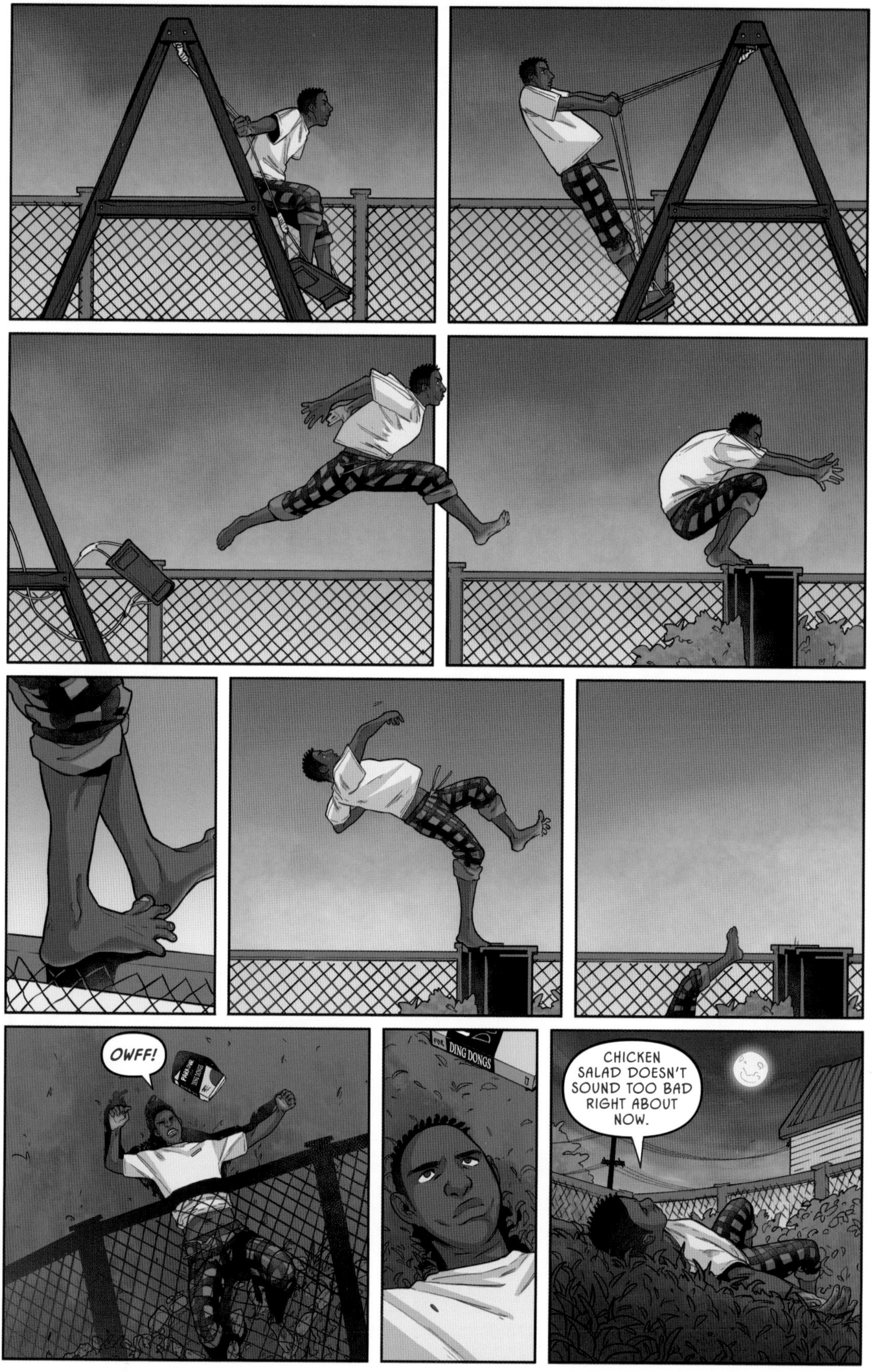
OWFF!
DING DONGS
CHICKEN SALAD DOESN'T SOUND TOO BAD RIGHT ABOUT NOW.

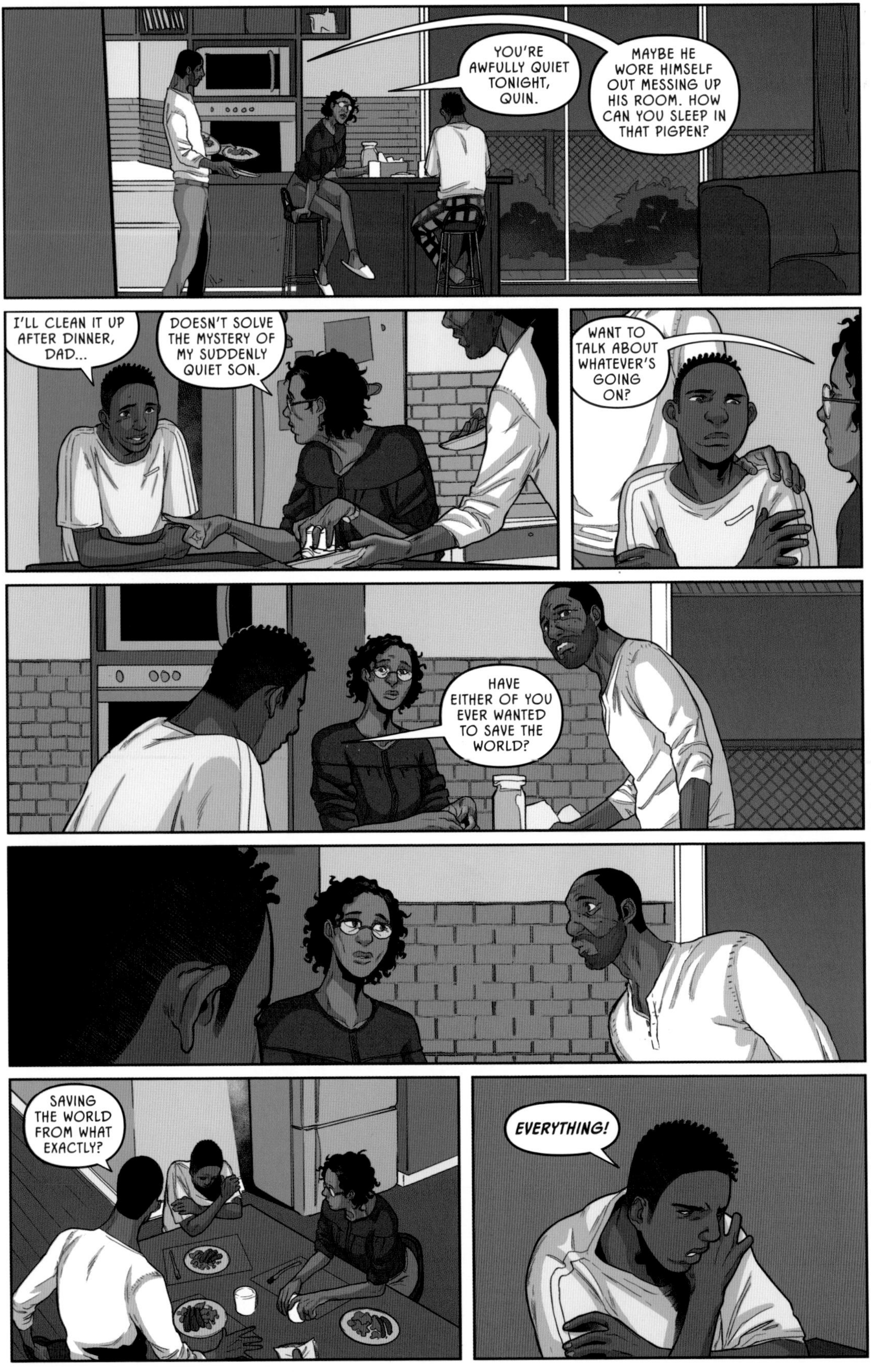
YOU'RE AWFULLY QUIET TONIGHT, QUIN.
MAYBE HE WORE HIMSELF OUT MESSING UP HIS ROOM. HOW CAN YOU SLEEP IN THAT PIGPEN?
I'LL CLEAN IT UP AFTER DINNER, DAD...
DOESN'T SOLVE THE MYSTERY OF MY SUDDENLY QUIET SON.
WANT TO TALK ABOUT WHATEVER'S GOING ON?
HAVE EITHER OF YOU EVER WANTED TO SAVE THE WORLD?
SAVING THE WORLD FROM WHAT EXACTLY?
EVERYTHING!

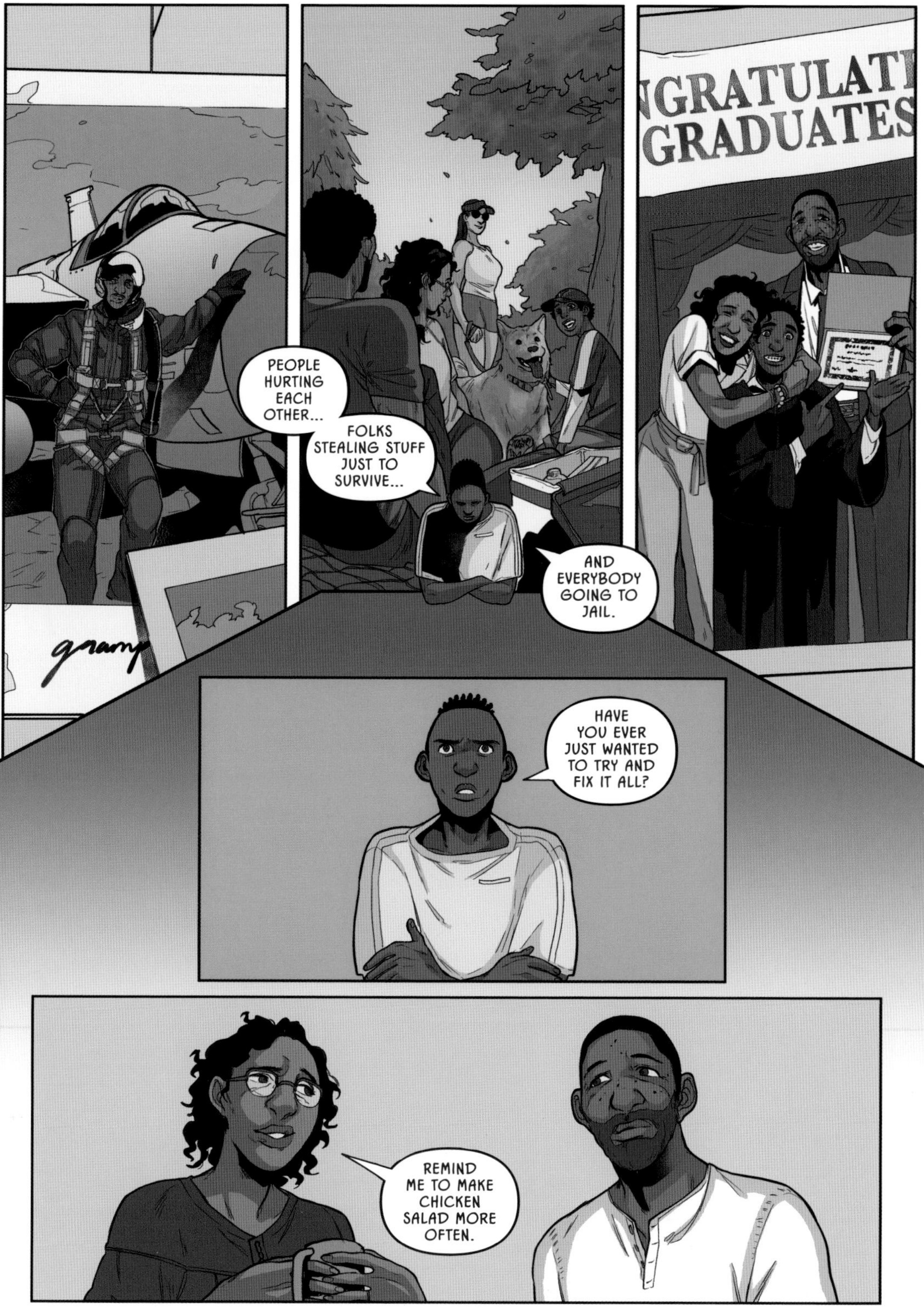
NGRATULATE
GRADUATES
grampa
PEOPLE HURTING EACH OTHER...
FOLKS STEALING STUFF JUST TO SURVIVE...
AND EVERYBODY GOING TO JAIL.
HAVE YOU EVER JUST WANTED TO TRY AND FIX IT ALL?
REMIND ME TO MAKE CHICKEN SALAD MORE OFTEN.

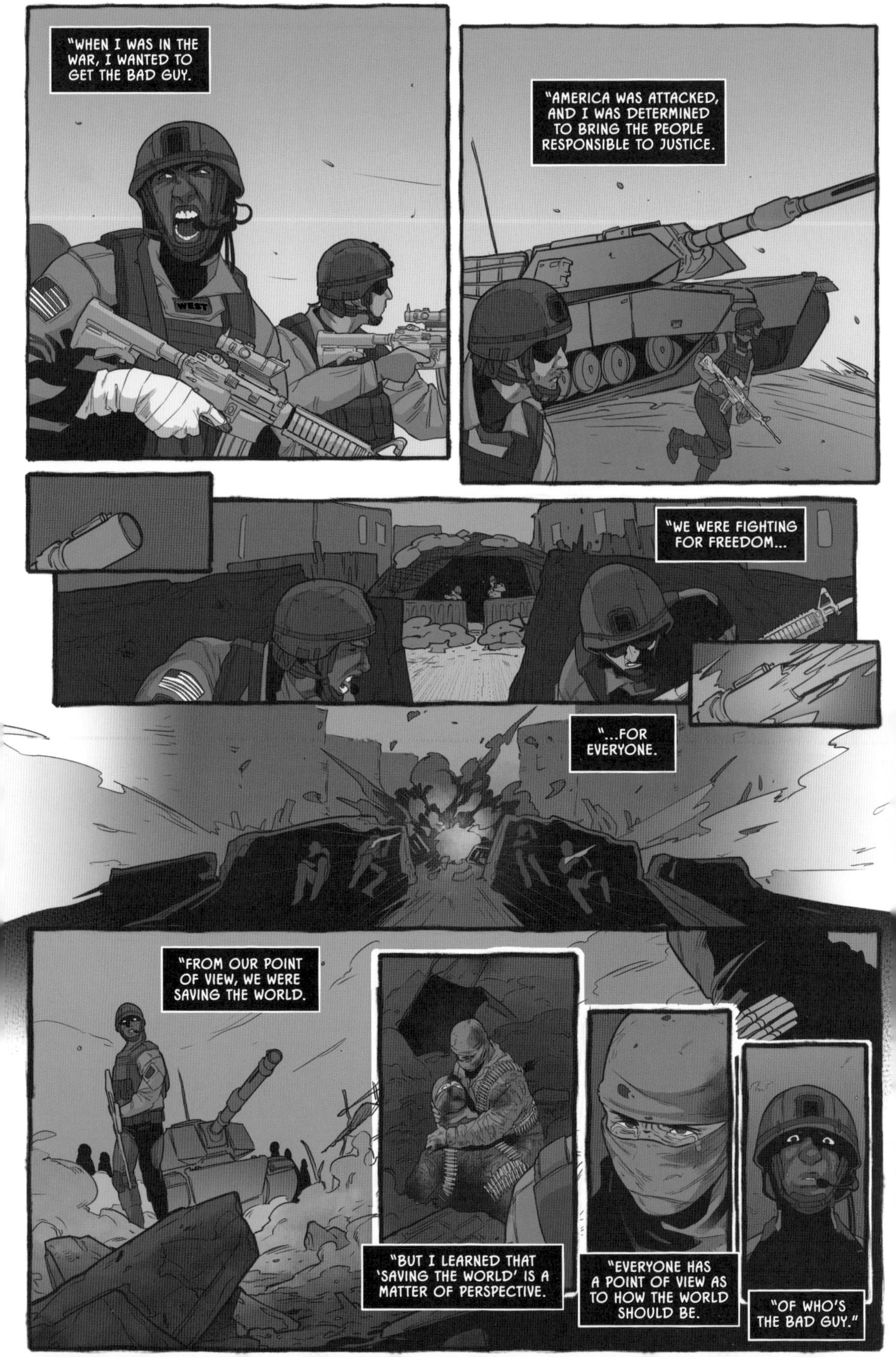
"WHEN I WAS IN THE WAR, I WANTED TO GET THE BAD GUY.
WEST
"AMERICA WAS ATTACKED, AND I WAS DETERMINED TO BRING THE PEOPLE RESPONSIBLE TO JUSTICE.
"WE WERE FIGHTING FOR FREEDOM...
"...FOR EVERYONE.
"FROM OUR POINT OF VIEW, WE WERE SAVING THE WORLD.
"BUT I LEARNED THAT 'SAVING THE WORLD' IS A MATTER OF PERSPECTIVE.
"EVERYONE HAS A POINT OF VIEW AS TO HOW THE WORLD SHOULD BE.
"OF WHO'S THE BAD GUY."

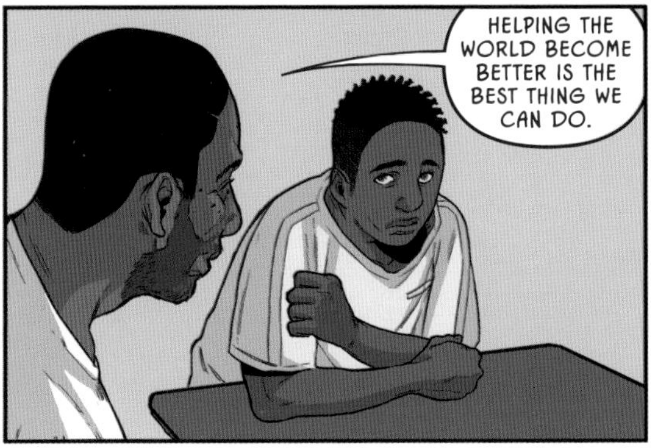
HELPING THE WORLD BECOME BETTER IS THE BEST THING WE CAN DO.

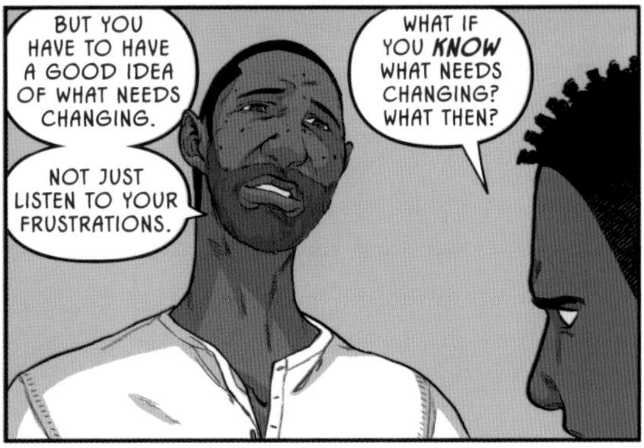
BUT YOU HAVE TO HAVE A GOOD IDEA OF WHAT NEEDS CHANGING.
NOT JUST LISTEN TO YOUR FRUSTRATIONS.
WHAT IF YOU **KNOW** WHAT NEEDS CHANGING? WHAT THEN?

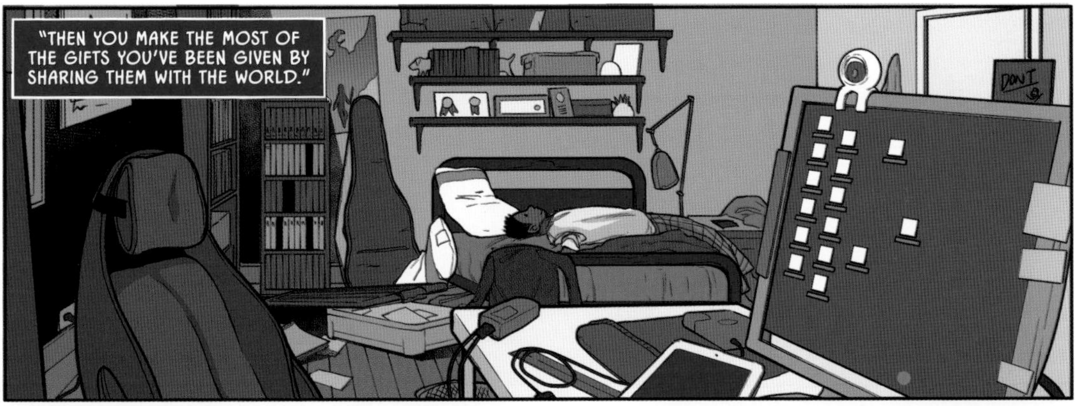
"THEN YOU MAKE THE MOST OF THE GIFTS YOU'VE BEEN GIVEN BY SHARING THEM WITH THE WORLD."

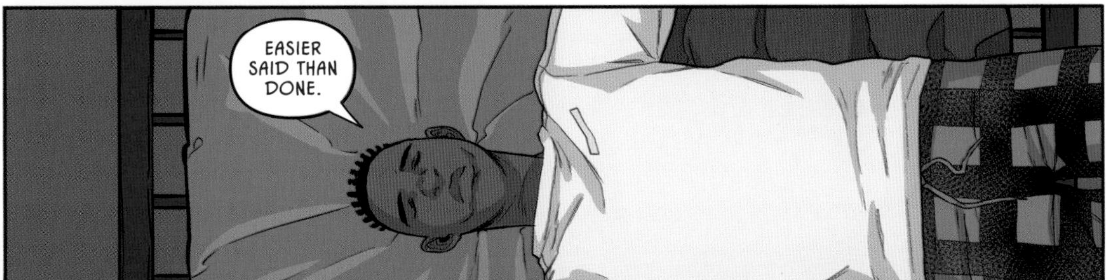
EASIER SAID THAN DONE.

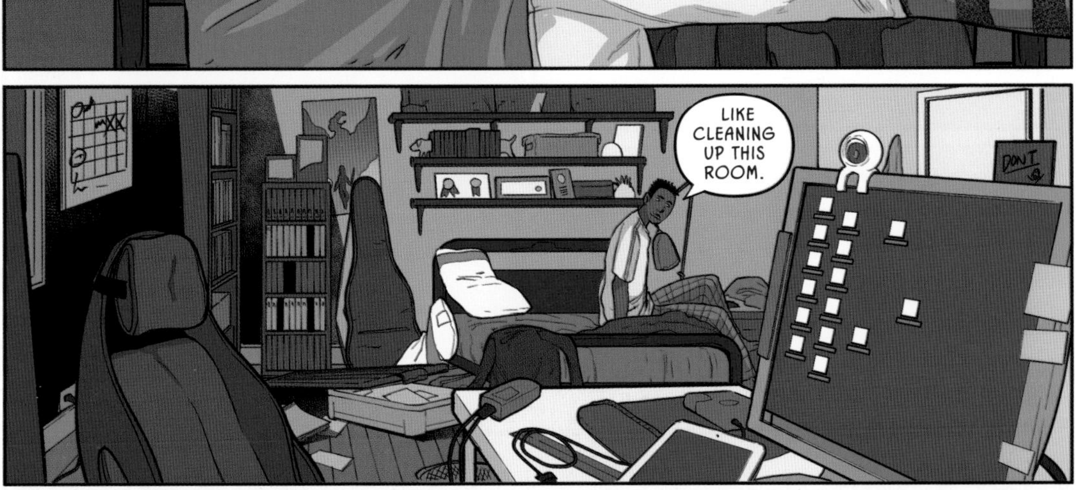
LIKE CLEANING UP THIS ROOM.

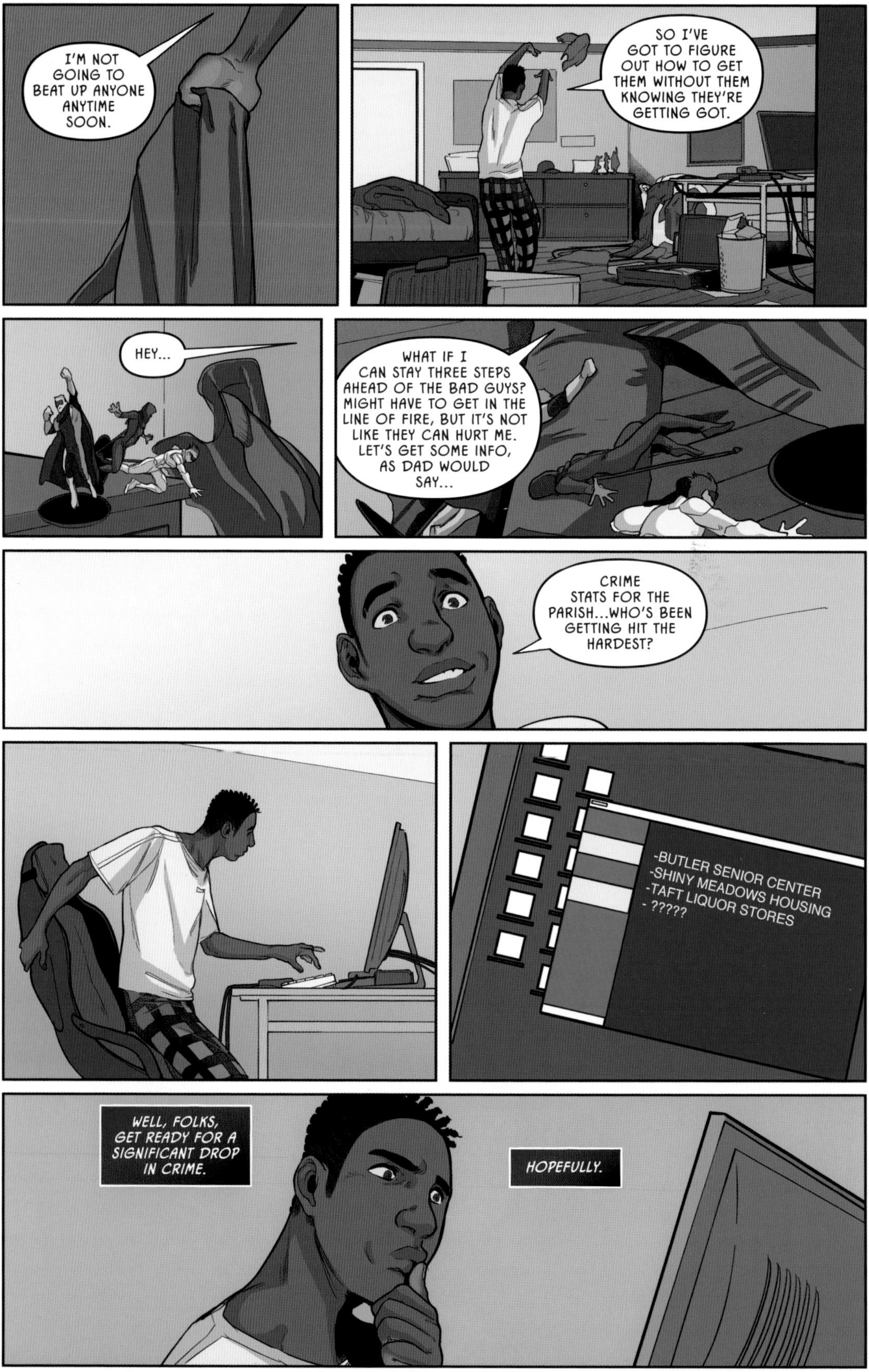
I'M NOT GOING TO BEAT UP ANYONE ANYTIME SOON.
SO I'VE GOT TO FIGURE OUT HOW TO GET THEM WITHOUT THEM KNOWING THEY'RE GETTING GOT.
HEY...
WHAT IF I CAN STAY THREE STEPS AHEAD OF THE BAD GUYS? MIGHT HAVE TO GET IN THE LINE OF FIRE, BUT IT'S NOT LIKE THEY CAN HURT ME. LET'S GET SOME INFO, AS DAD WOULD SAY...
CRIME STATS FOR THE PARISH...WHO'S BEEN GETTING HIT THE HARDEST?
-BUTLER SENIOR CENTER
-SHINY MEADOWS HOUSING
-TAFT LIQUOR STORES
- ?????
WELL, FOLKS, GET READY FOR A SIGNIFICANT DROP IN CRIME.
HOPEFULLY.

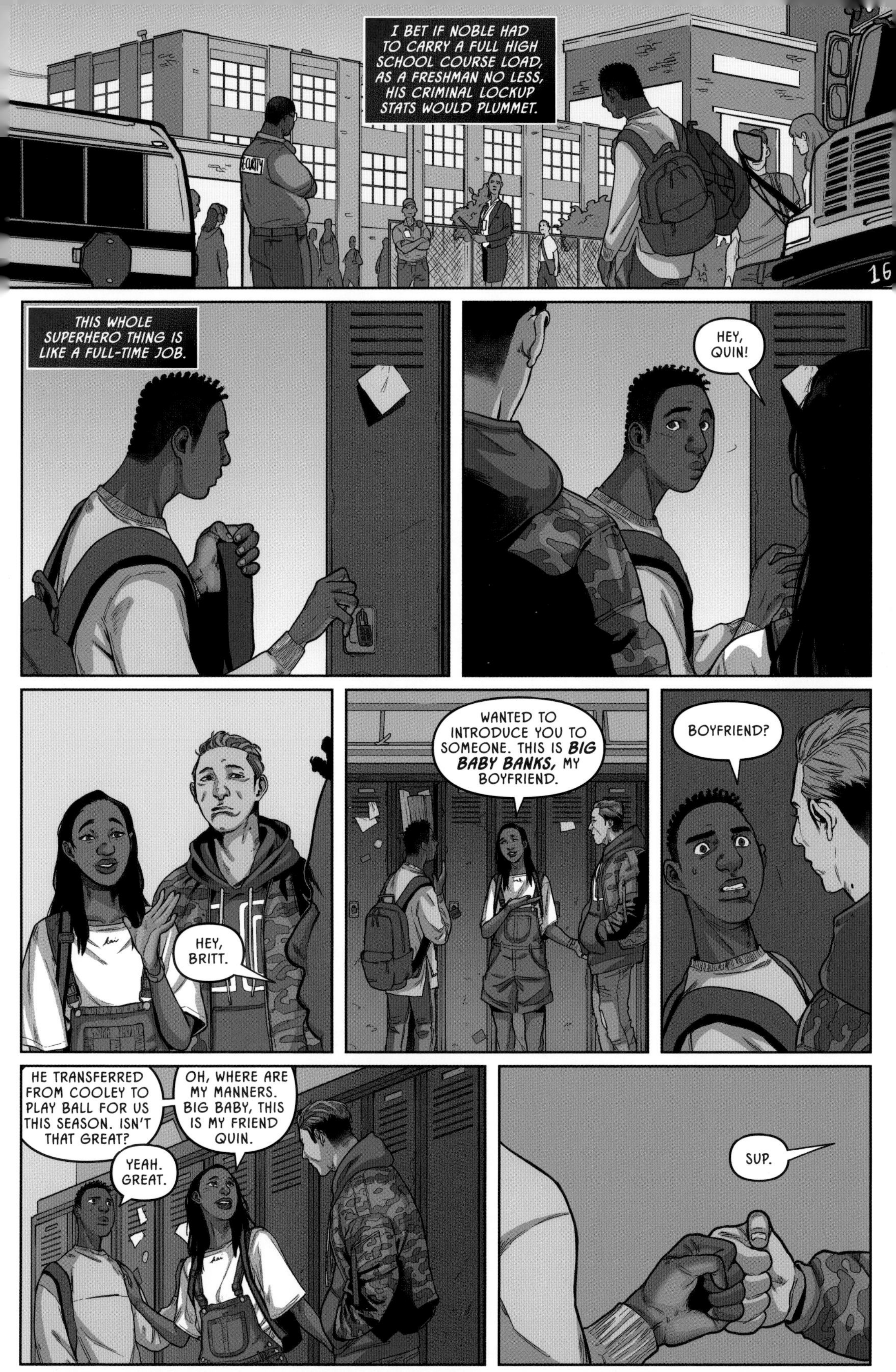
I BET IF NOBLE HAD TO CARRY A FULL HIGH SCHOOL COURSE LOAD, AS A FRESHMAN NO LESS, HIS CRIMINAL LOCKUP STATS WOULD PLUMMET.
SECURITY
THIS WHOLE SUPERHERO THING IS LIKE A FULL-TIME JOB.
HEY, QUIN!
HEY, BRITT.
WANTED TO INTRODUCE YOU TO SOMEONE. THIS IS **BIG BABY BANKS,** MY BOYFRIEND.
BOYFRIEND?
HE TRANSFERRED FROM COOLEY TO PLAY BALL FOR US THIS SEASON. ISN'T THAT GREAT?
OH, WHERE ARE MY MANNERS. BIG BABY, THIS IS MY FRIEND QUIN.
YEAH. GREAT.
SUP.

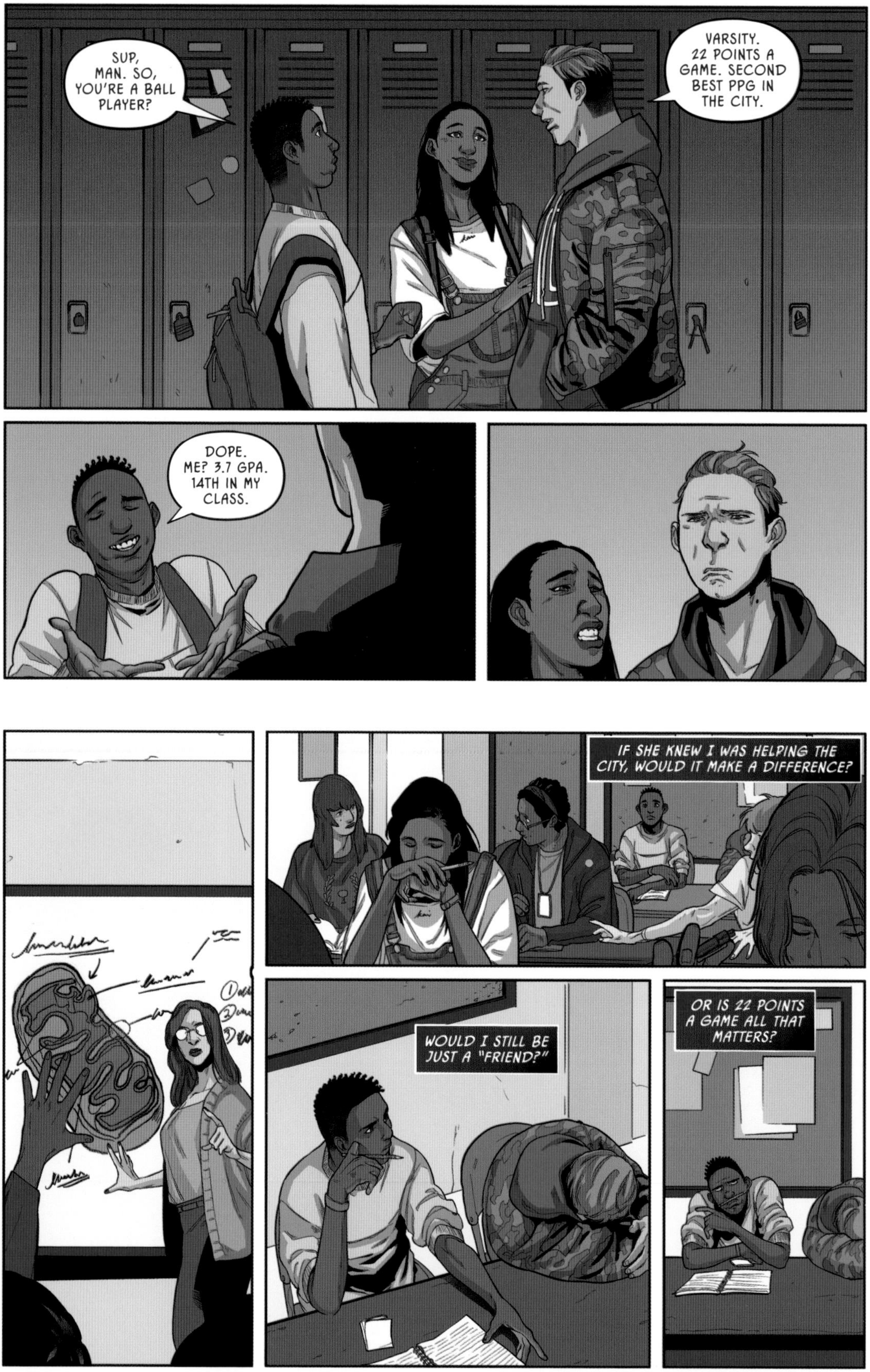
SUP, MAN. SO, YOU'RE A BALL PLAYER?
VARSITY. 22 POINTS A GAME. SECOND BEST PPG IN THE CITY.
DOPE. ME? 3.7 GPA. 14TH IN MY CLASS.
IF SHE KNEW I WAS HELPING THE CITY, WOULD IT MAKE A DIFFERENCE?
WOULD I STILL BE JUST A "FRIEND?"
OR IS 22 POINTS A GAME ALL THAT MATTERS?

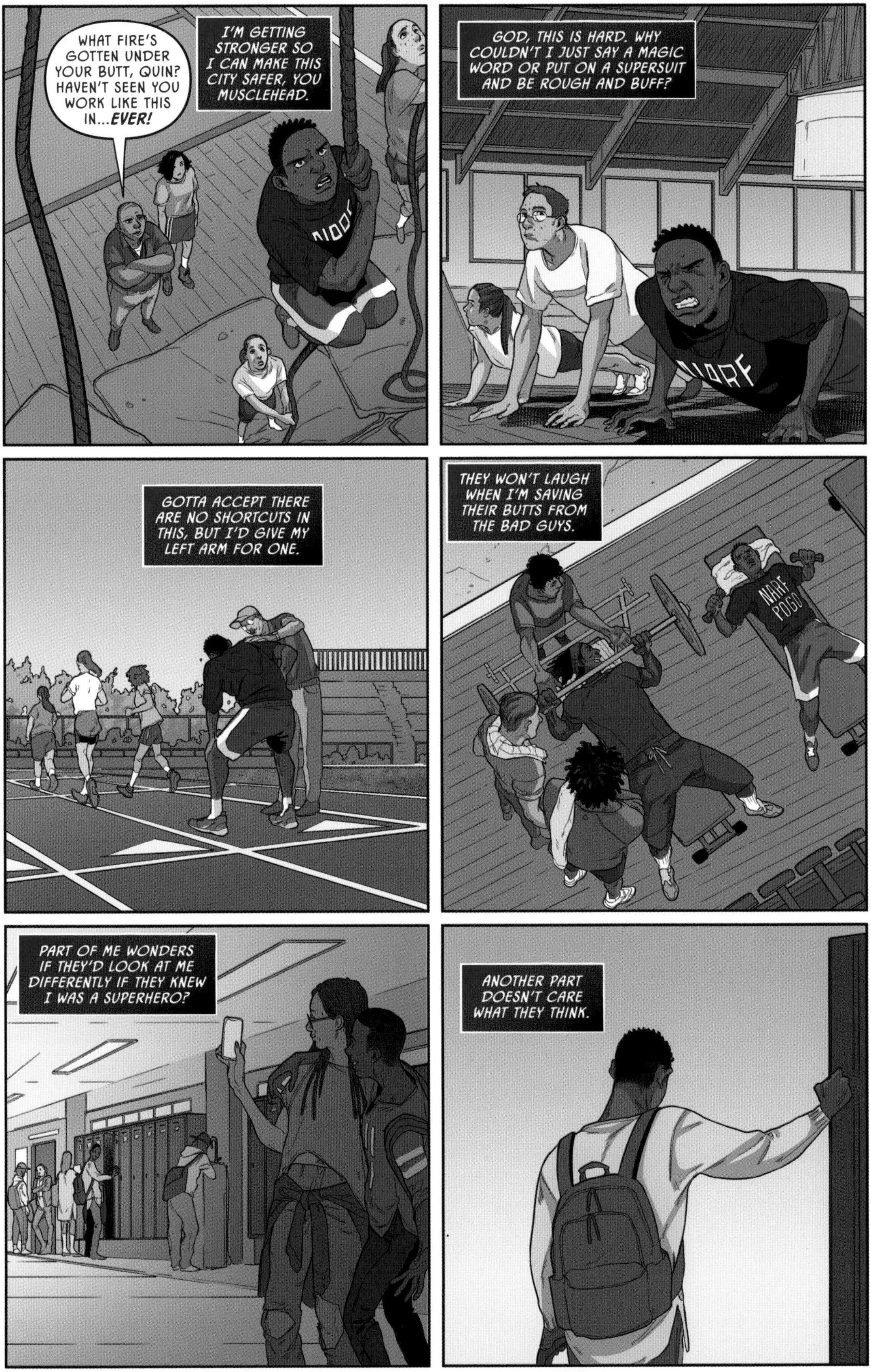
WHAT FIRE'S GOTTEN UNDER YOUR BUTT, QUIN? HAVEN'T SEEN YOU WORK LIKE THIS IN...EVER!
I'M GETTING STRONGER SO I CAN MAKE THIS CITY SAFER, YOU MUSCLEHEAD.
GOD, THIS IS HARD. WHY COULDN'T I JUST SAY A MAGIC WORD OR PUT ON A SUPERSUIT AND BE ROUGH AND BUFF?
NARF
GOTTA ACCEPT THERE ARE NO SHORTCUTS IN THIS, BUT I'D GIVE MY LEFT ARM FOR ONE.
THEY WON'T LAUGH WHEN I'M SAVING THEIR BUTTS FROM THE BAD GUYS.
NARF POGO
PART OF ME WONDERS IF THEY'D LOOK AT ME DIFFERENTLY IF THEY KNEW I WAS A SUPERHERO?
ANOTHER PART DOESN'T CARE WHAT THEY THINK.

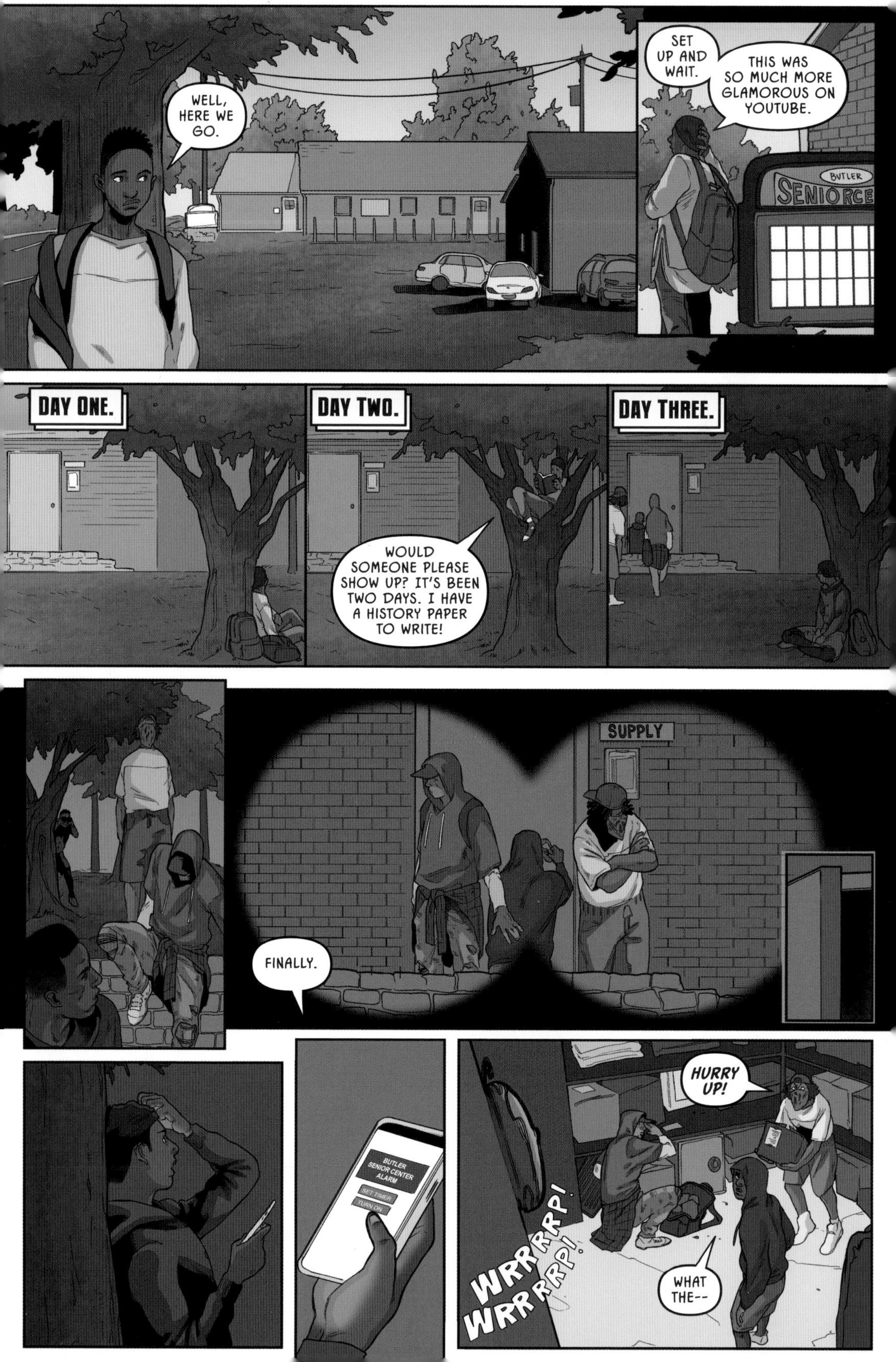
WELL, HERE WE GO.
SET UP AND WAIT.
THIS WAS SO MUCH MORE GLAMOROUS ON YOUTUBE.
BUTLER SENIOR CE
DAY ONE.
DAY TWO.
WOULD SOMEONE PLEASE SHOW UP? IT'S BEEN TWO DAYS. I HAVE A HISTORY PAPER TO WRITE!
DAY THREE.
SUPPLY
FINALLY.
BUTLER SENIOR CENTER ALARM
SET TIMER
TURN ON
HURRY UP!
WRRRRRP! WRRRRRP!
WHAT THE--

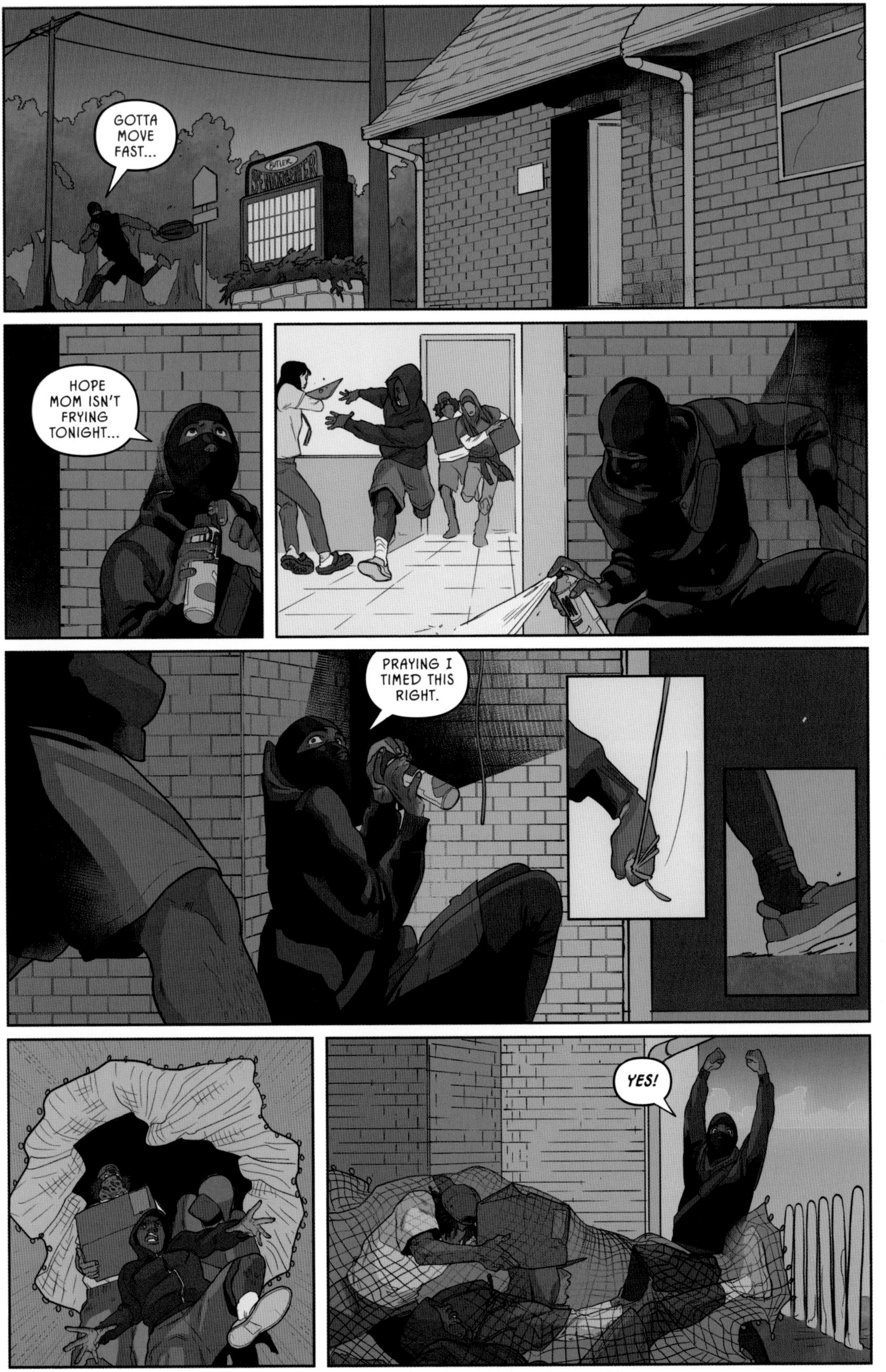
GOTTA MOVE FAST...
HOPE MOM ISN'T FRYING TONIGHT...
PRAYING I TIMED THIS RIGHT.
YES!

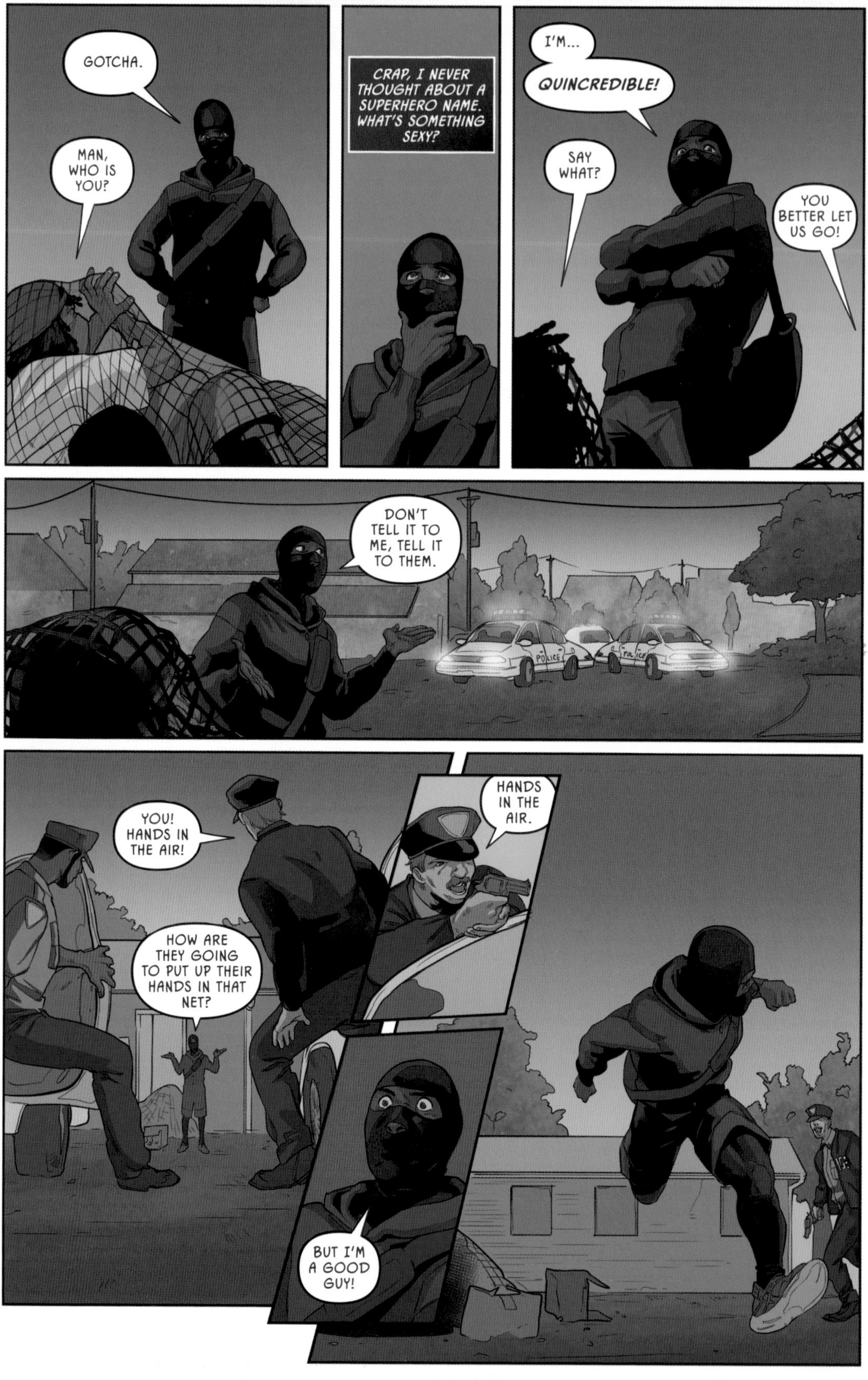
GOTCHA.
MAN, WHO IS YOU?
CRAP, I NEVER THOUGHT ABOUT A SUPERHERO NAME. WHAT'S SOMETHING SEXY?
I'M...
QUINCREDIBLE!
SAY WHAT?
YOU BETTER LET US GO!
DON'T TELL IT TO ME, TELL IT TO THEM.
POLICE
POLICE
YOU! HANDS IN THE AIR!
HOW ARE THEY GOING TO PUT UP THEIR HANDS IN THAT NET?
HANDS IN THE AIR.
BUT I'M A GOOD GUY!

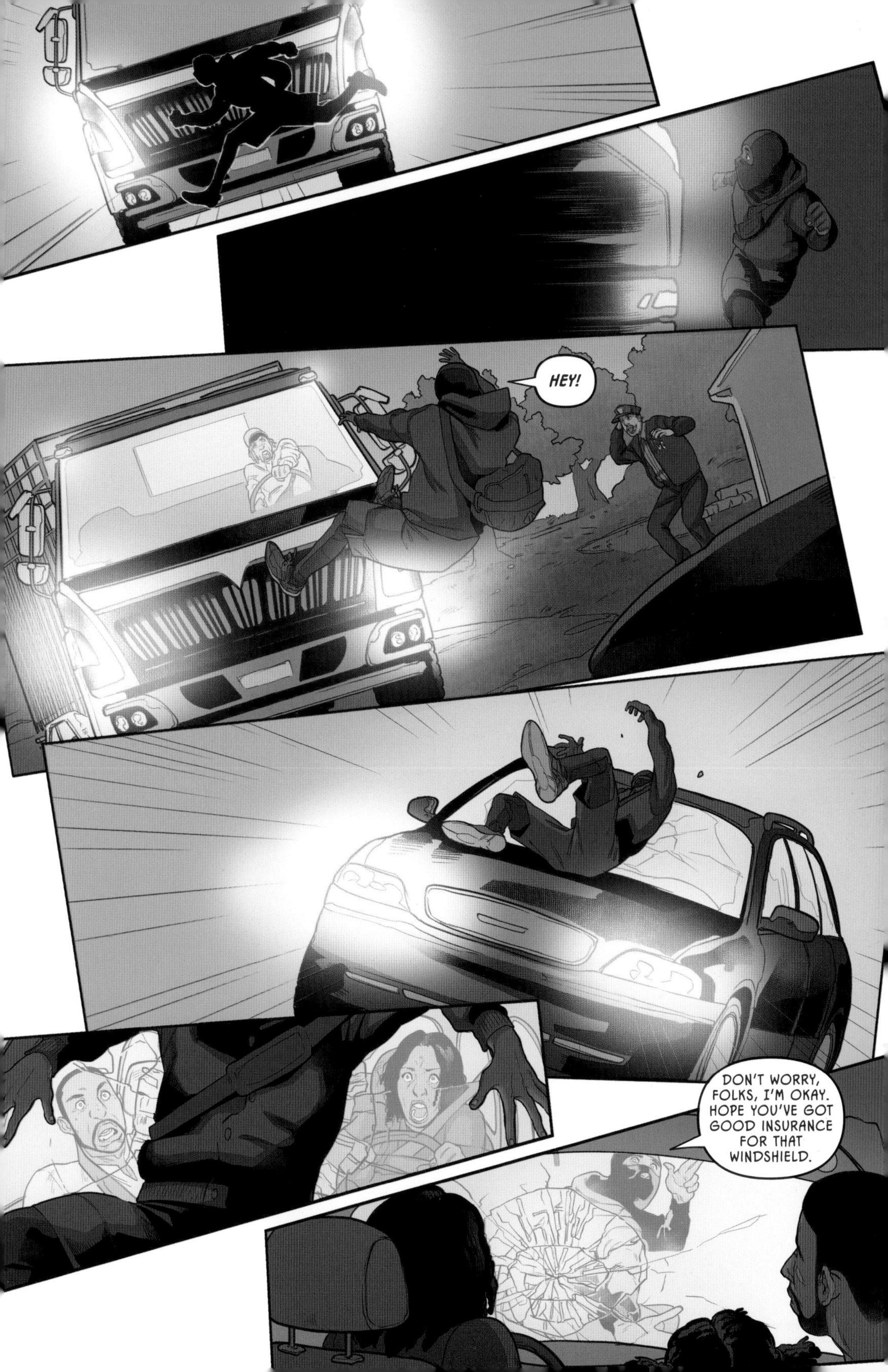
HEY!
DON'T WORRY, FOLKS, I'M OKAY. HOPE YOU'VE GOT GOOD INSURANCE FOR THAT WINDSHIELD.

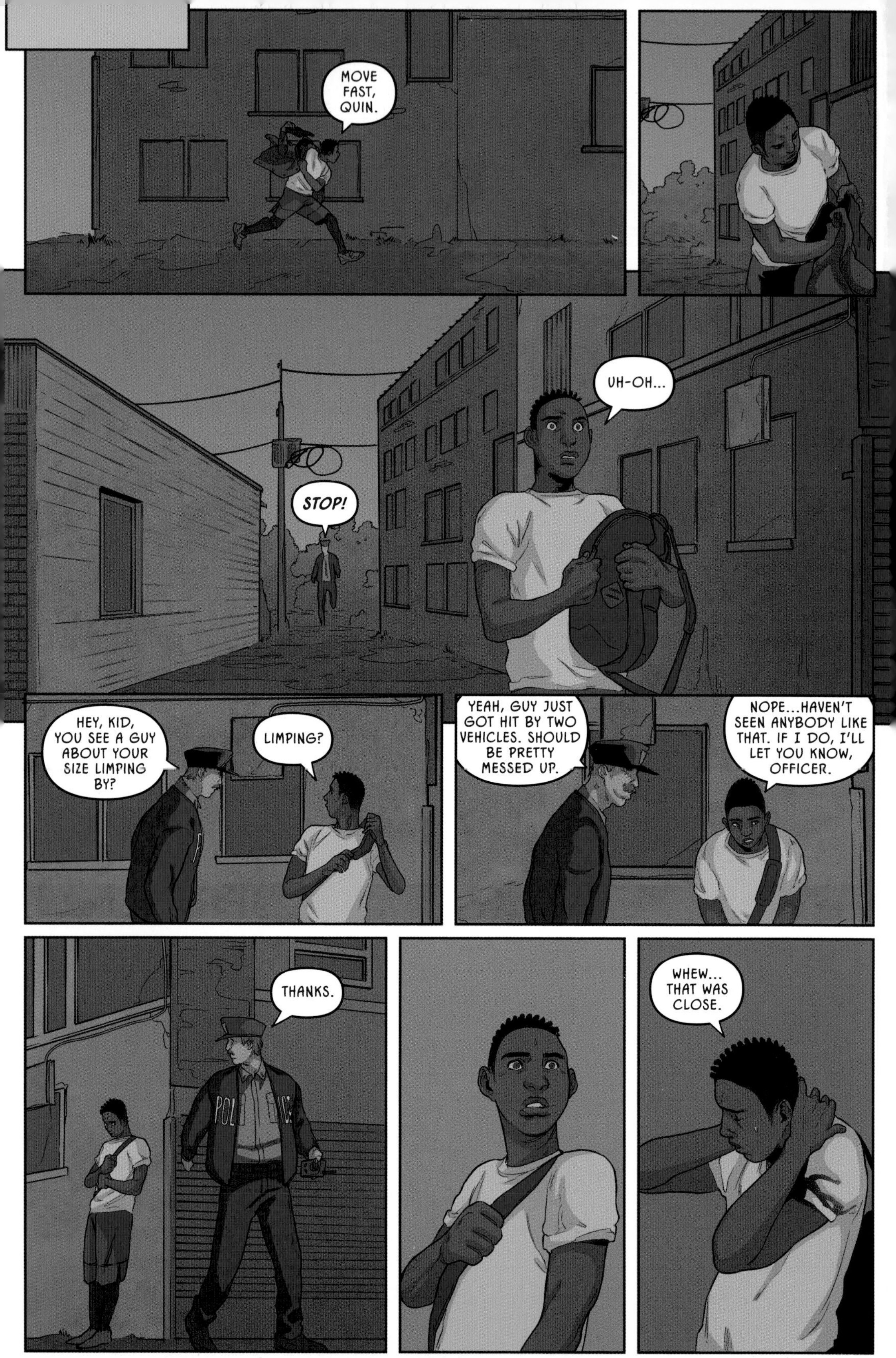
MOVE FAST, QUIN.
UH-OH...
STOP!
HEY, KID, YOU SEE A GUY ABOUT YOUR SIZE LIMPING BY?
LIMPING?
YEAH, GUY JUST GOT HIT BY TWO VEHICLES. SHOULD BE PRETTY MESSED UP.
NOPE...HAVEN'T SEEN ANYBODY LIKE THAT. IF I DO, I'LL LET YOU KNOW, OFFICER.
THANKS.
WHEW... THAT WAS CLOSE.

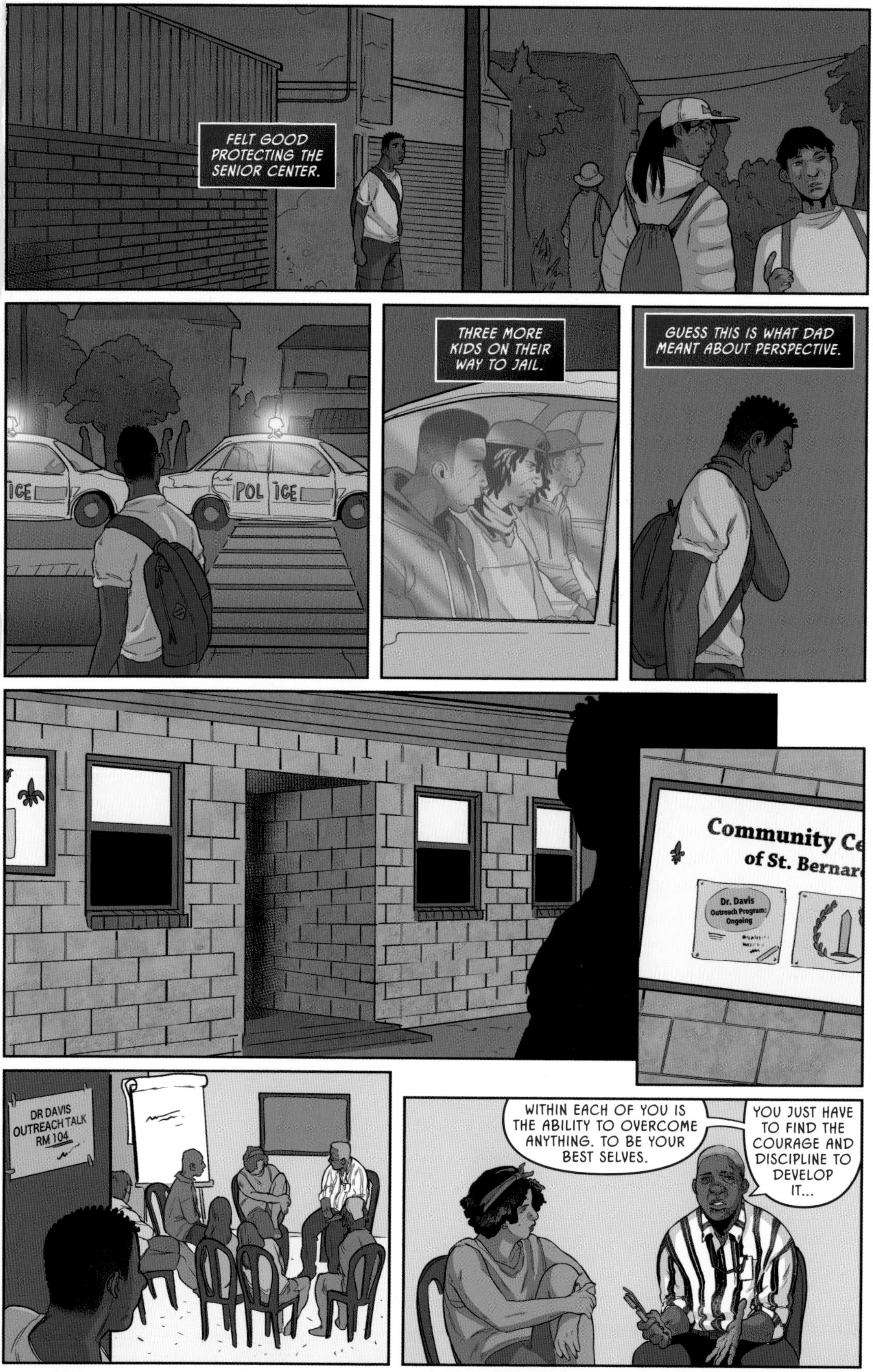
FELT GOOD PROTECTING THE SENIOR CENTER.
POLICE
THREE MORE KIDS ON THEIR WAY TO JAIL.
GUESS THIS IS WHAT DAD MEANT ABOUT PERSPECTIVE.
Community Ce
of St. Bernar
Dr. Davis
Outreach Program:
Ongoing
DR DAVIS
OUTREACH TALK
RM 104
WITHIN EACH OF YOU IS THE ABILITY TO OVERCOME ANYTHING. TO BE YOUR BEST SELVES.
YOU JUST HAVE TO FIND THE COURAGE AND DISCIPLINE TO DEVELOP IT...

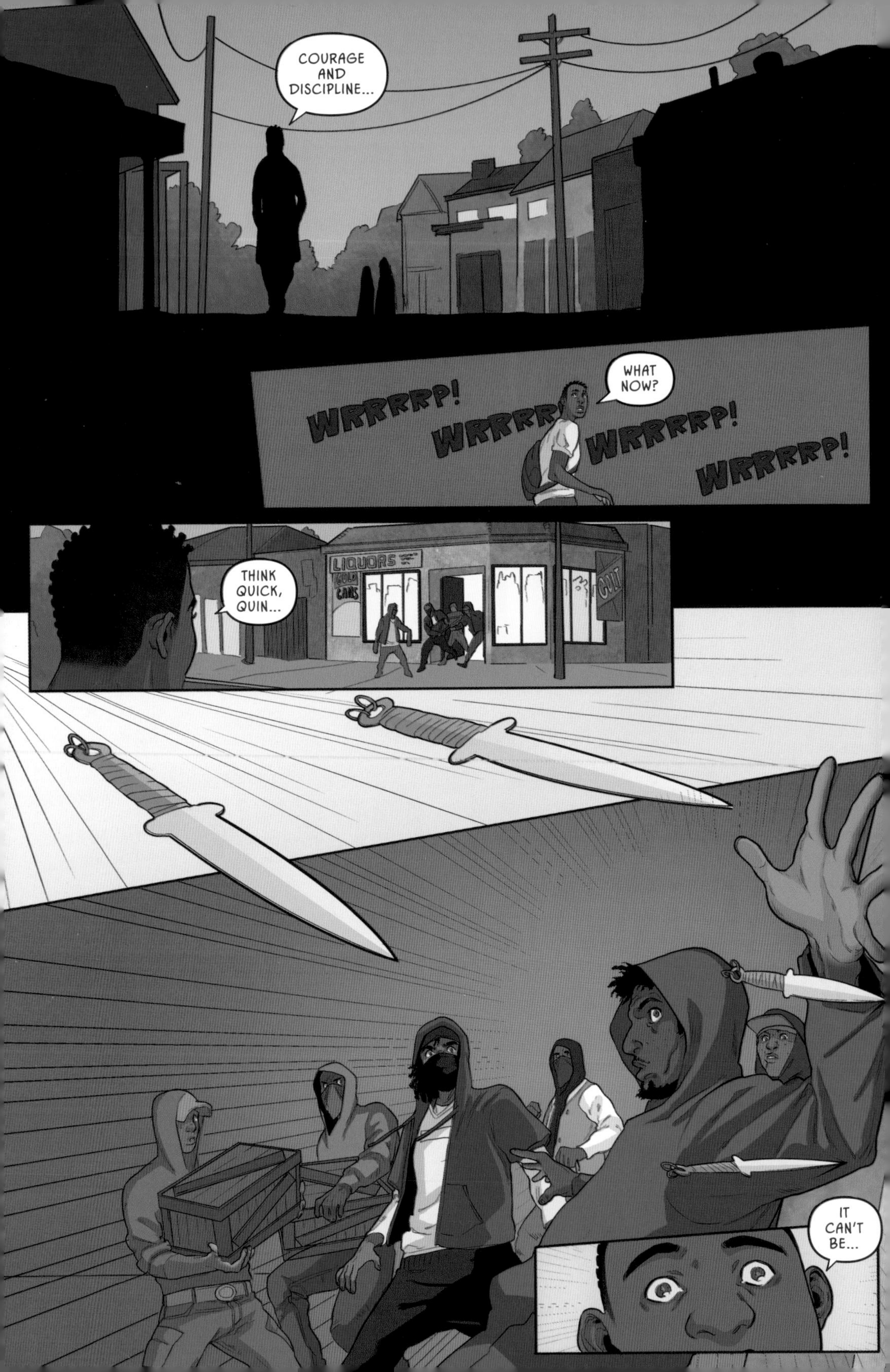
COURAGE AND DISCIPLINE...
WRRRRP!
WRRRRP!
WHAT NOW?
WRRRRP!
WRRRRP!
LIQUORS
GOLD CANS
COLT
THINK QUICK, QUIN...
IT CAN'T BE...

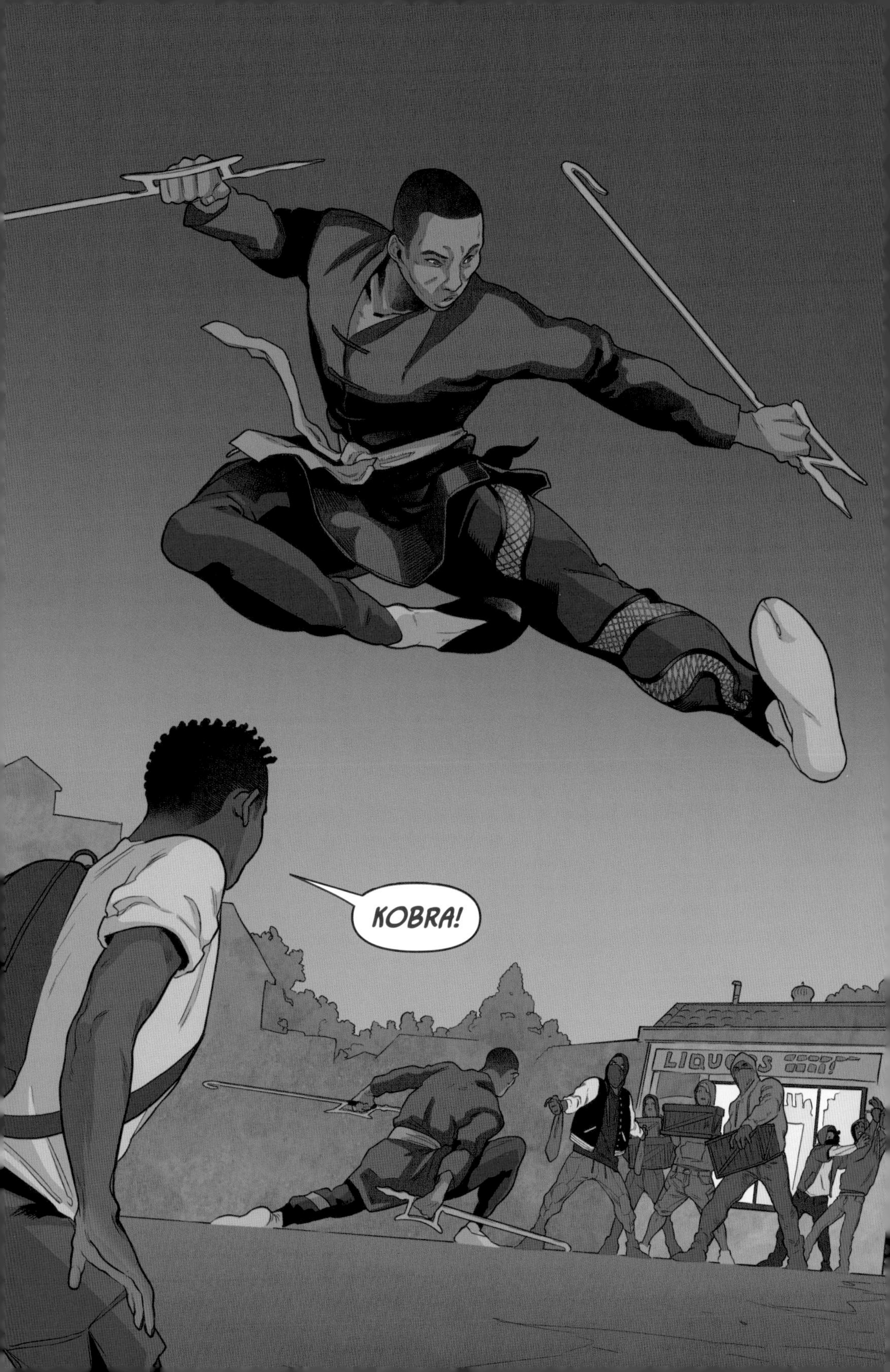
KOBRA!

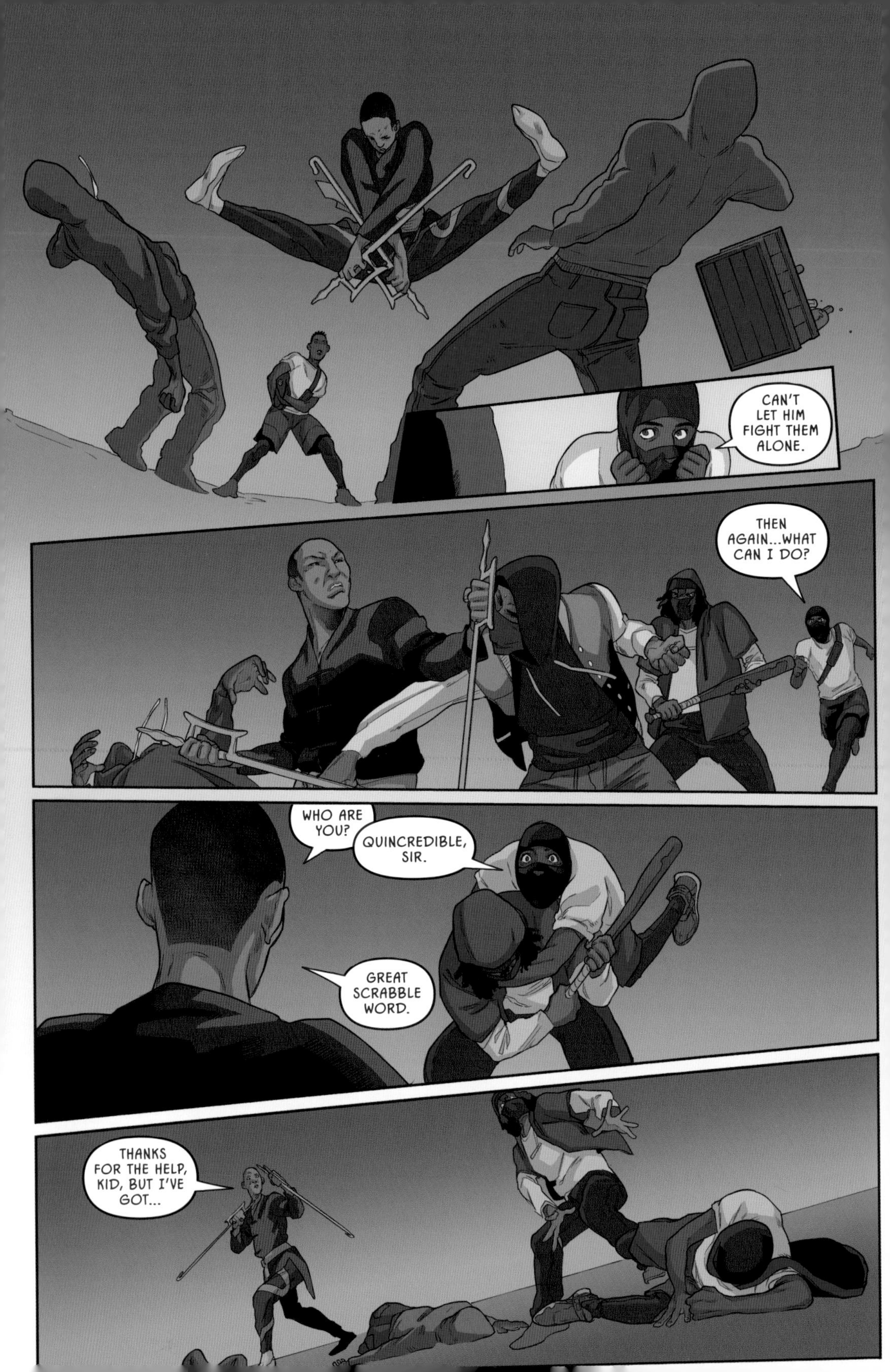
CAN'T LET HIM FIGHT THEM ALONE.
THEN AGAIN...WHAT CAN I DO?
WHO ARE YOU?
QUINCREDIBLE, SIR.
GREAT SCRABBLE WORD.
THANKS FOR THE HELP, KID, BUT I'VE GOT...

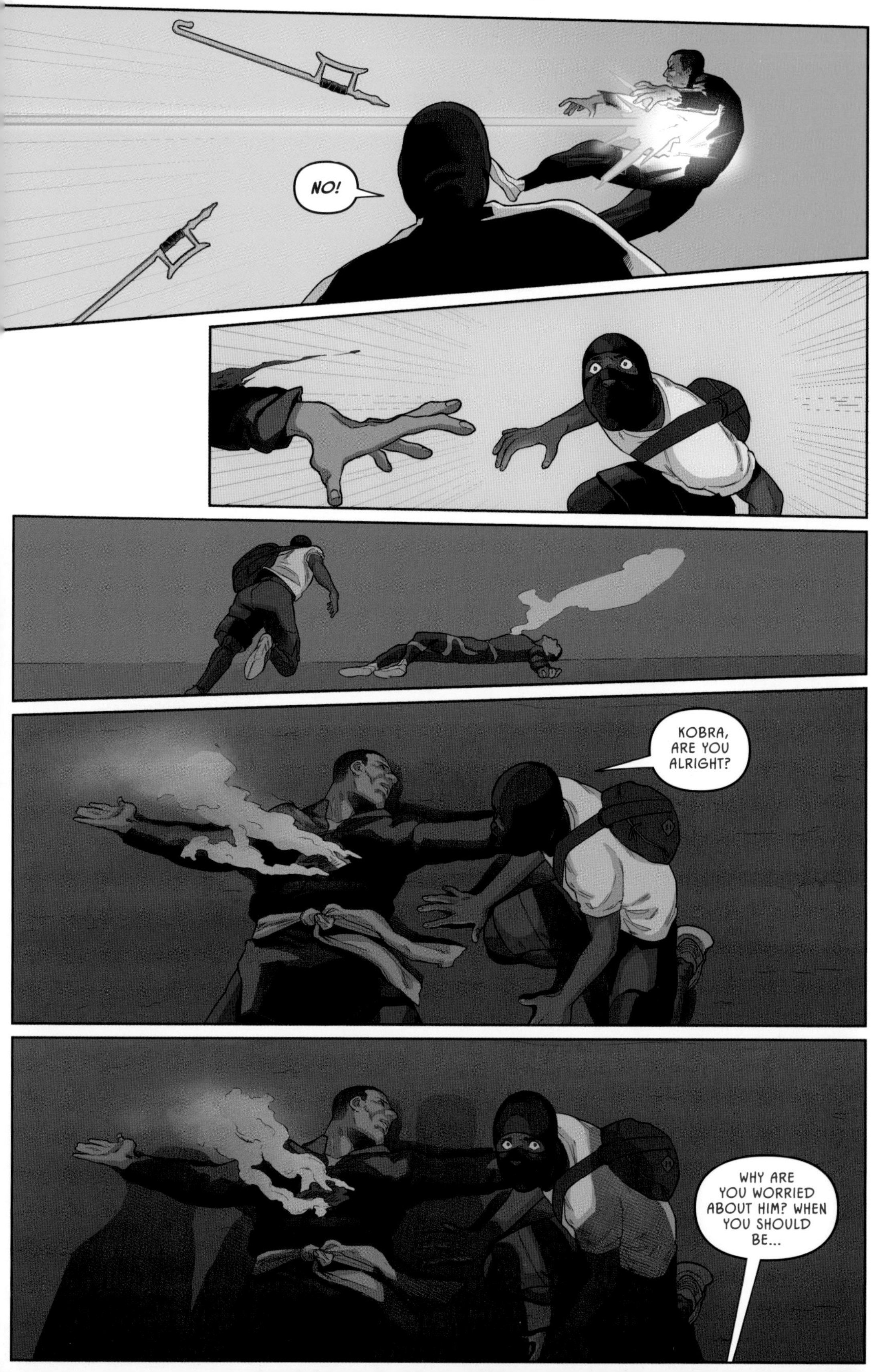
NO!
KOBRA, ARE YOU ALRIGHT?
WHY ARE YOU WORRIED ABOUT HIM? WHEN YOU SHOULD BE...

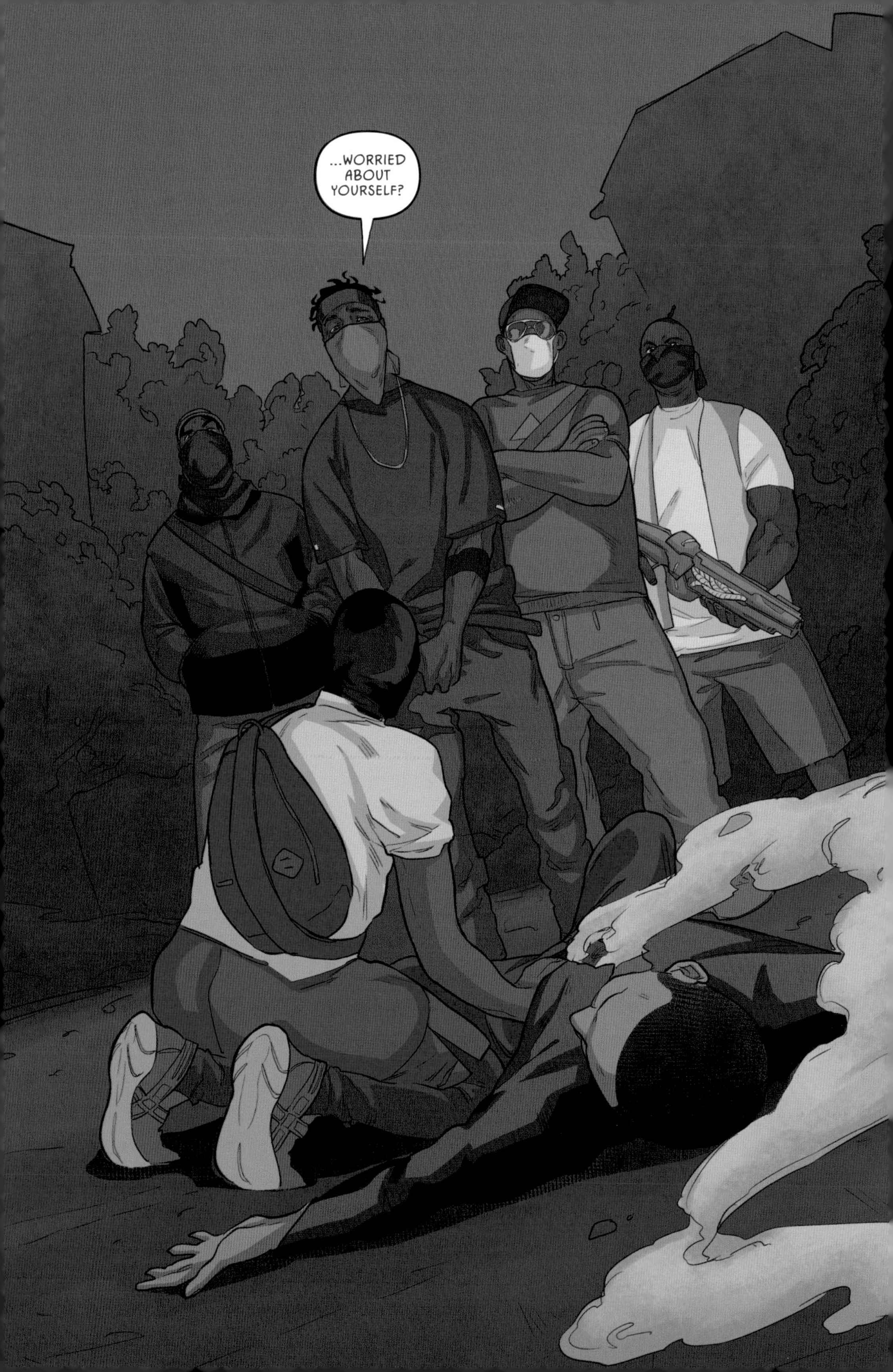
...WORRIED ABOUT YOURSELF?

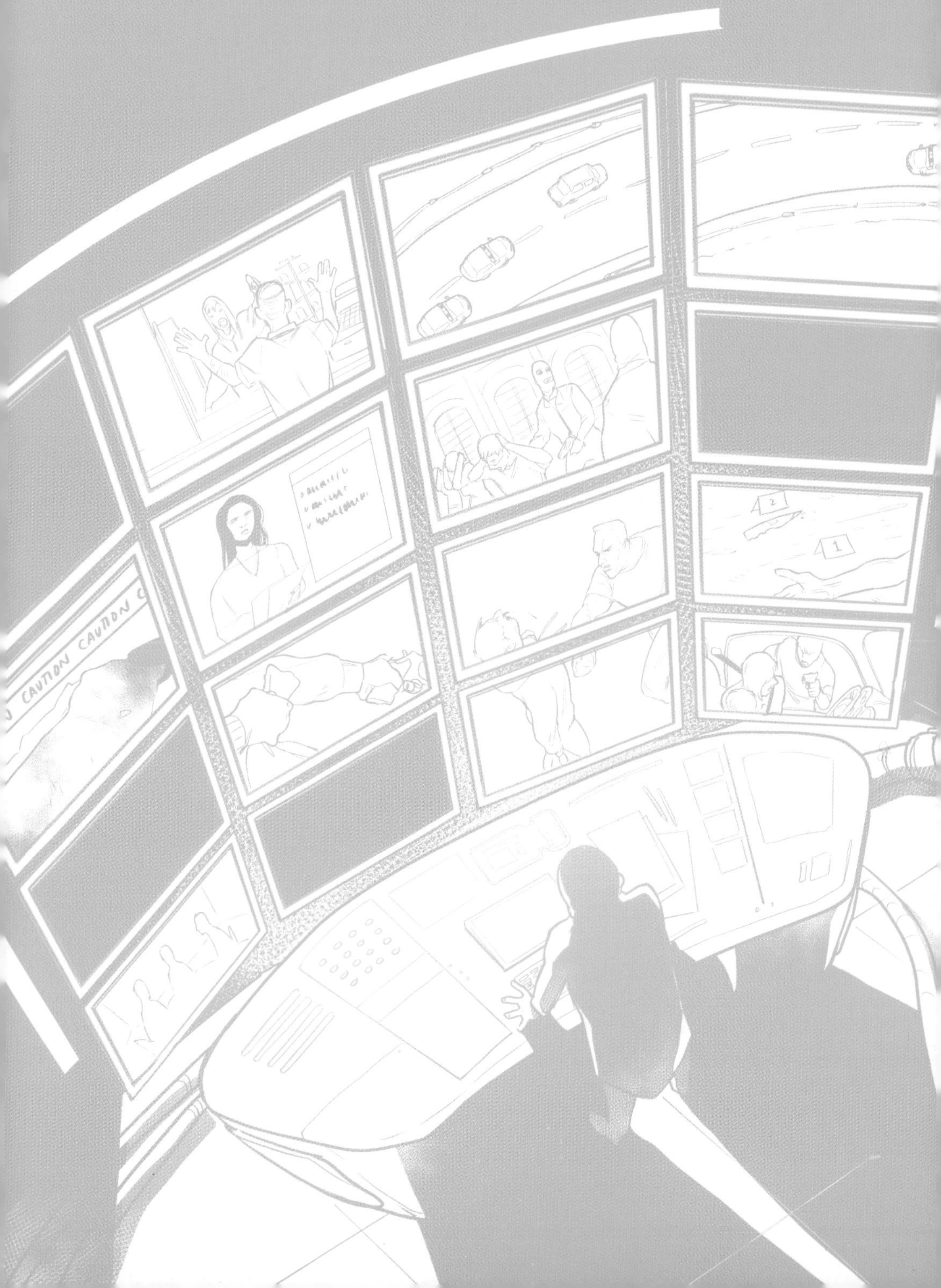
CAUTION CAUTION C

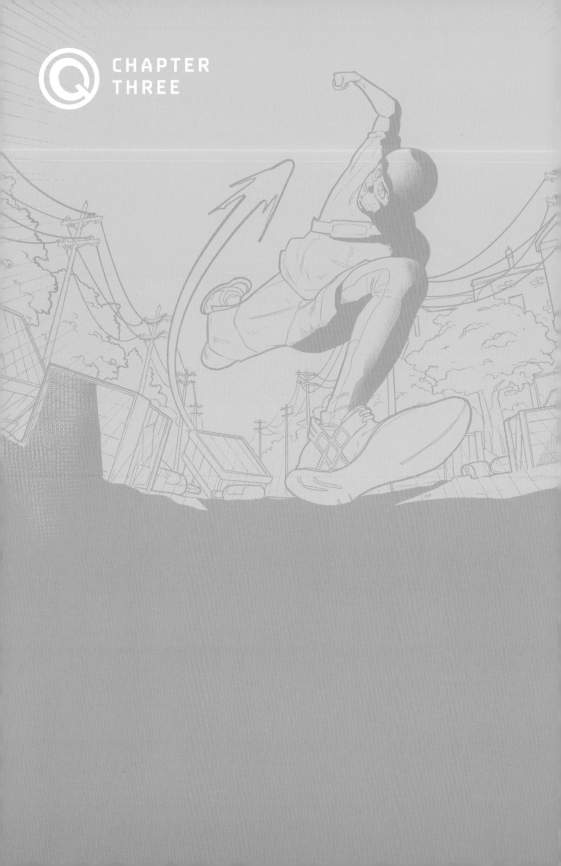

CHAPTER THREE

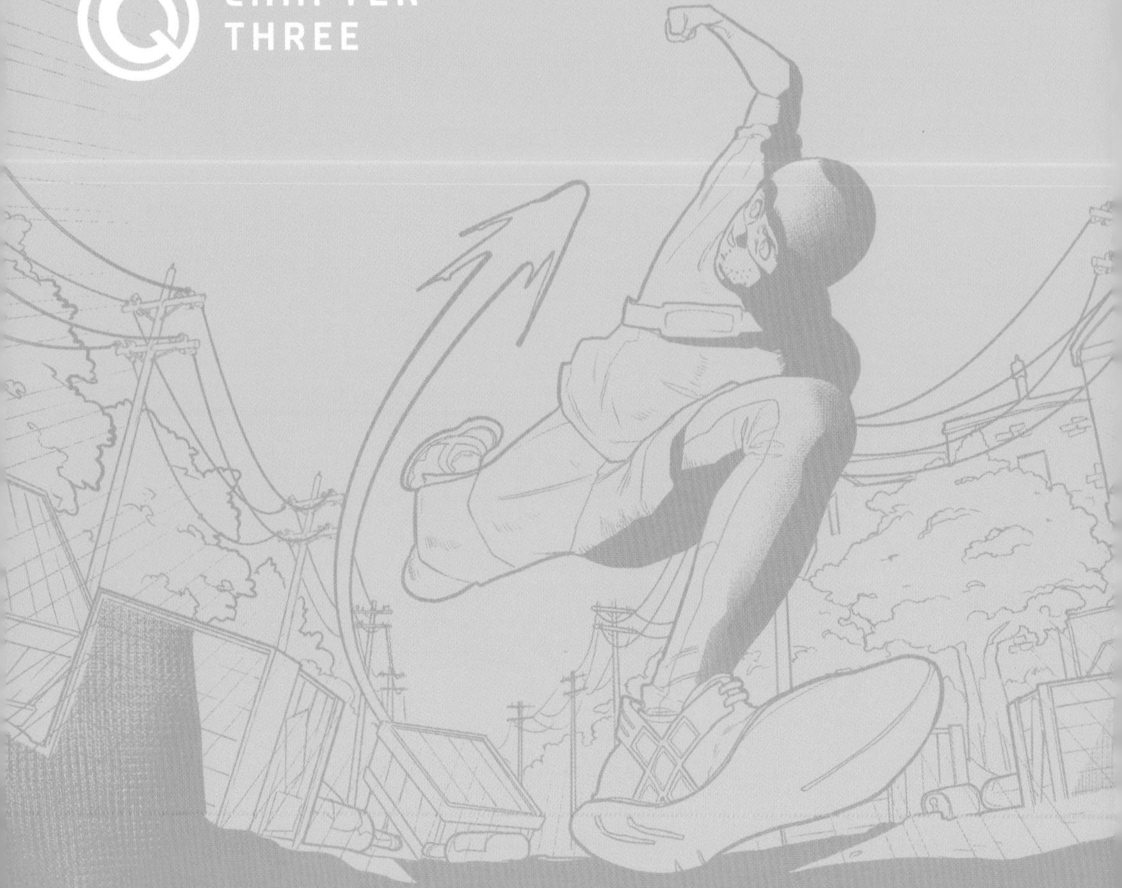

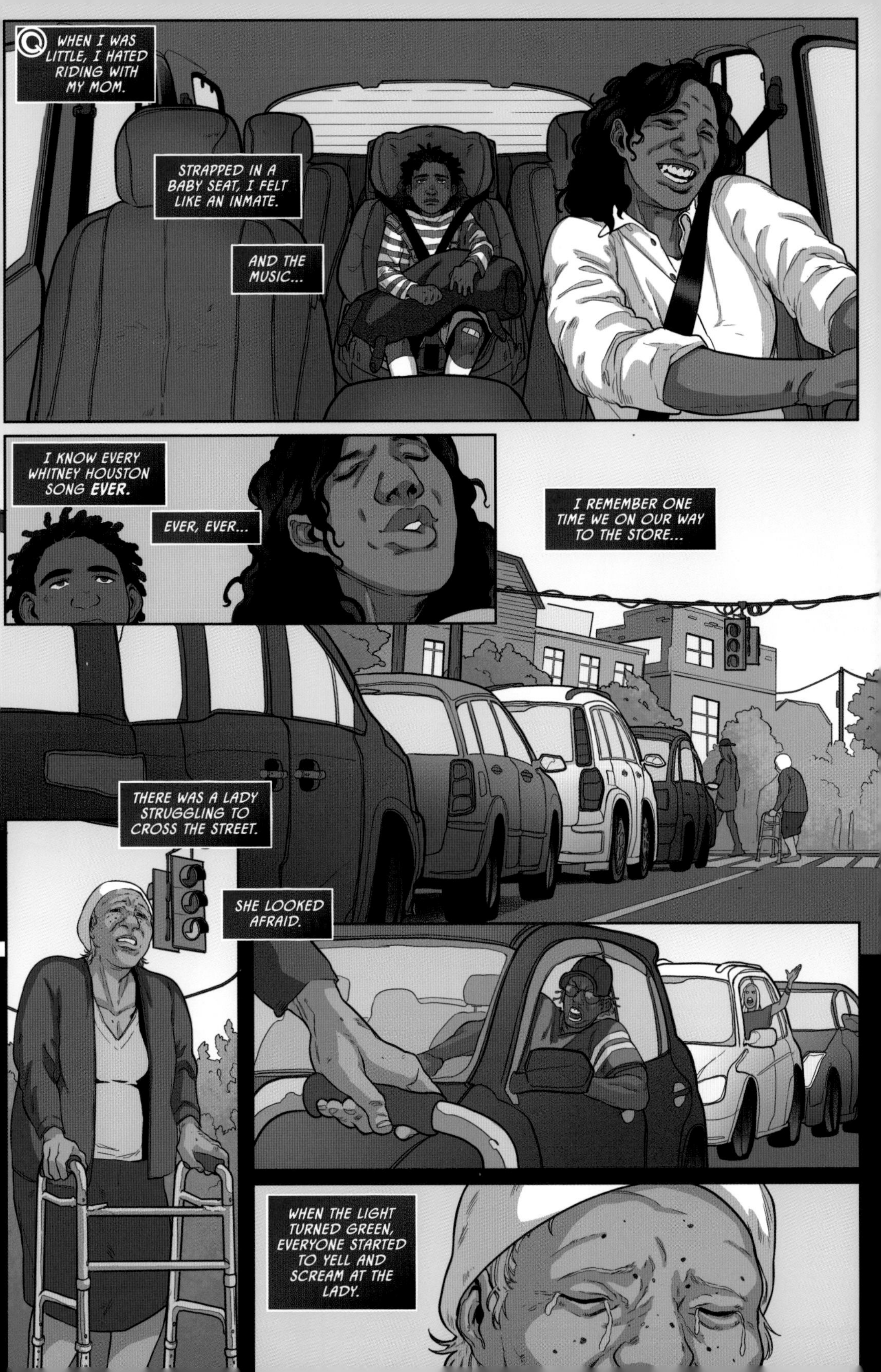
WHEN I WAS LITTLE, I HATED RIDING WITH MY MOM.
STRAPPED IN A BABY SEAT, I FELT LIKE AN INMATE.
AND THE MUSIC...
I KNOW EVERY WHITNEY HOUSTON SONG EVER.
EVER, EVER...
I REMEMBER ONE TIME WE ON OUR WAY TO THE STORE...
THERE WAS A LADY STRUGGLING TO CROSS THE STREET.
SHE LOOKED AFRAID.
WHEN THE LIGHT TURNED GREEN, EVERYONE STARTED TO YELL AND SCREAM AT THE LADY.

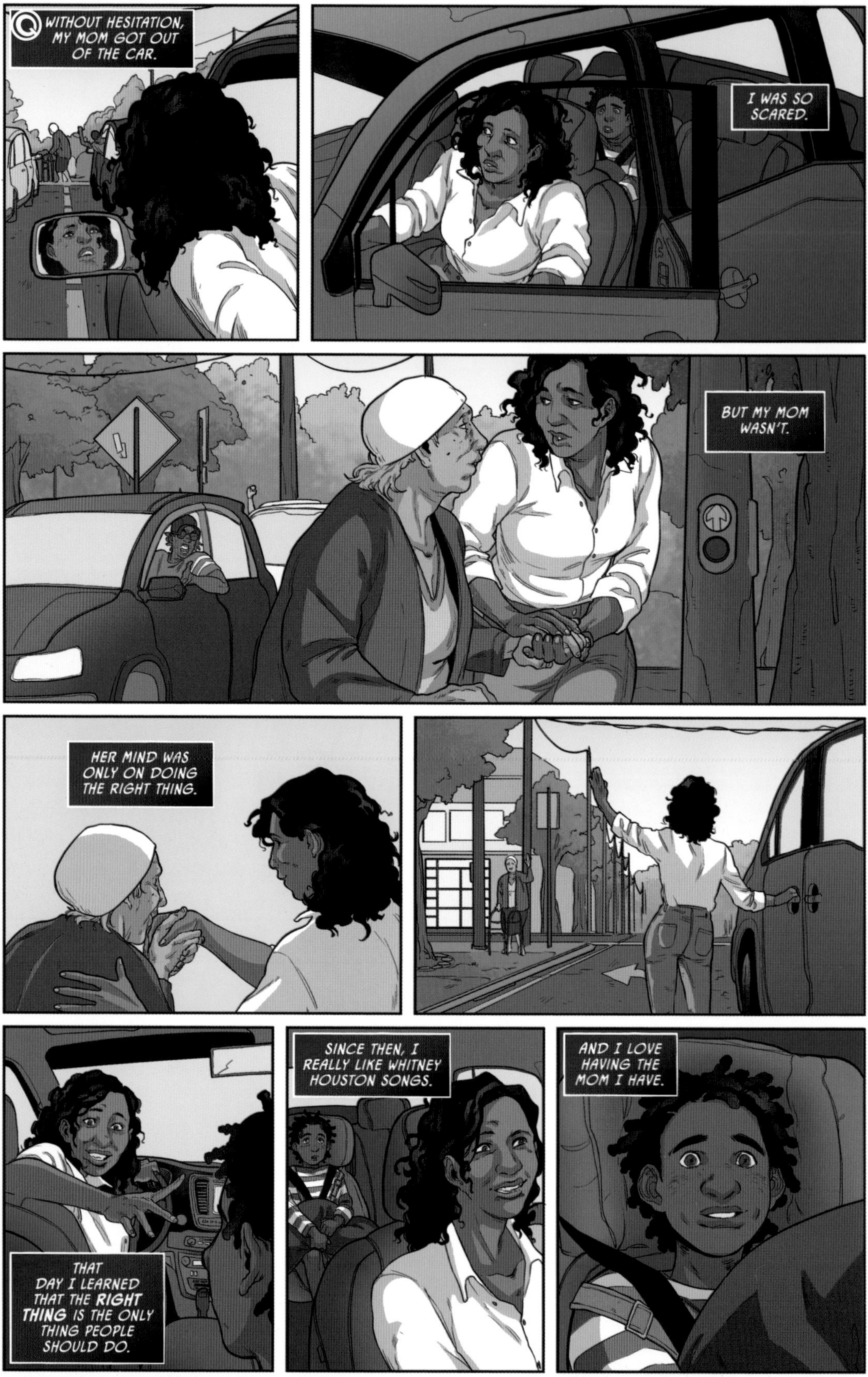
WITHOUT HESITATION, MY MOM GOT OUT OF THE CAR.
I WAS SO SCARED.
BUT MY MOM WASN'T.
HER MIND WAS ONLY ON DOING THE RIGHT THING.
THAT DAY I LEARNED THAT THE RIGHT THING IS THE ONLY THING PEOPLE SHOULD DO.
SINCE THEN, I REALLY LIKE WHITNEY HOUSTON SONGS.
AND I LOVE HAVING THE MOM I HAVE.

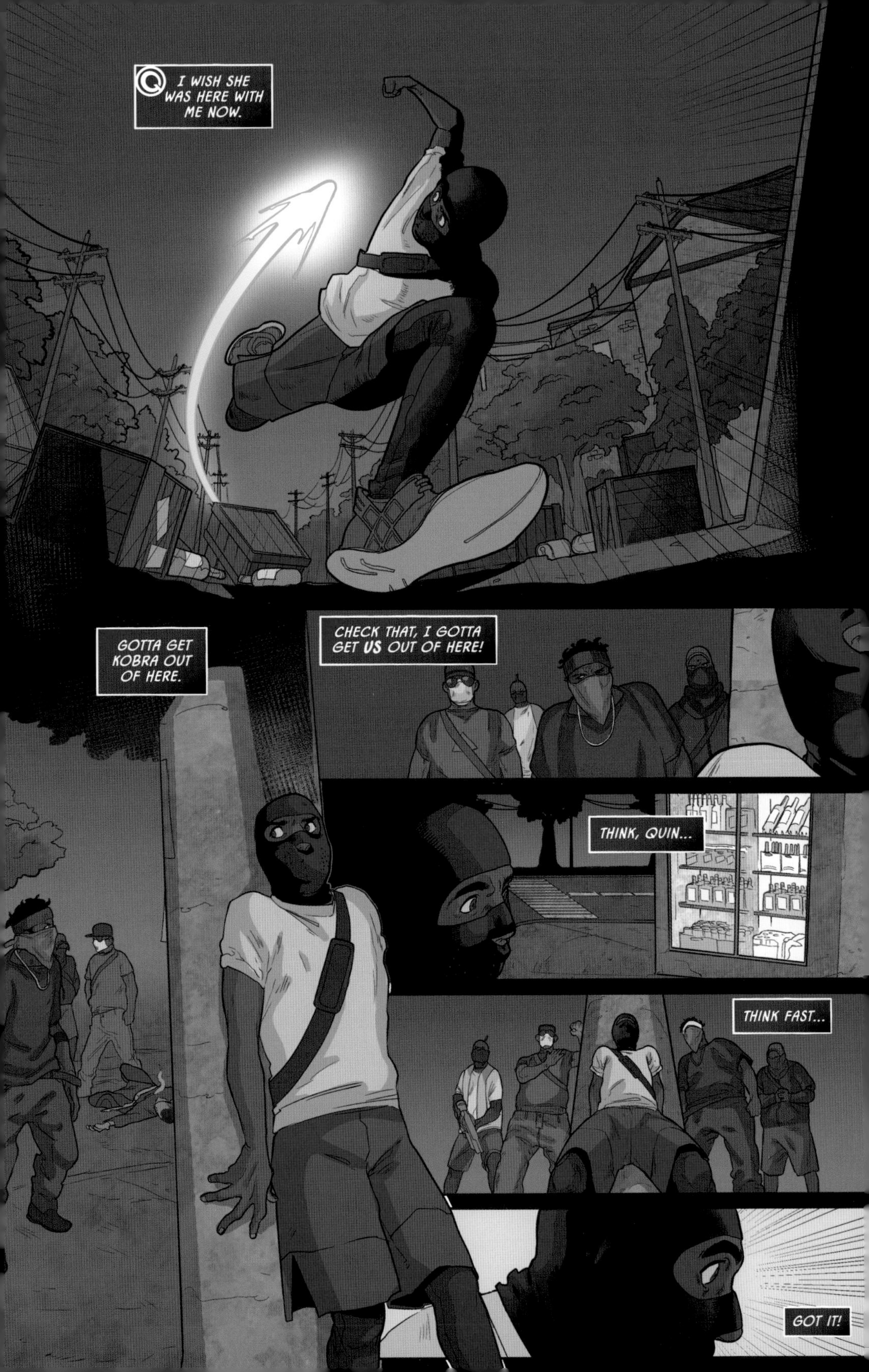
I WISH SHE WAS HERE WITH ME NOW.
GOTTA GET KOBRA OUT OF HERE.
CHECK THAT, I GOTTA GET US OUT OF HERE!
THINK, QUIN...
THINK FAST...
GOT IT!

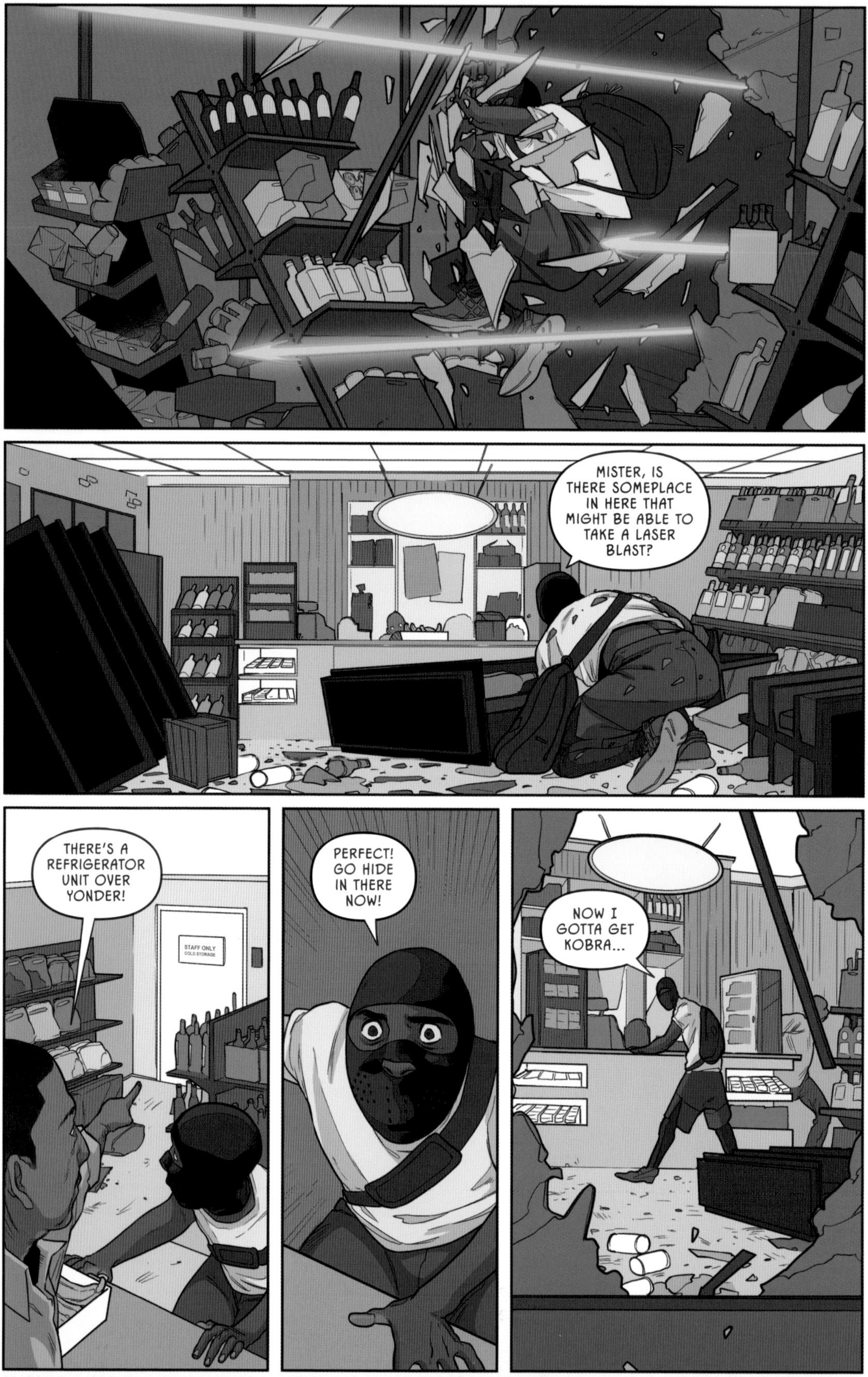
MISTER, IS THERE SOMEPLACE IN HERE THAT MIGHT BE ABLE TO TAKE A LASER BLAST?
THERE'S A REFRIGERATOR UNIT OVER YONDER!
STAFF ONLY
COLD STORAGE
PERFECT! GO HIDE IN THERE NOW!
NOW I GOTTA GET KOBRA...

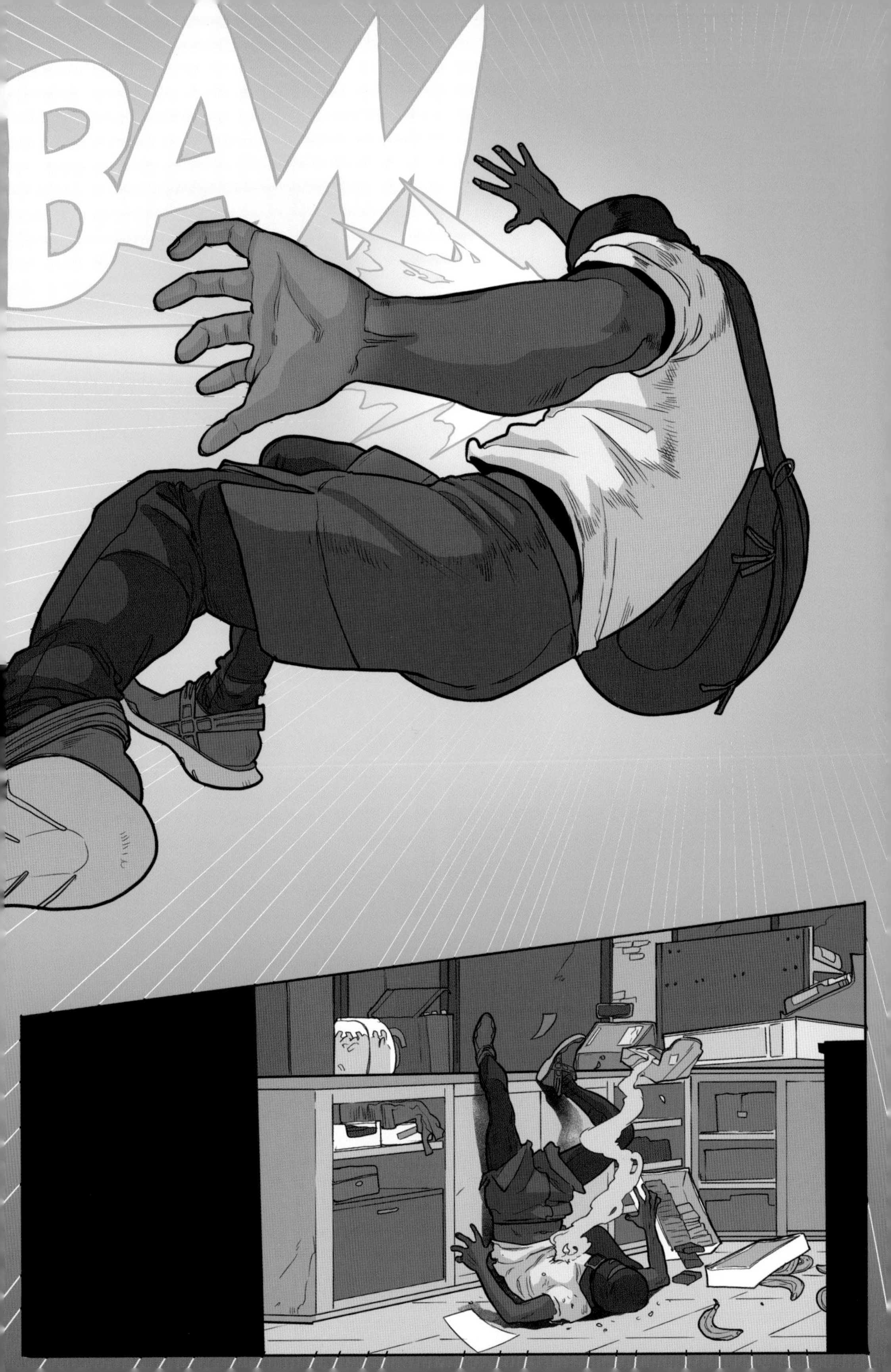
BAM

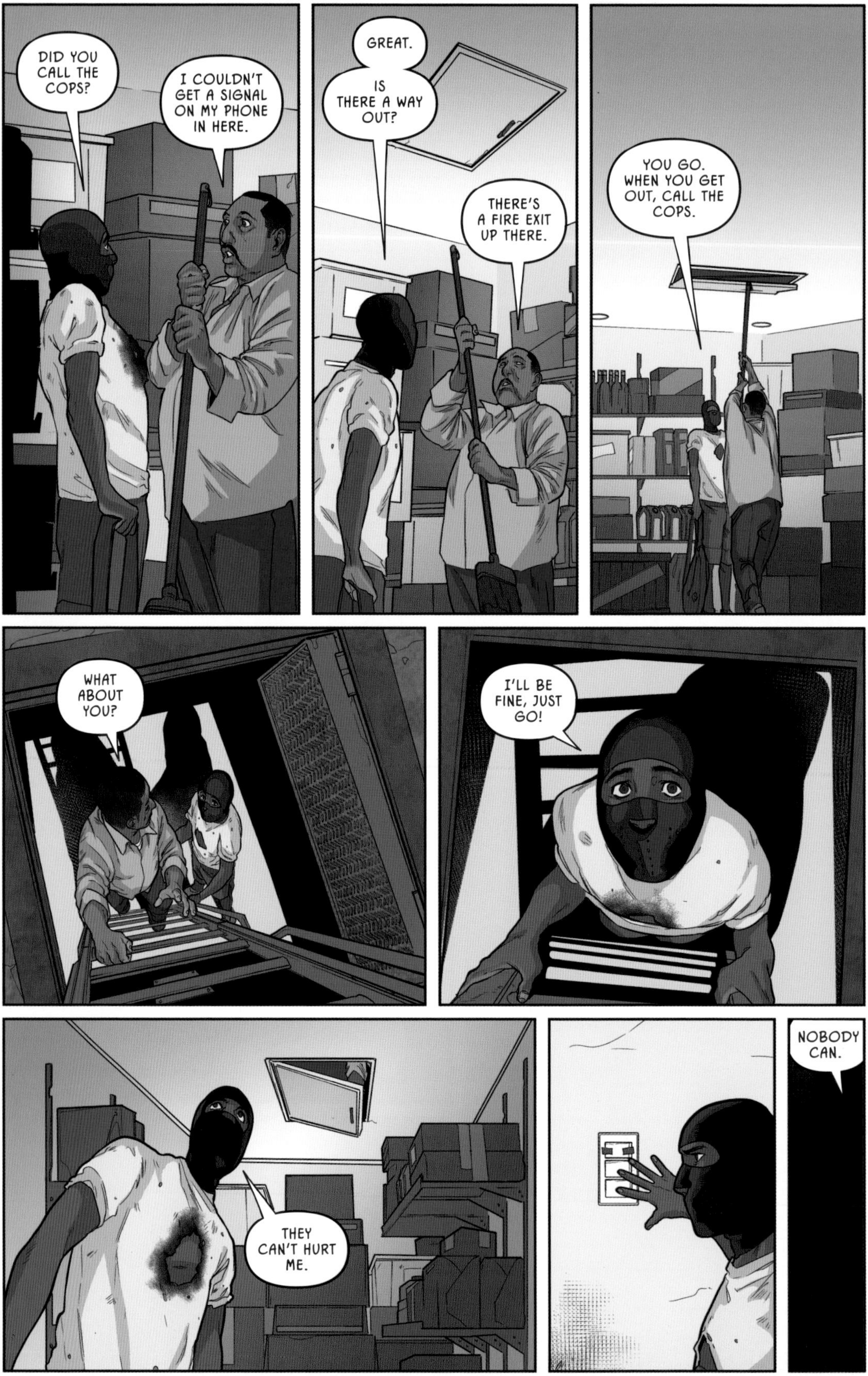
DID YOU CALL THE COPS?
I COULDN'T GET A SIGNAL ON MY PHONE IN HERE.
GREAT.
IS THERE A WAY OUT?
THERE'S A FIRE EXIT UP THERE.
YOU GO. WHEN YOU GET OUT, CALL THE COPS.
WHAT ABOUT YOU?
I'LL BE FINE, JUST GO!
THEY CAN'T HURT ME.
NOBODY CAN.

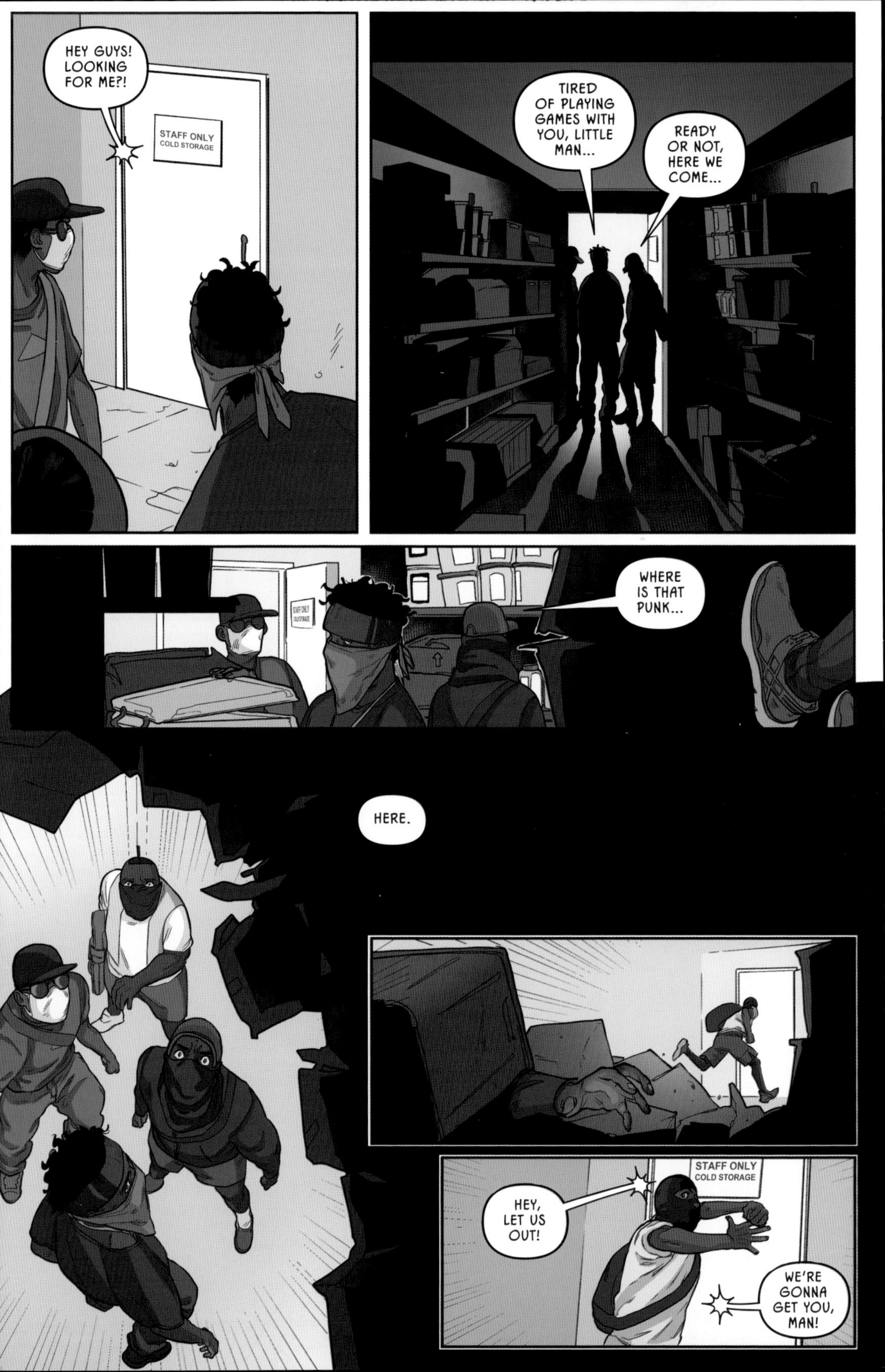
HEY GUYS! LOOKING FOR ME?!
STAFF ONLY
COLD STORAGE
TIRED OF PLAYING GAMES WITH YOU, LITTLE MAN...
READY OR NOT, HERE WE COME...
STAFF ONLY
COLD STORAGE
WHERE IS THAT PUNK...
HERE.
STAFF ONLY
COLD STORAGE
HEY, LET US OUT!
WE'RE GONNA GET YOU, MAN!

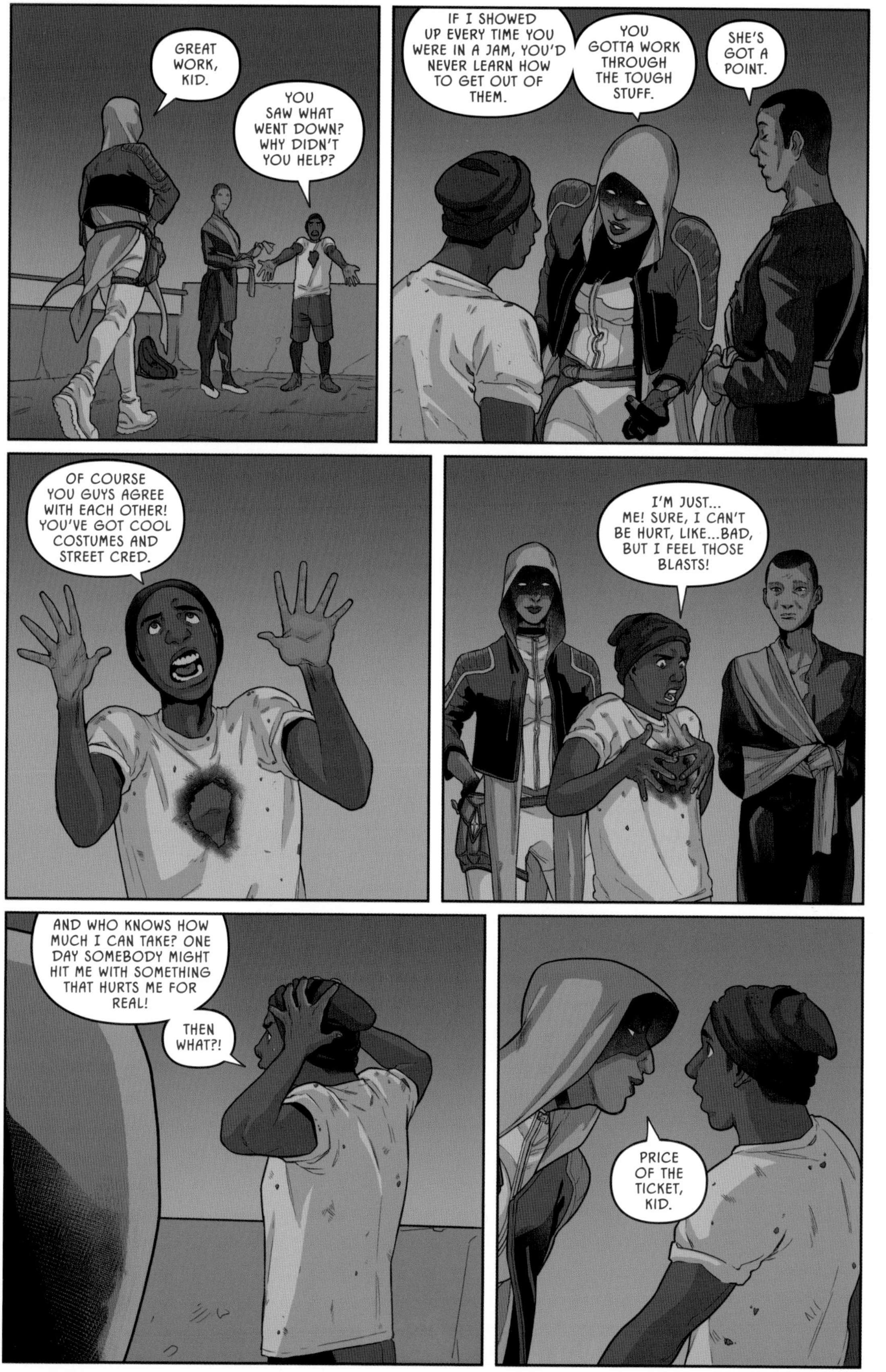
GREAT WORK, KID.
YOU SAW WHAT WENT DOWN? WHY DIDN'T YOU HELP?
IF I SHOWED UP EVERY TIME YOU WERE IN A JAM, YOU'D NEVER LEARN HOW TO GET OUT OF THEM.
YOU GOTTA WORK THROUGH THE TOUGH STUFF.
SHE'S GOT A POINT.
OF COURSE YOU GUYS AGREE WITH EACH OTHER! YOU'VE GOT COOL COSTUMES AND STREET CRED.
I'M JUST... ME! SURE, I CAN'T BE HURT, LIKE...BAD, BUT I FEEL THOSE BLASTS!
AND WHO KNOWS HOW MUCH I CAN TAKE? ONE DAY SOMEBODY MIGHT HIT ME WITH SOMETHING THAT HURTS ME FOR REAL!
THEN WHAT?!
PRICE OF THE TICKET, KID.

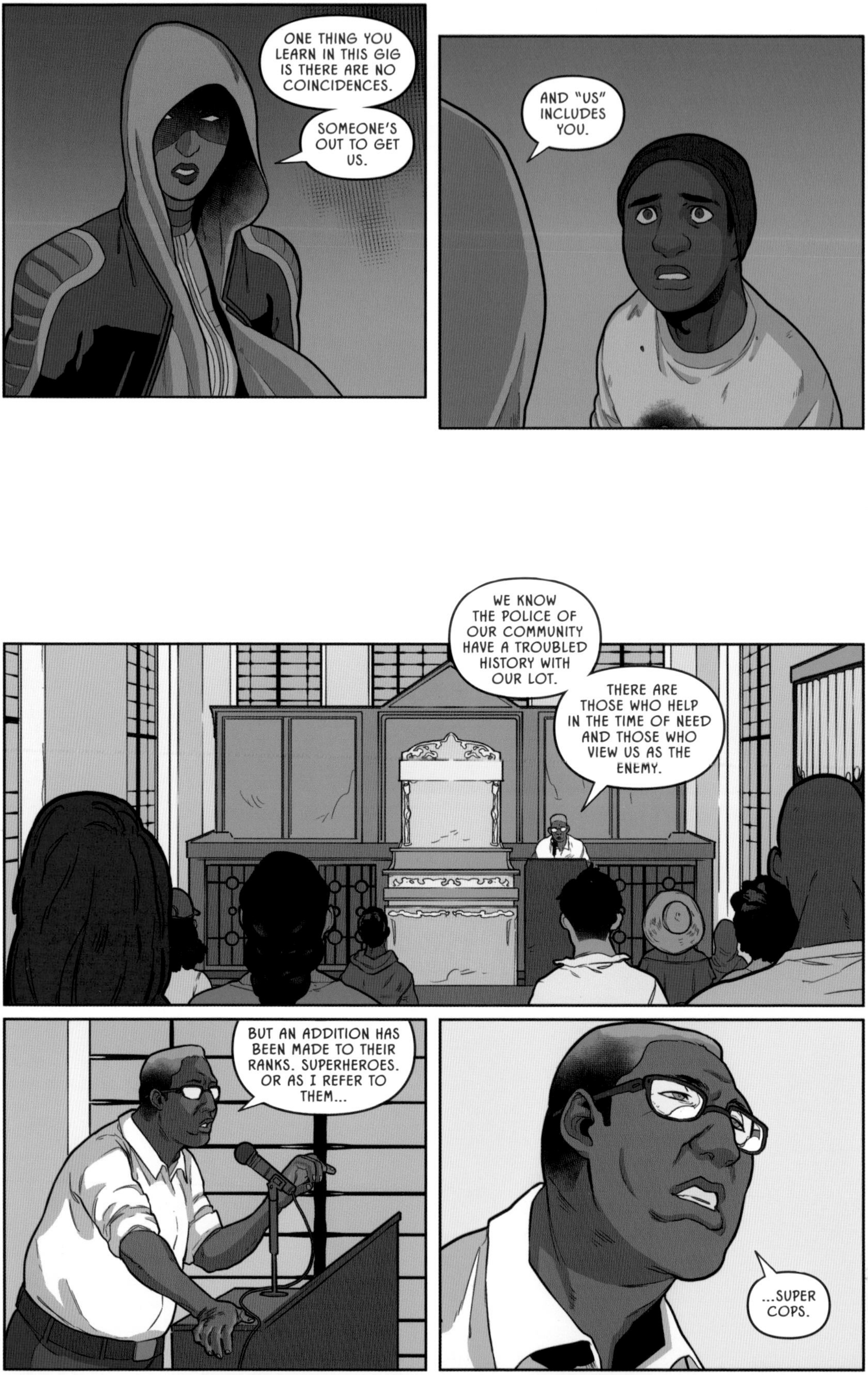
ONE THING YOU LEARN IN THIS GIG IS THERE ARE NO COINCIDENCES.
SOMEONE'S OUT TO GET US.
AND "US" INCLUDES YOU.
WE KNOW THE POLICE OF OUR COMMUNITY HAVE A TROUBLED HISTORY WITH OUR LOT.
THERE ARE THOSE WHO HELP IN THE TIME OF NEED AND THOSE WHO VIEW US AS THE ENEMY.
BUT AN ADDITION HAS BEEN MADE TO THEIR RANKS. SUPERHEROES. OR AS I REFER TO THEM...
...SUPER COPS.

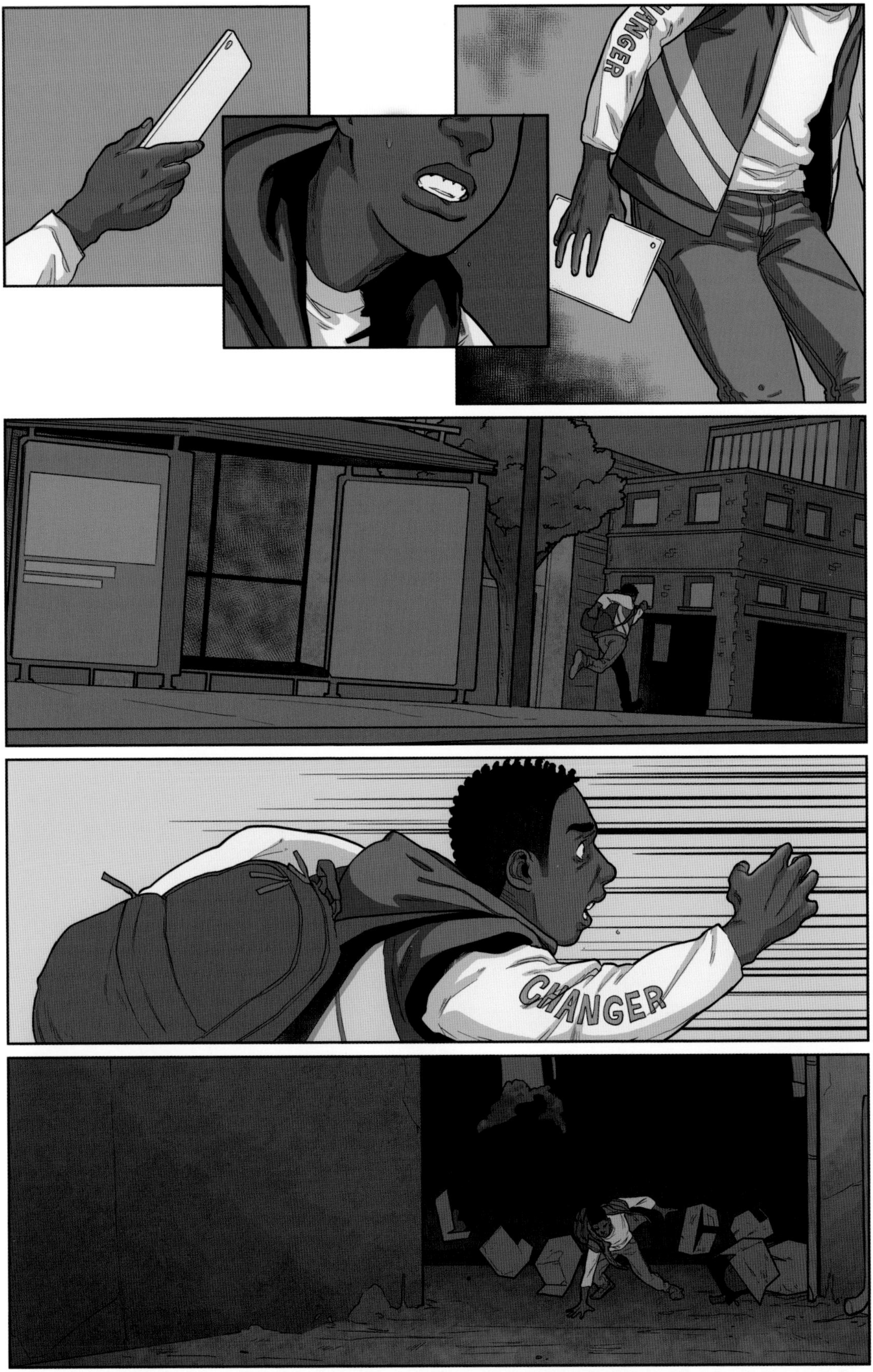

CHANGER
CHANGER

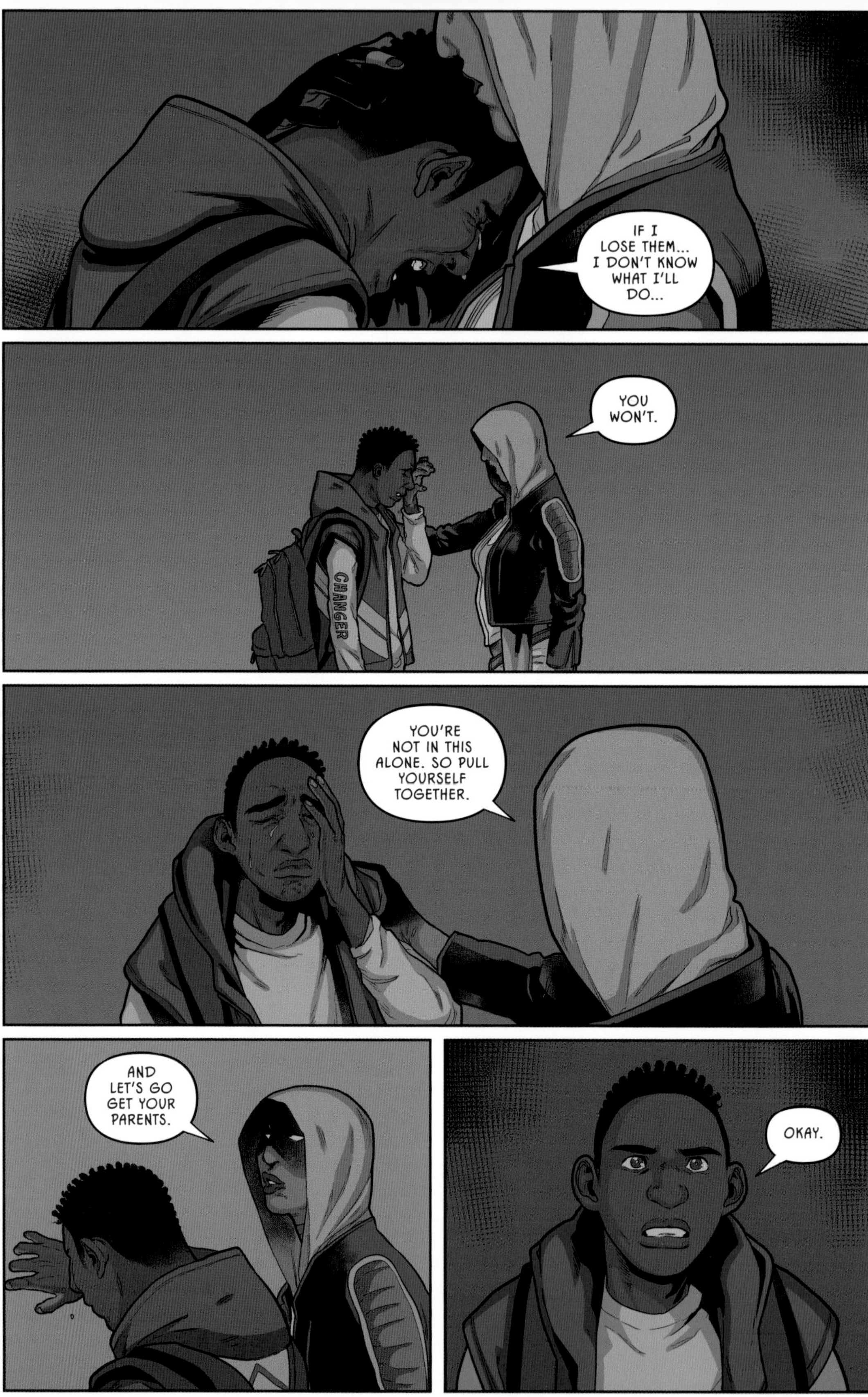
IF I LOSE THEM... I DON'T KNOW WHAT I'LL DO...
YOU WON'T.
CHANGER
YOU'RE NOT IN THIS ALONE. SO PULL YOURSELF TOGETHER.
AND LET'S GO GET YOUR PARENTS.
OKAY.

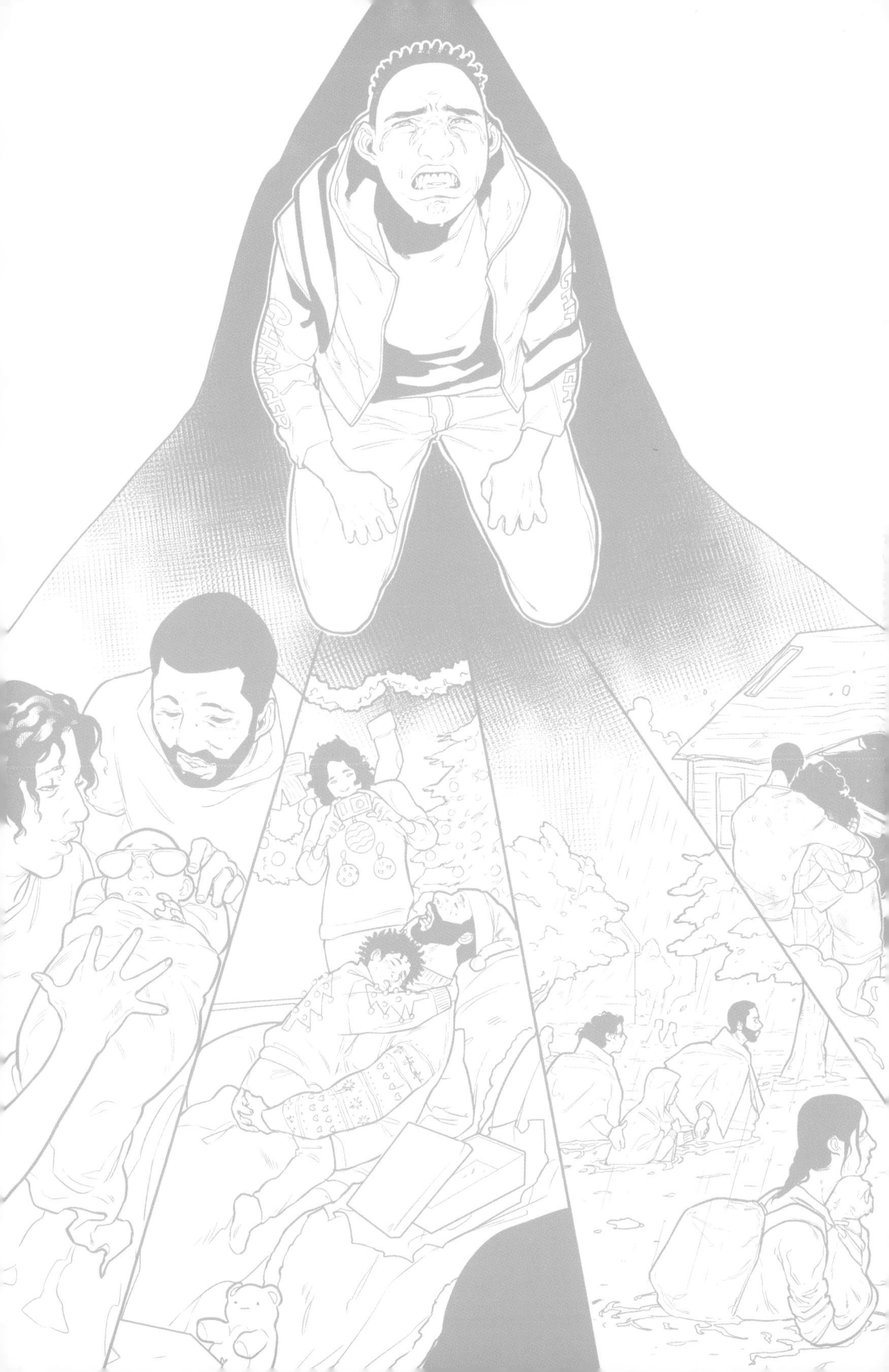

CHAPTER FOUR

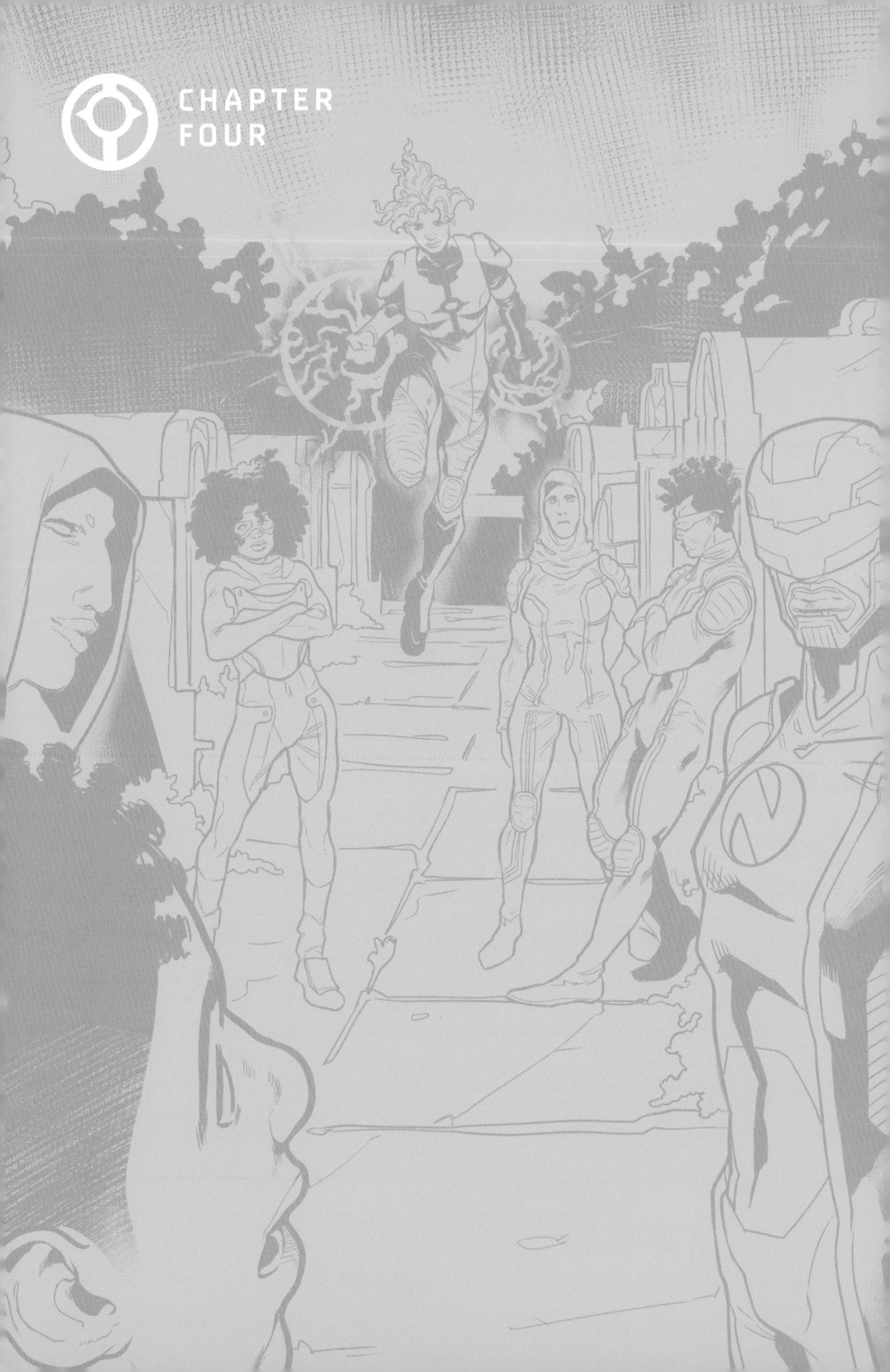

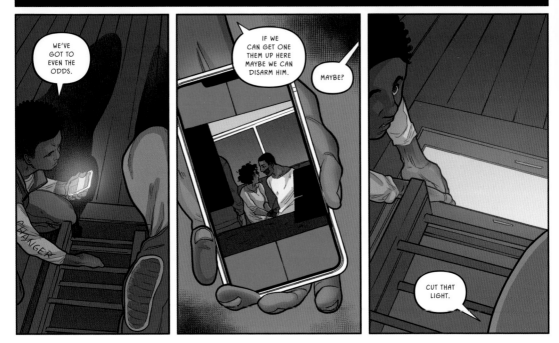

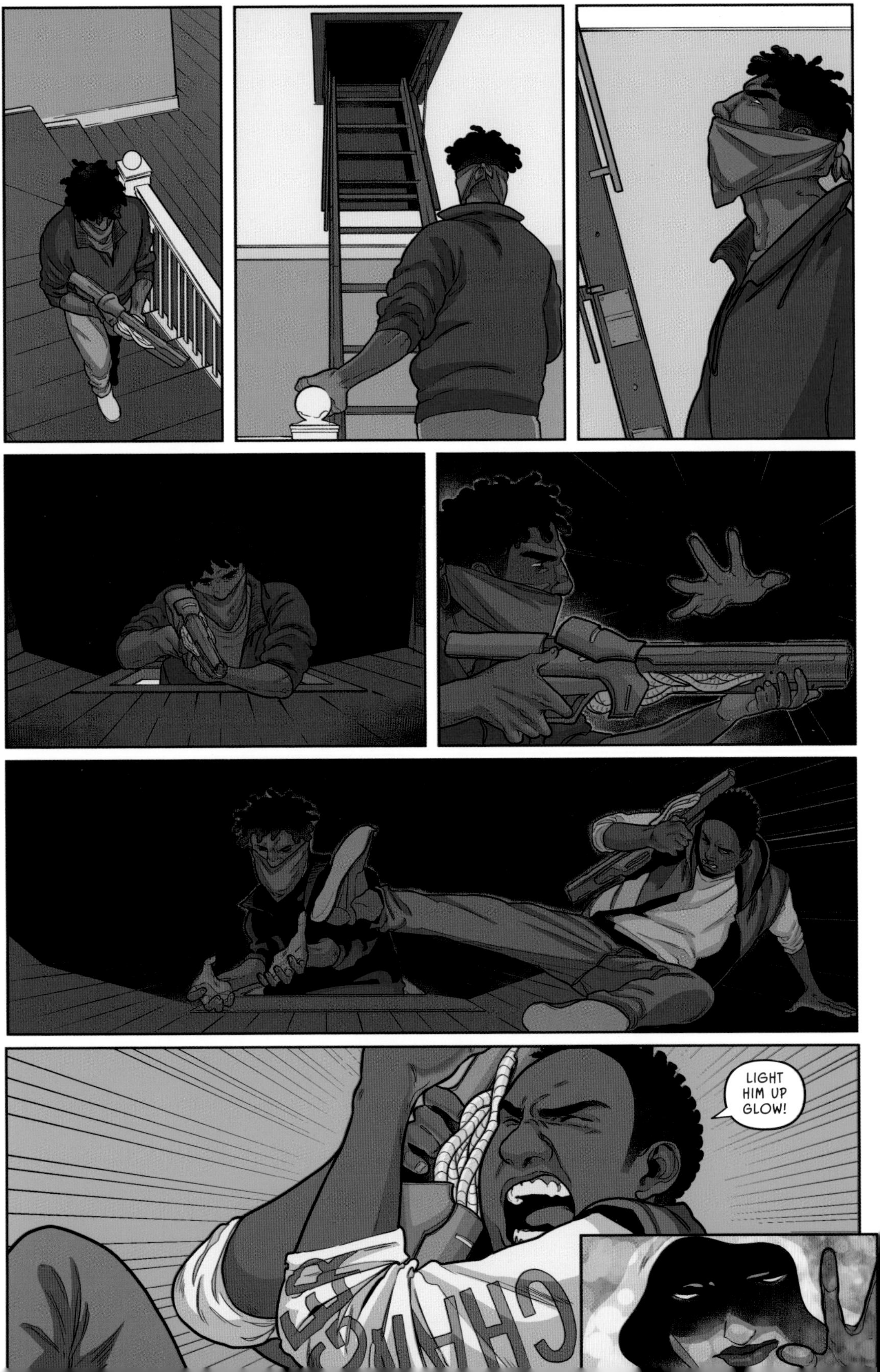
LIGHT HIM UP GLOW!

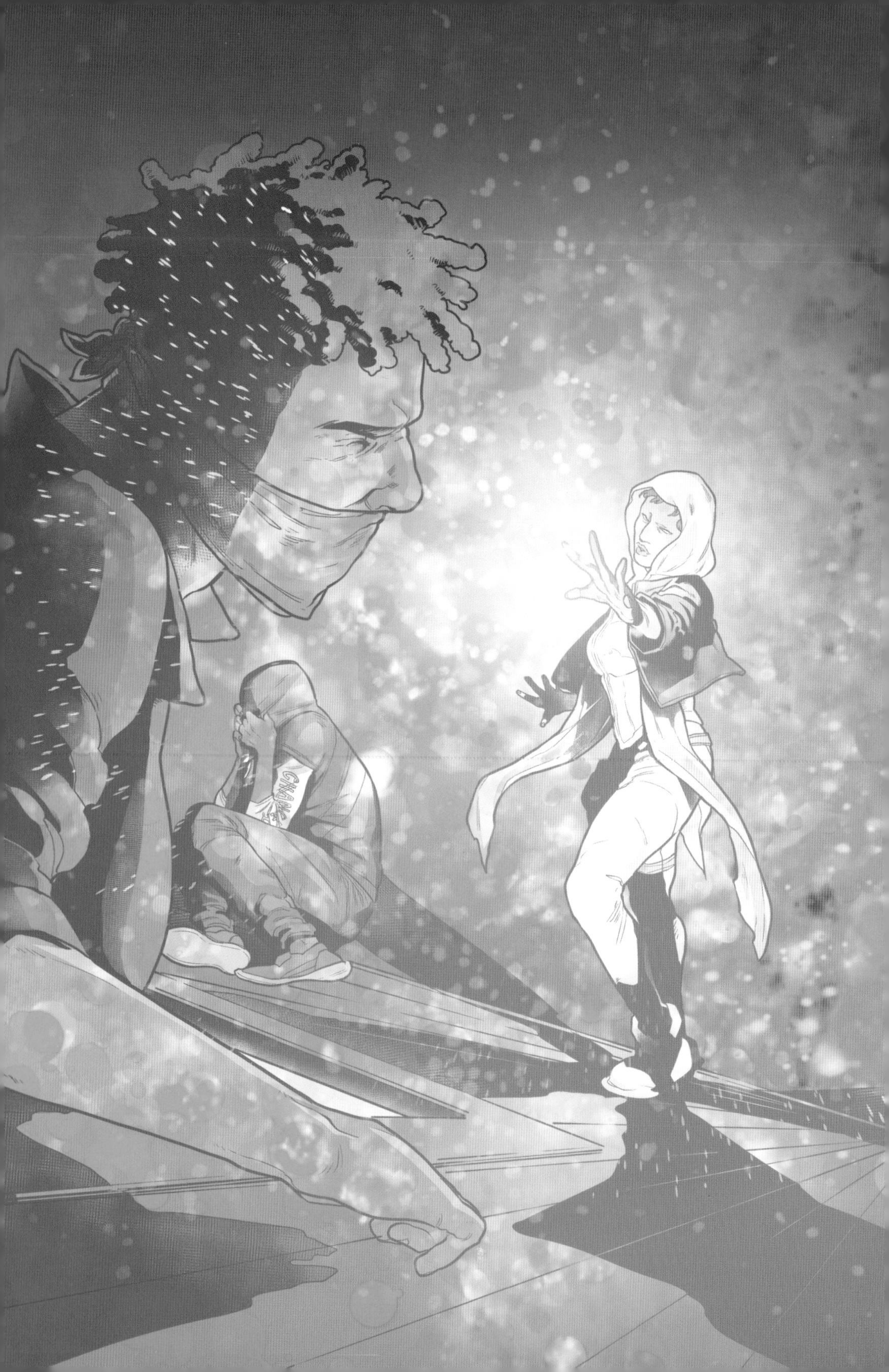

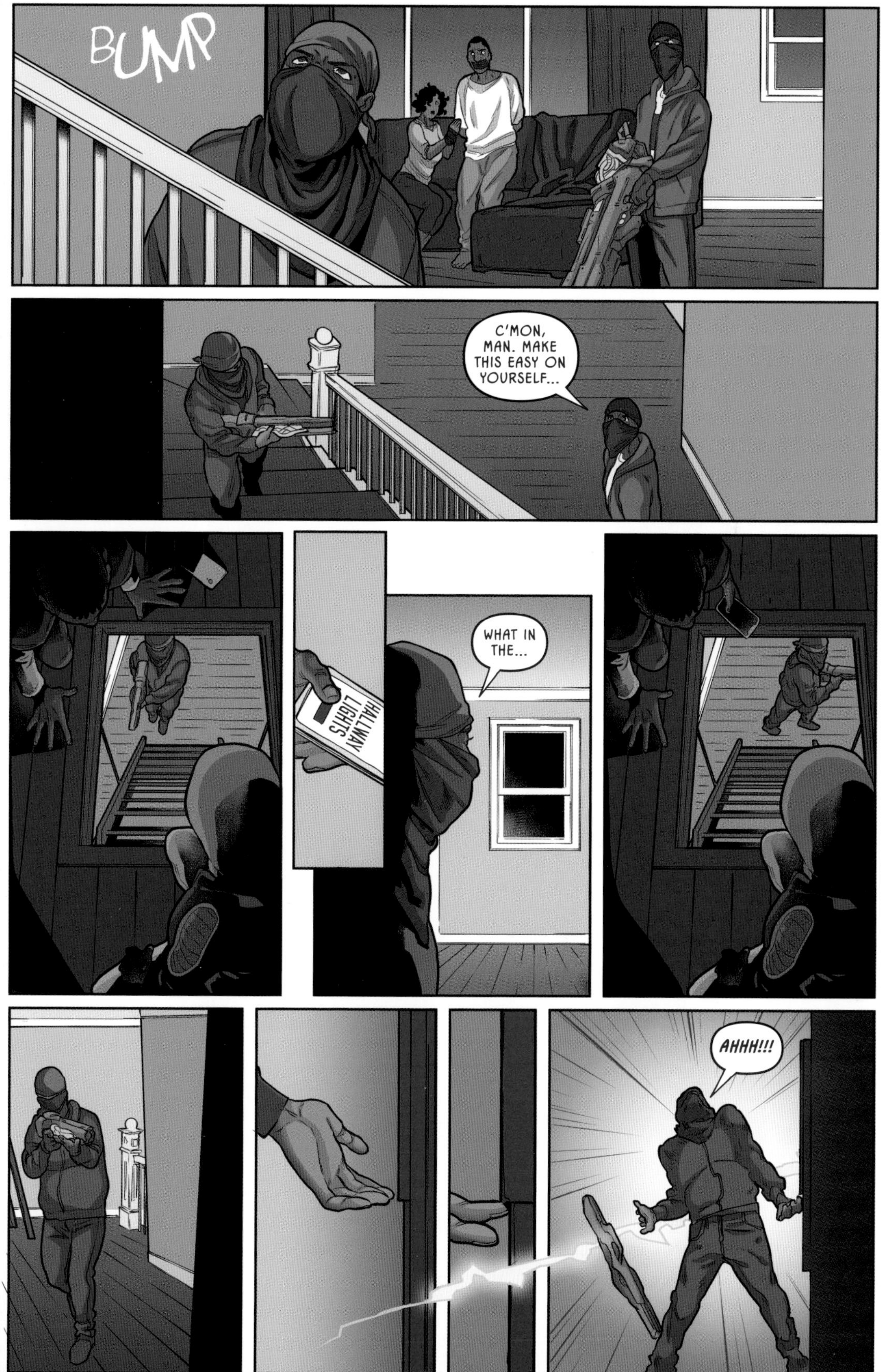
BUMP
C'MON, MAN. MAKE THIS EASY ON YOURSELF...
HALLWAY LIGHTS
WHAT IN THE...
AHHH!!!

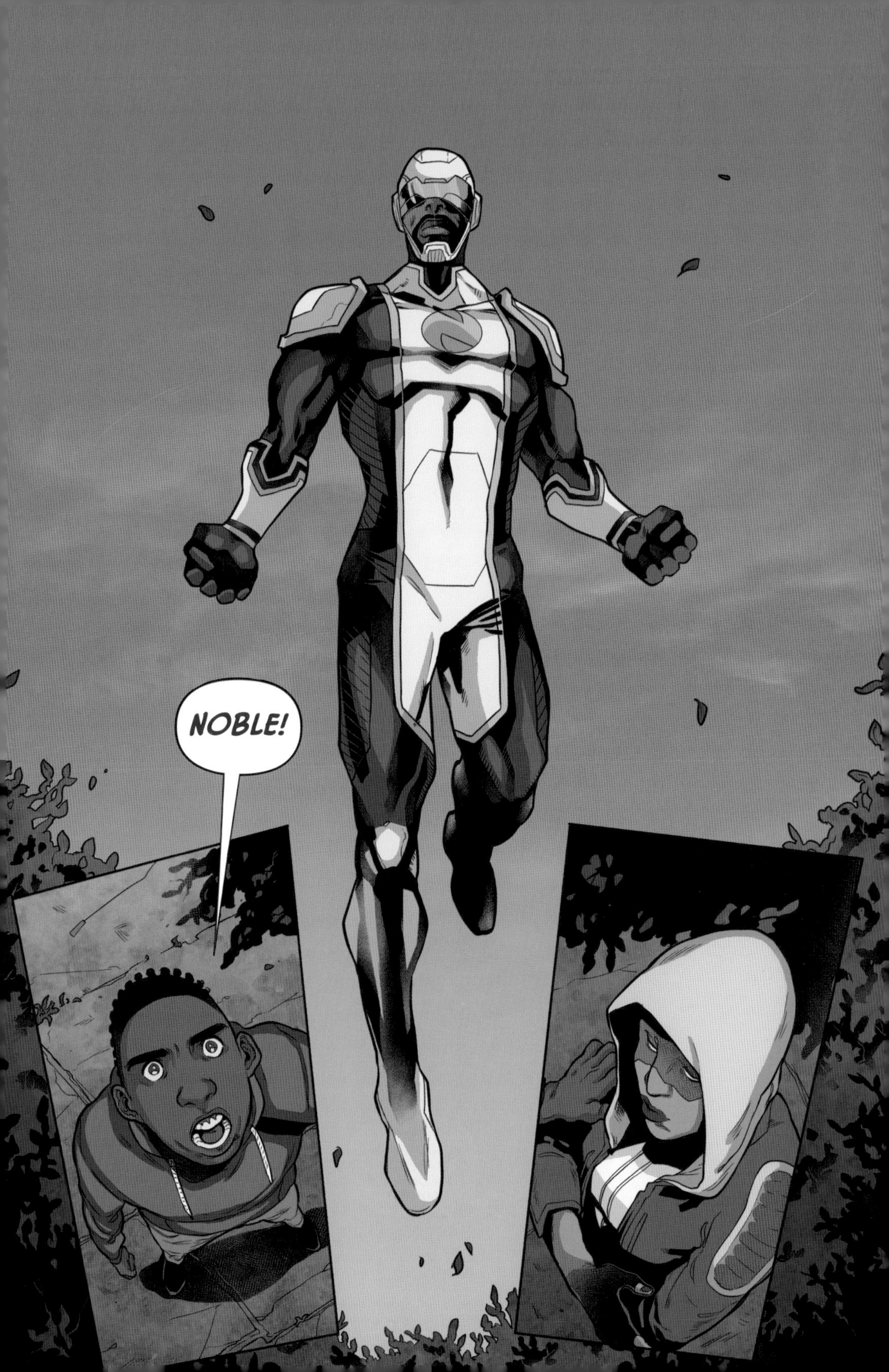
NOBLE!

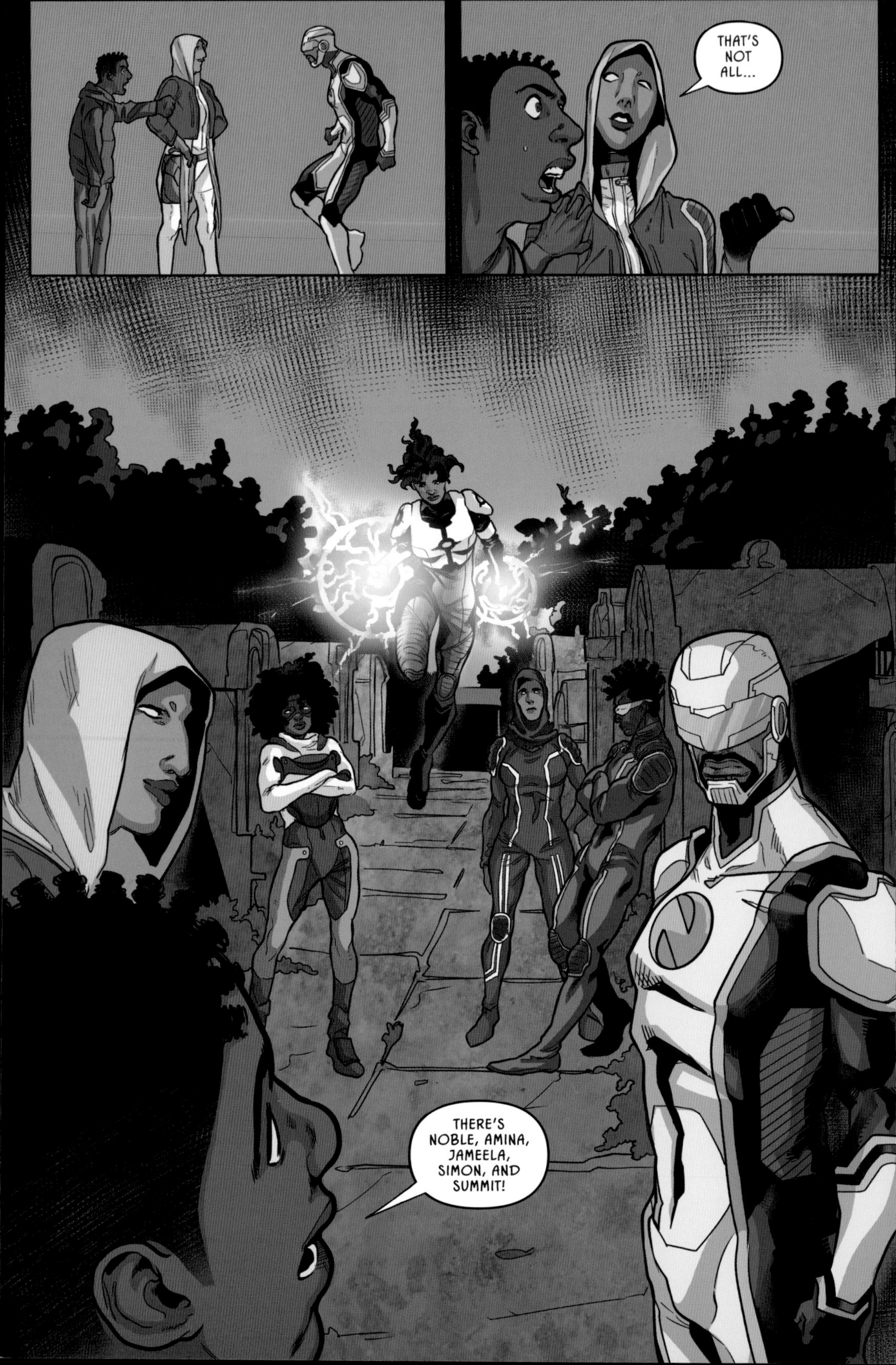
THAT'S NOT ALL...
THERE'S NOBLE, AMINA, JAMEELA, SIMON, AND SUMMIT!

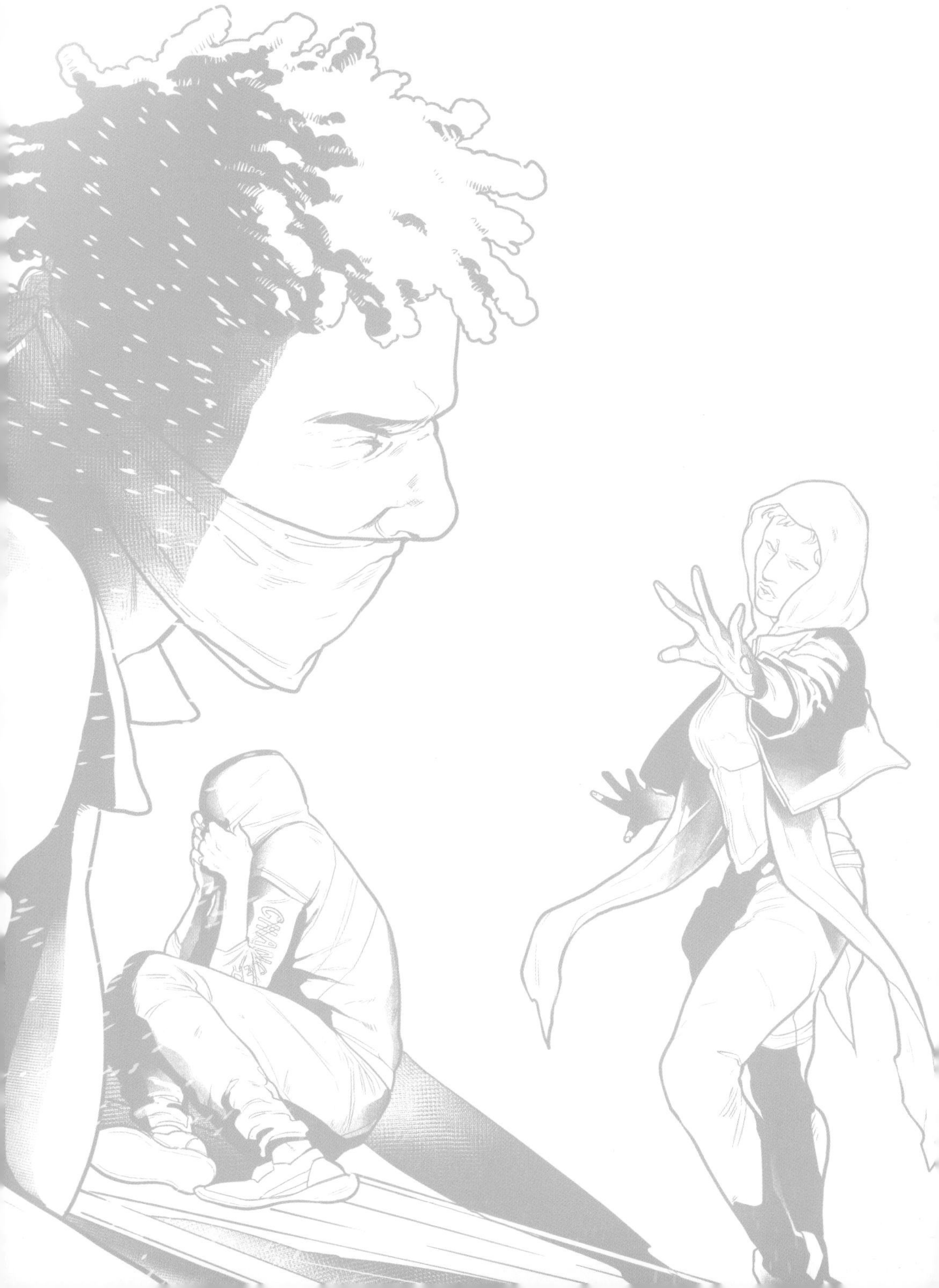

CHAPTER FIVE

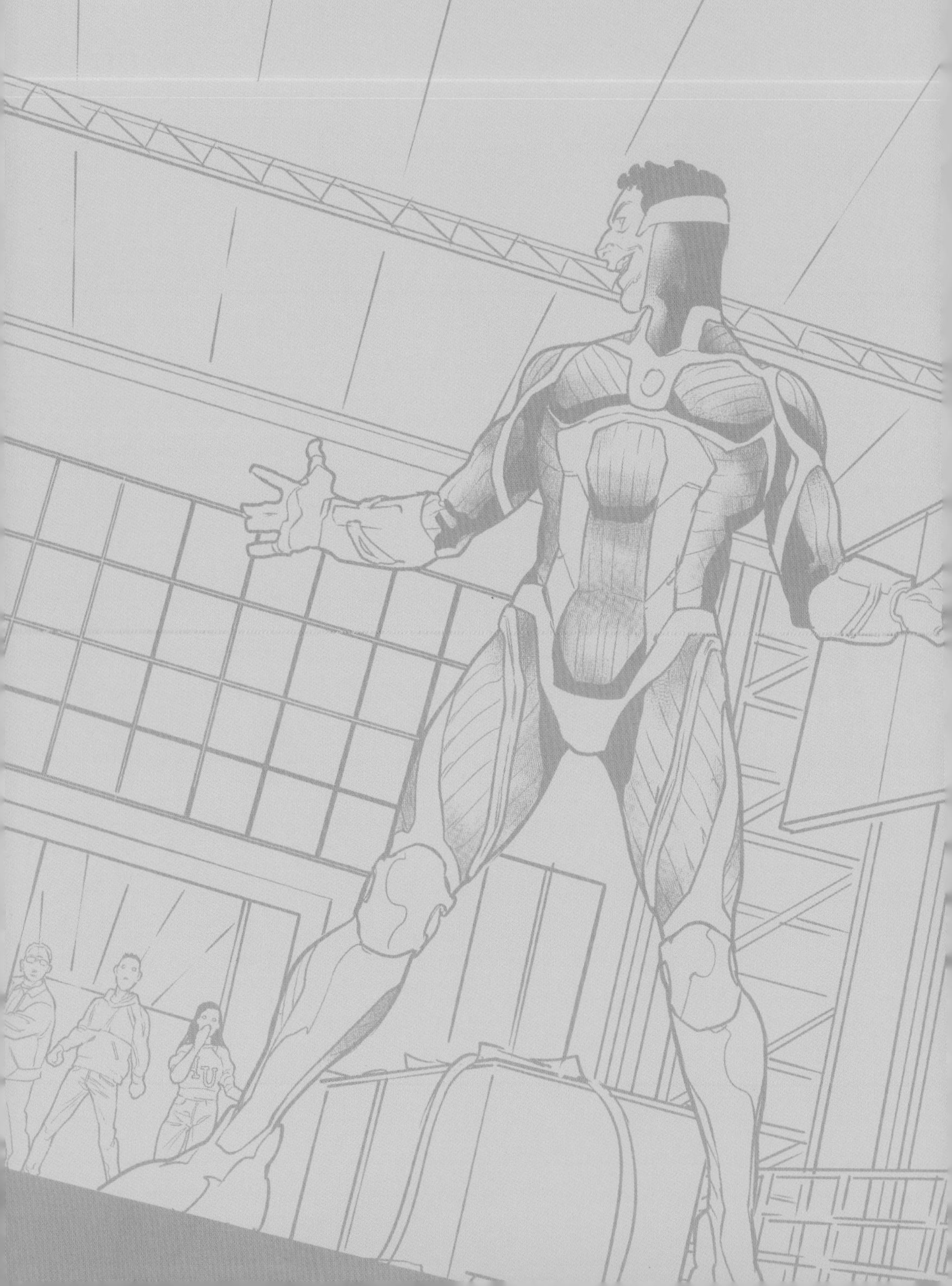

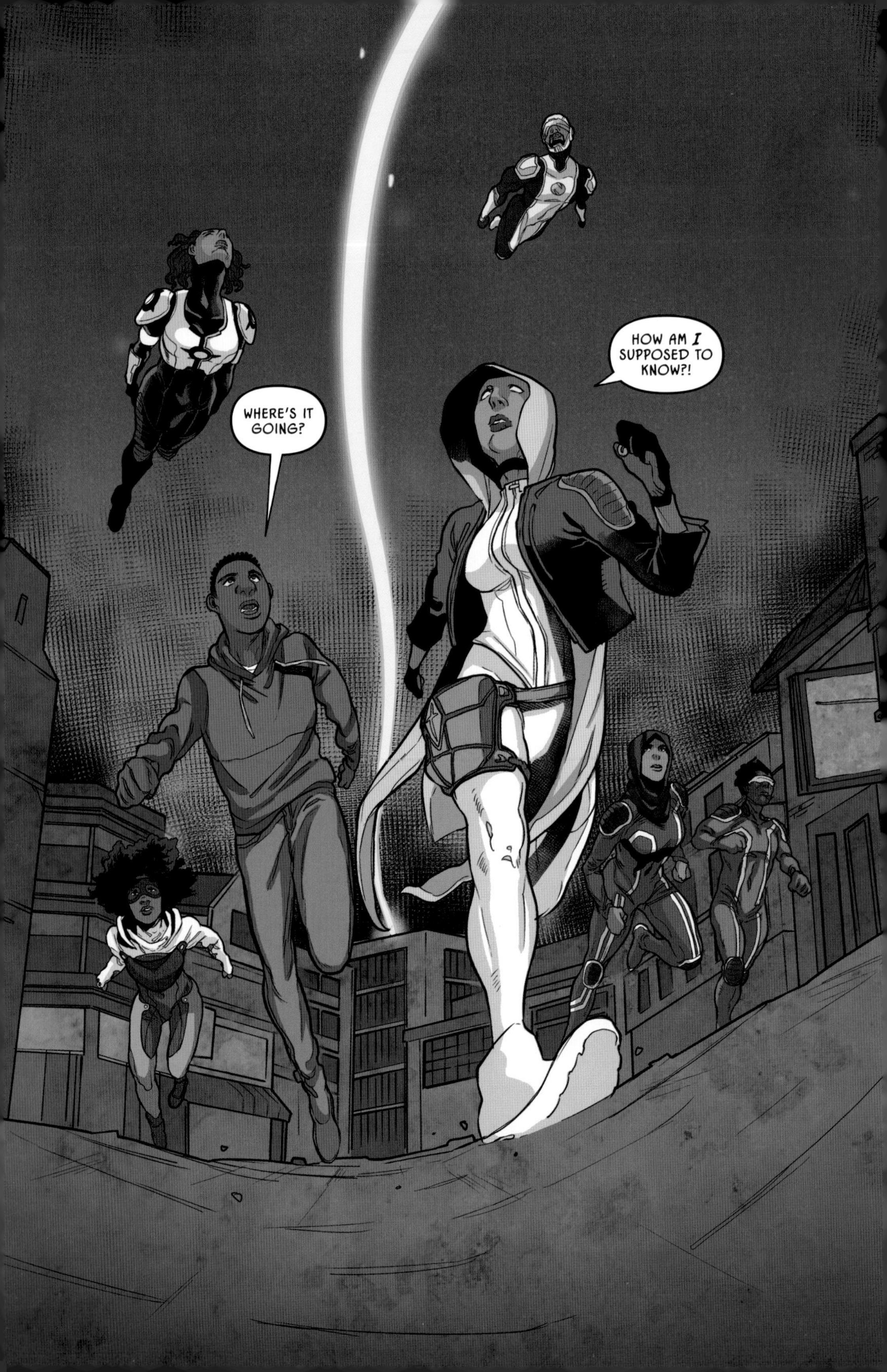
WHERE'S IT GOING?
HOW AM I SUPPOSED TO KNOW?!

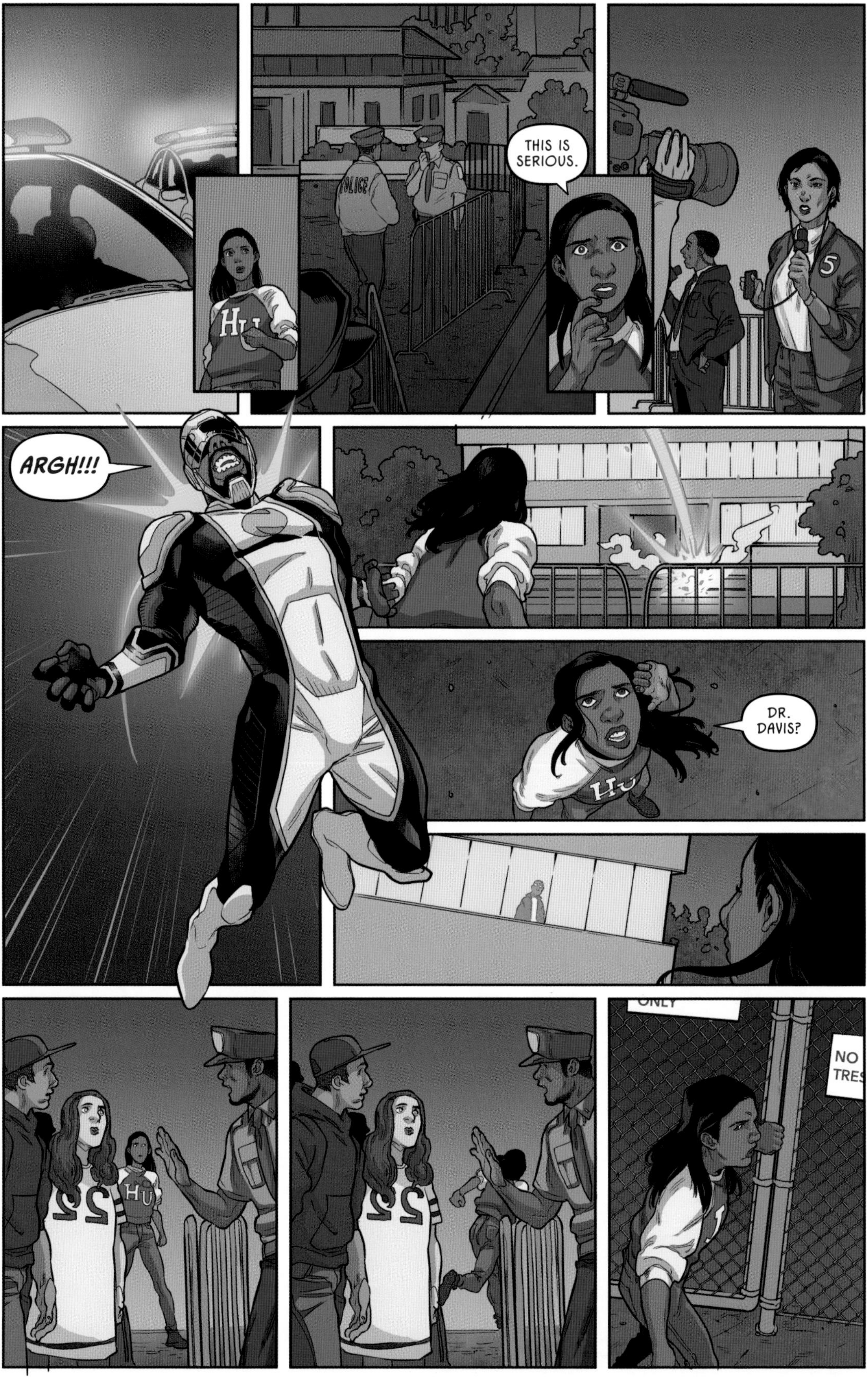
THIS IS SERIOUS.
ARGH!!!
DR. DAVIS?
ONLY
NO TRES

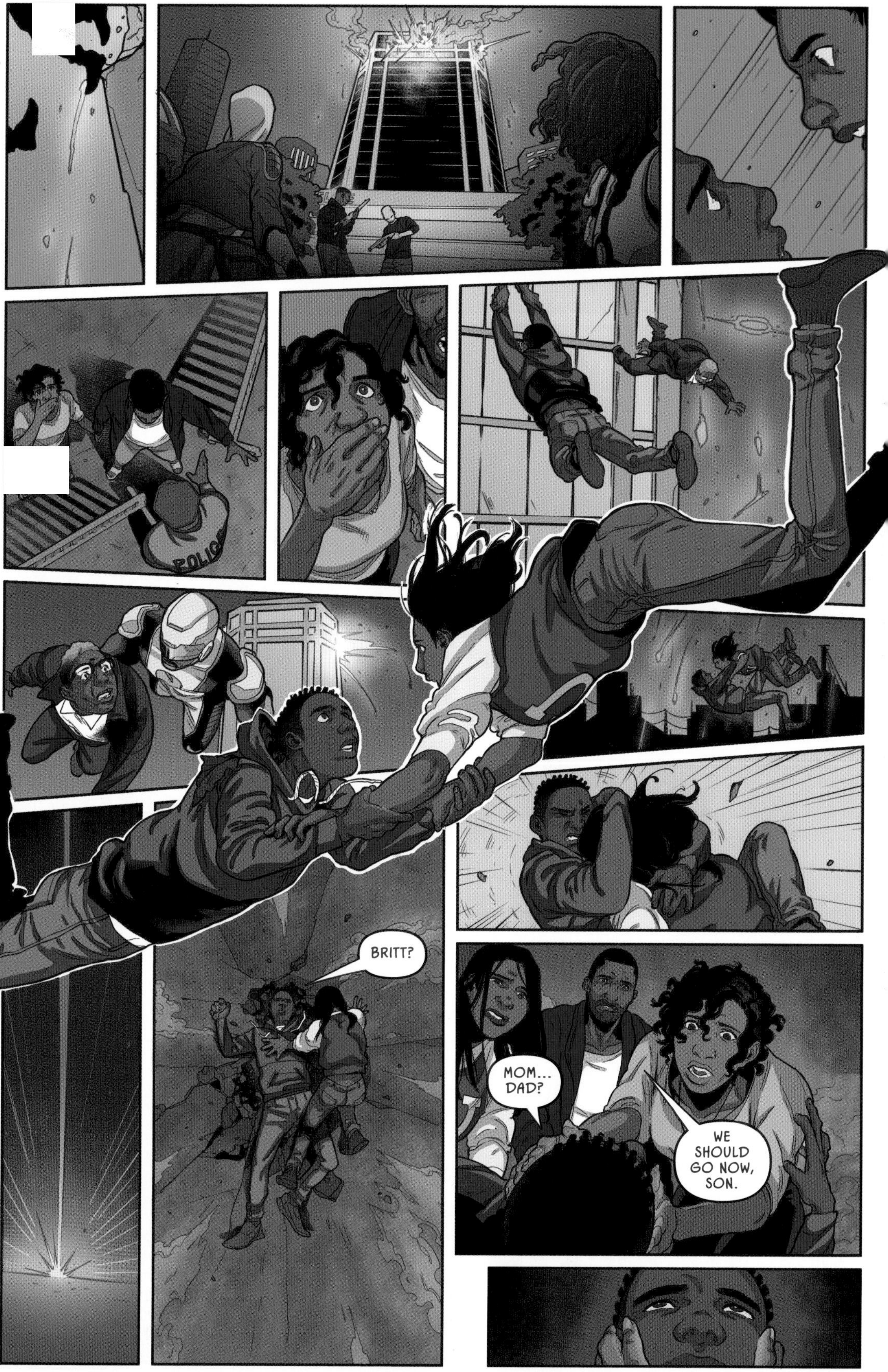
POLICE
BRITT?
MOM... DAD?
WE SHOULD GO NOW, SON.

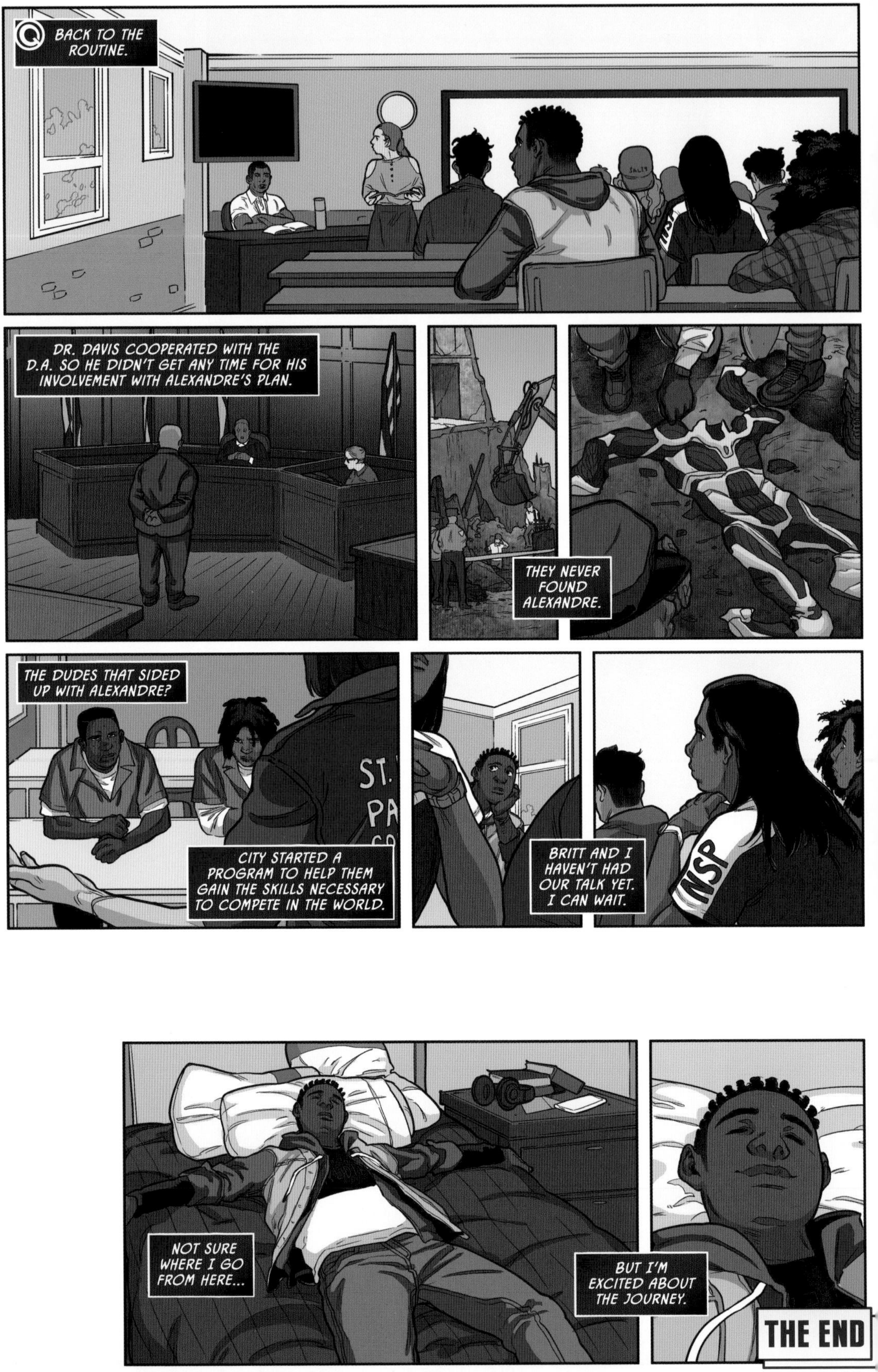
BACK TO THE ROUTINE.
DR. DAVIS COOPERATED WITH THE D.A. SO HE DIDN'T GET ANY TIME FOR HIS INVOLVEMENT WITH ALEXANDRE'S PLAN.
THEY NEVER FOUND ALEXANDRE.
THE DUDES THAT SIDED UP WITH ALEXANDRE?
CITY STARTED A PROGRAM TO HELP THEM GAIN THE SKILLS NECESSARY TO COMPETE IN THE WORLD.
BRITT AND I HAVEN'T HAD OUR TALK YET. I CAN WAIT.
NOT SURE WHERE I GO FROM HERE...
BUT I'M EXCITED ABOUT THE JOURNEY.
THE END

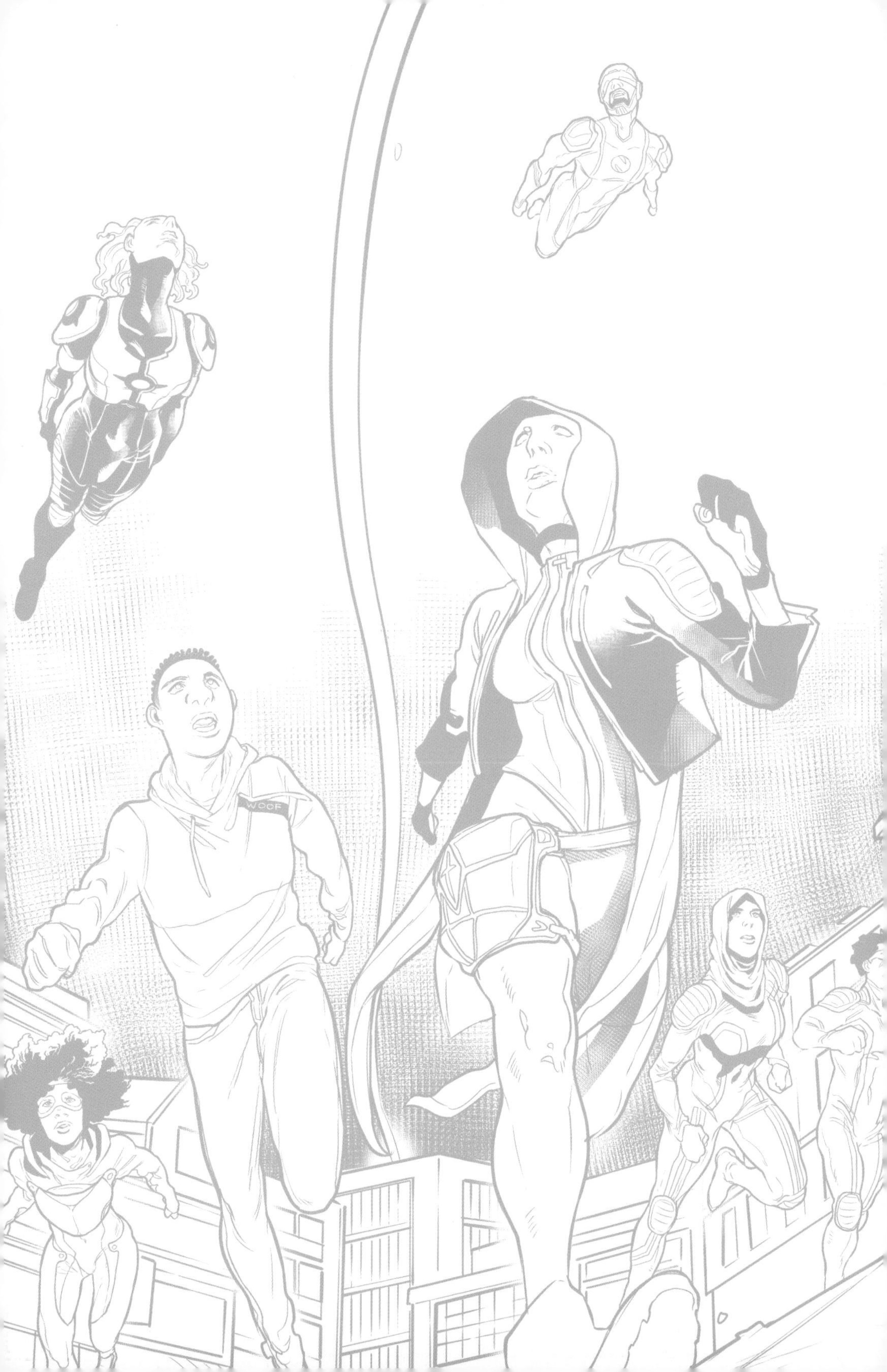
WOOF

COVER GALLERY

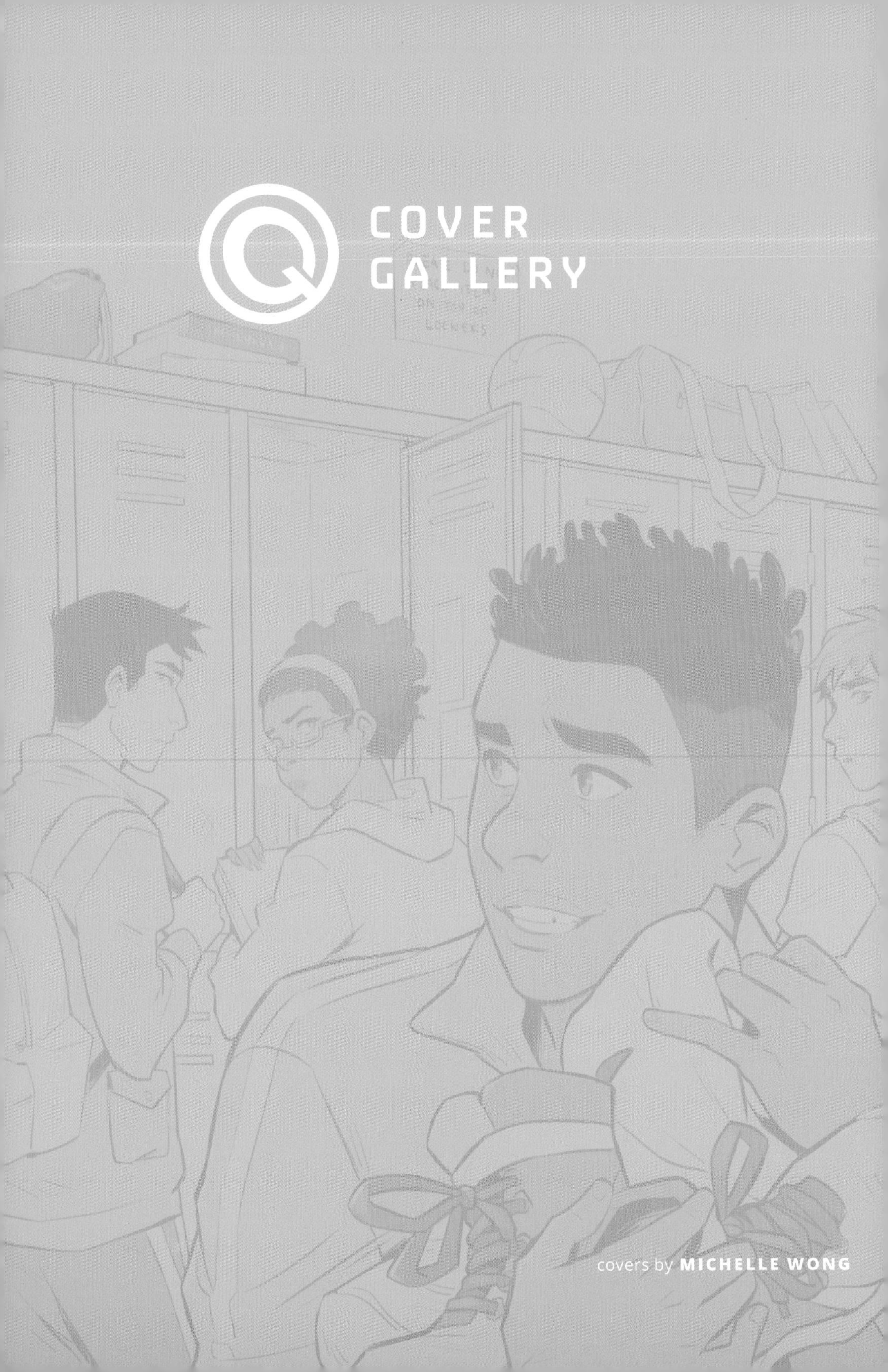

covers by **MICHELLE WONG**

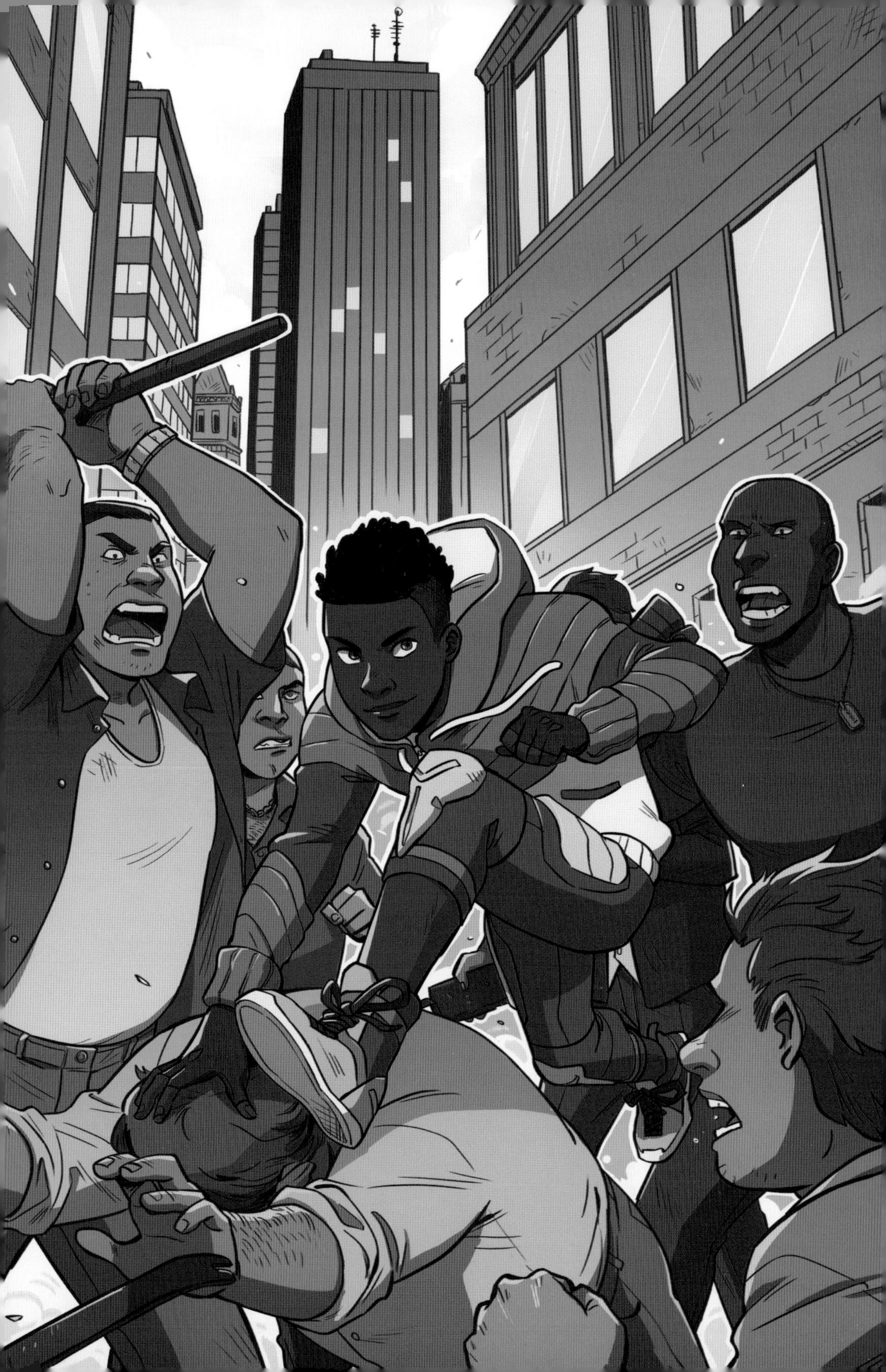

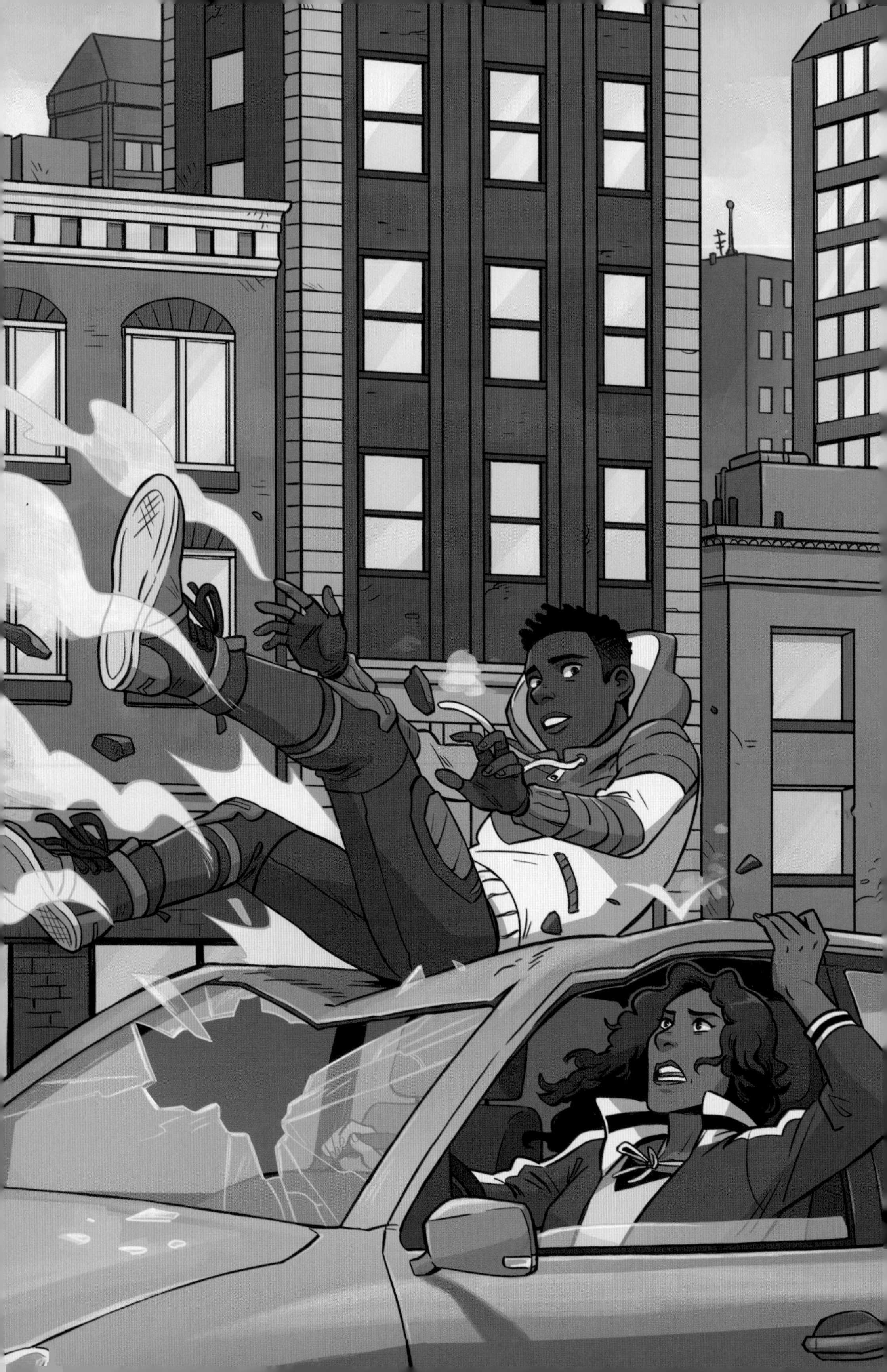

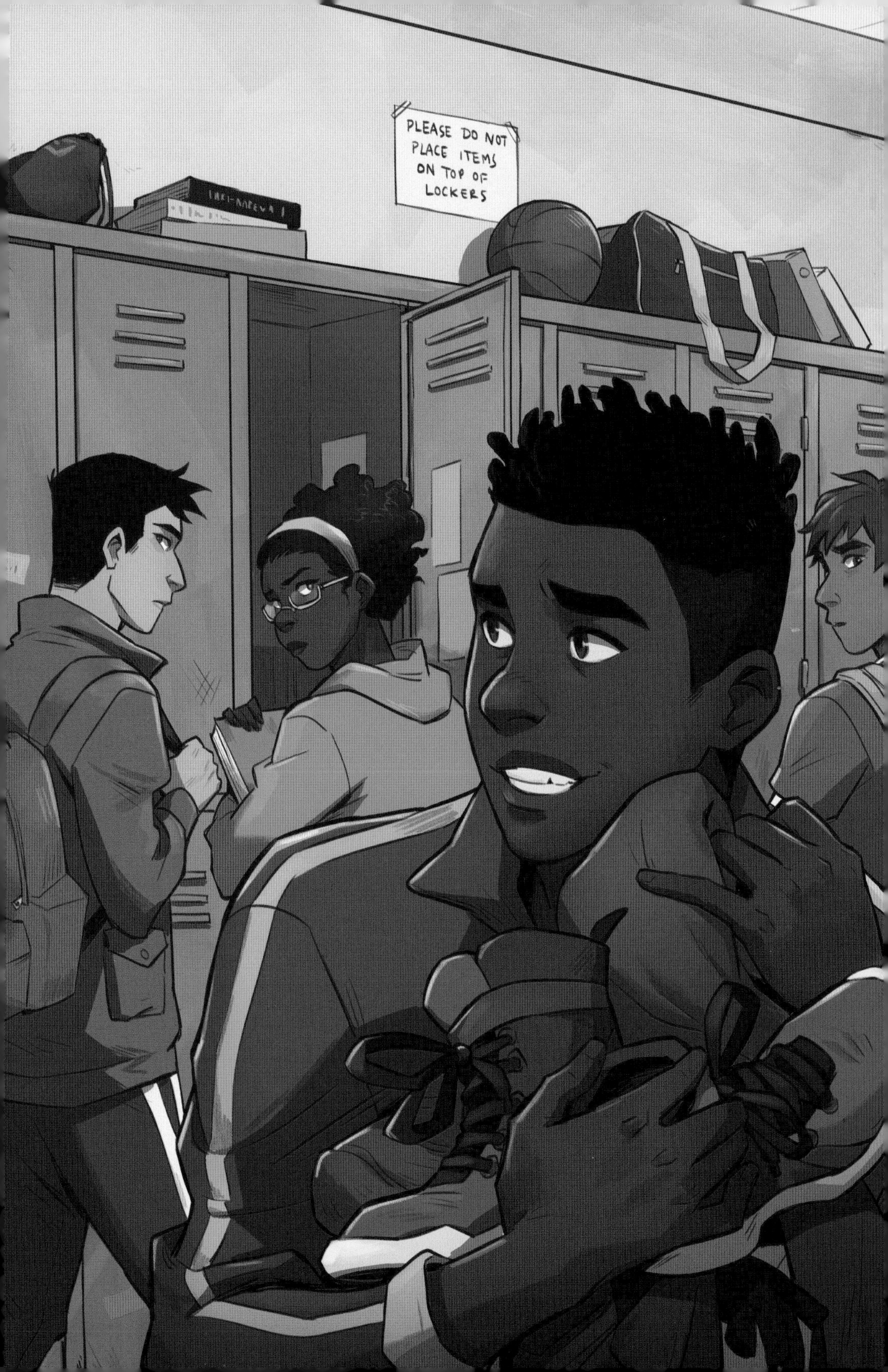
PLEASE DO NOT PLACE ITEMS ON TOP OF LOCKERS

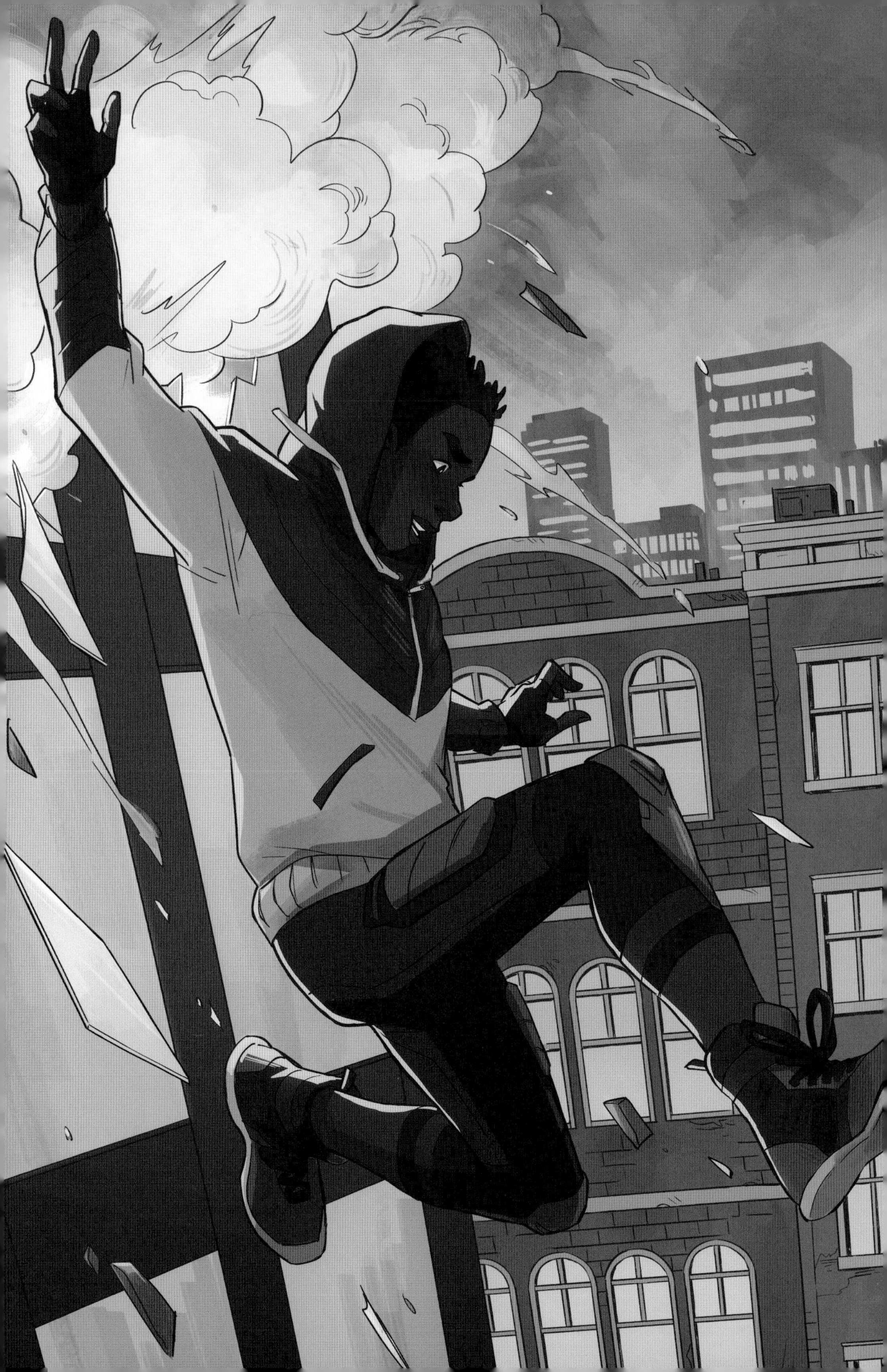

MAKING OF QUINCREDIBLE

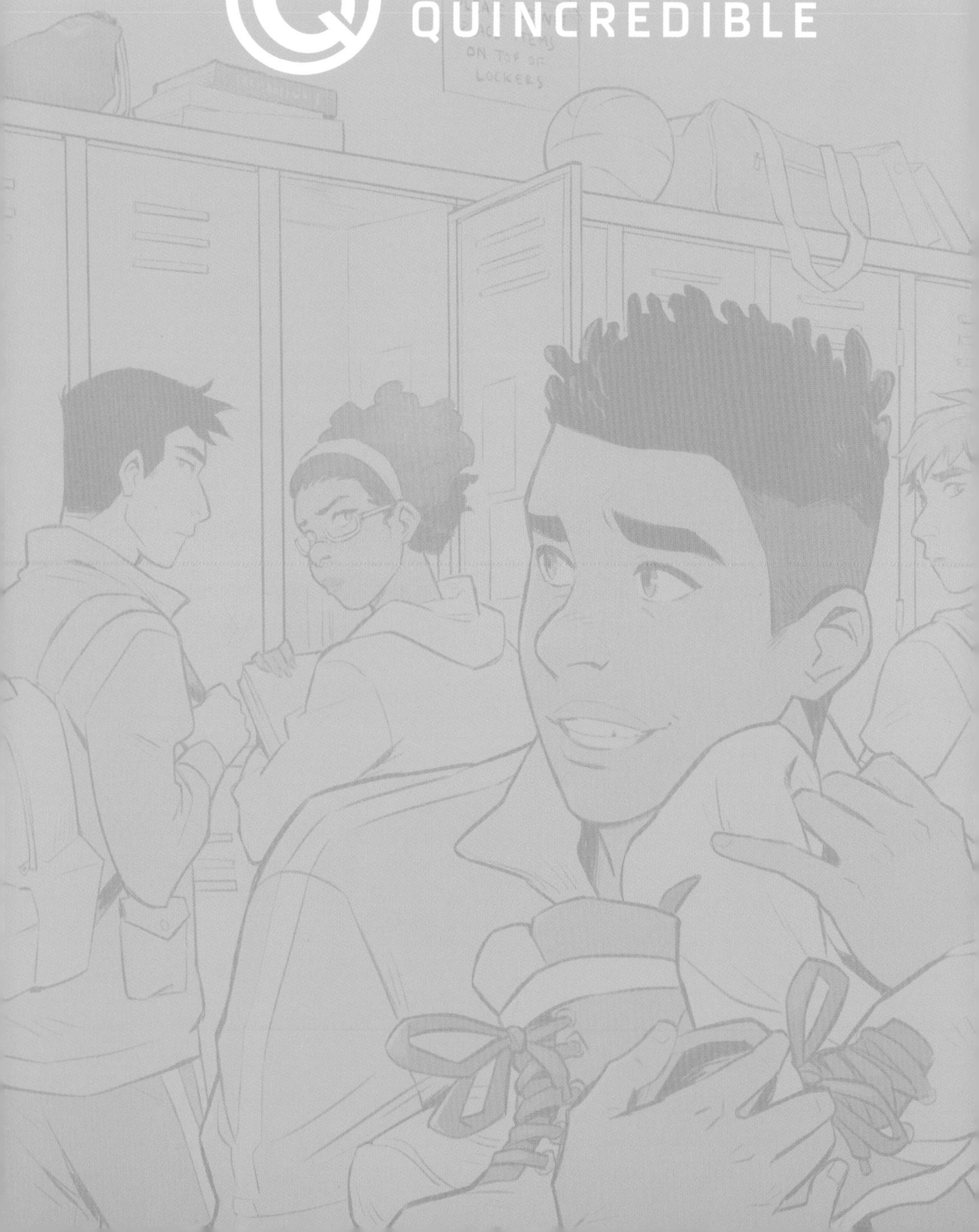
ON TOP OF
LOCKERS

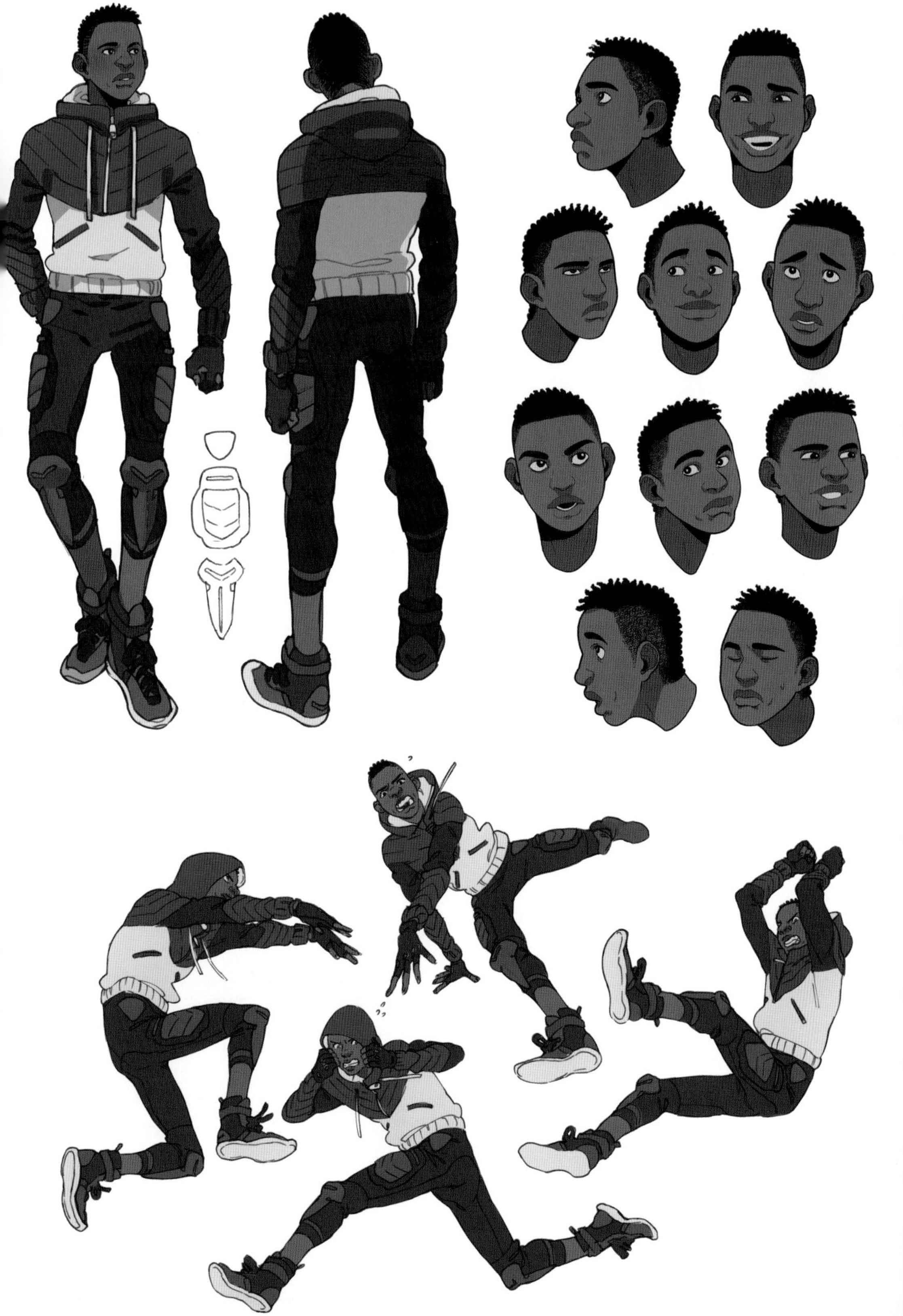

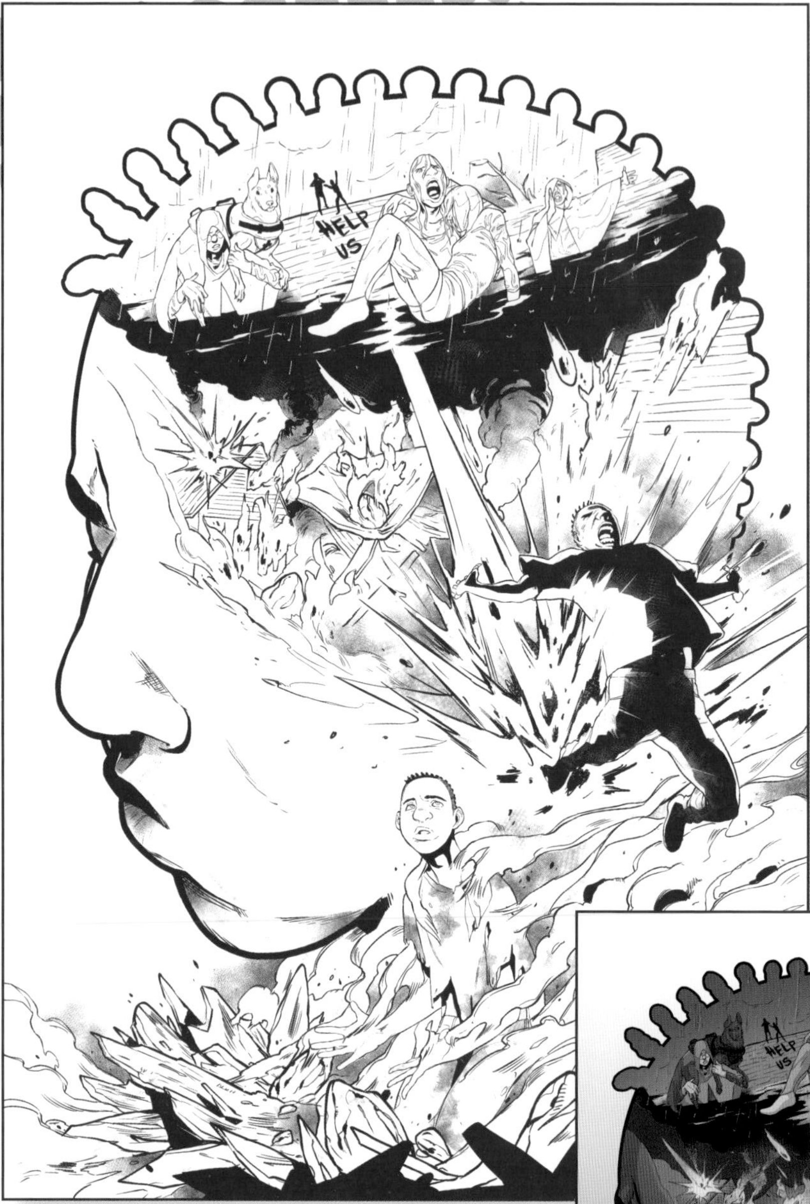
HELP
US

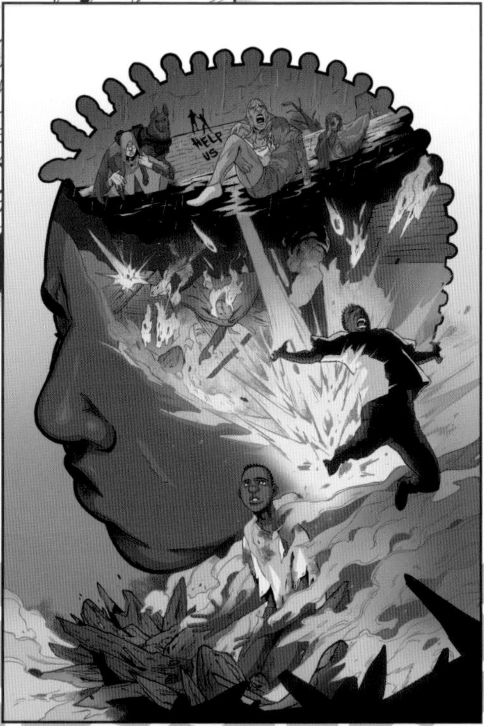
HELP
US

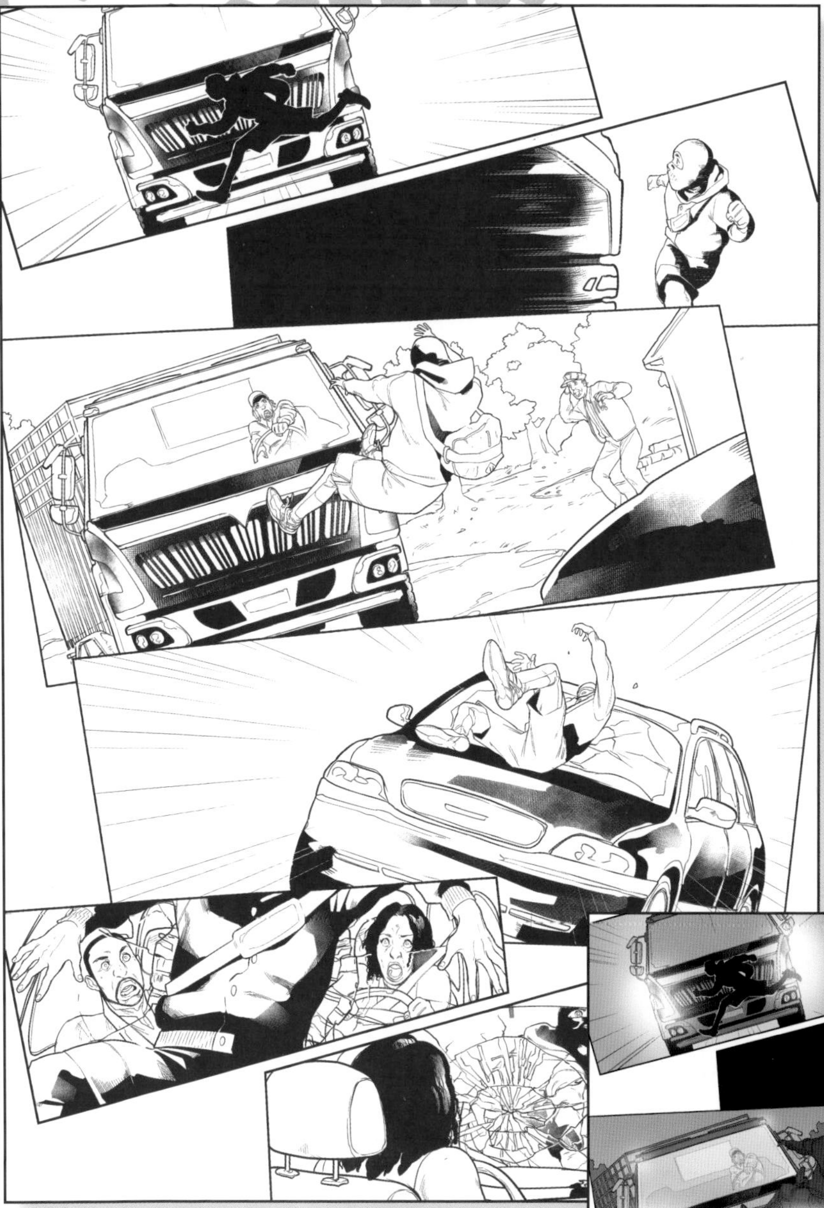
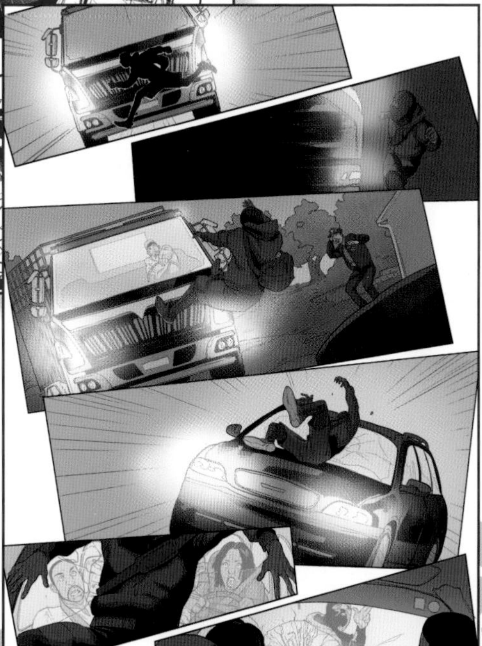

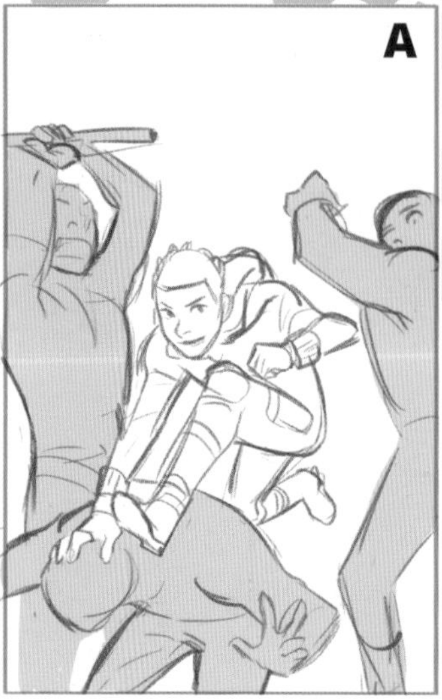
A

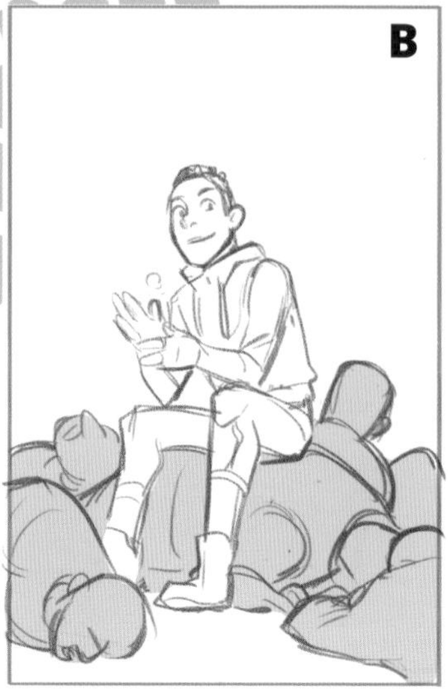
B

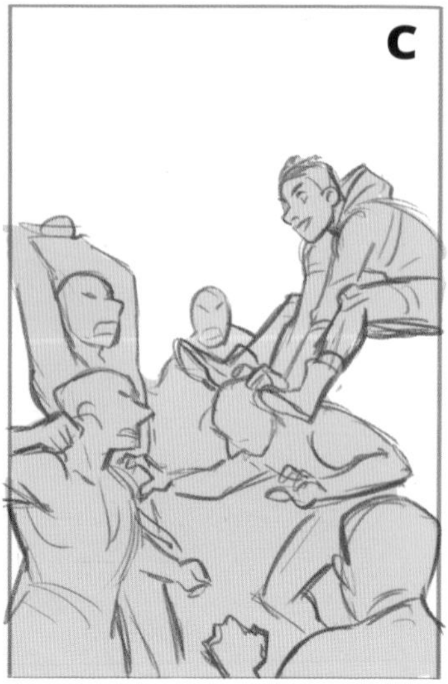
C

CONCEPT SKETCHES

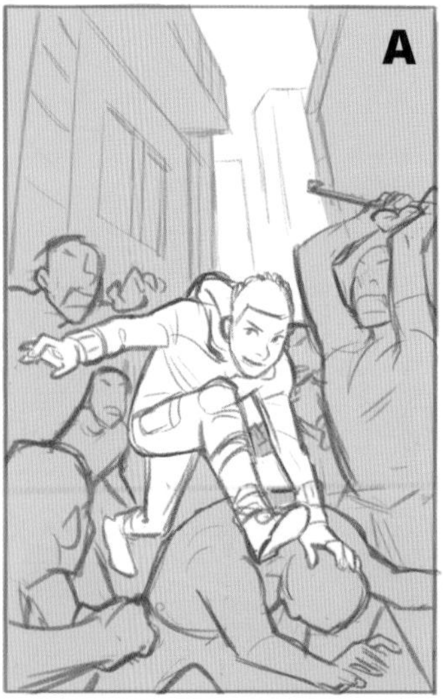
A

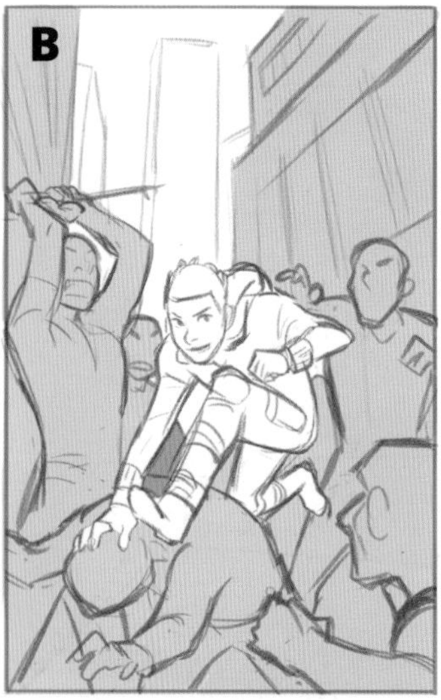
B

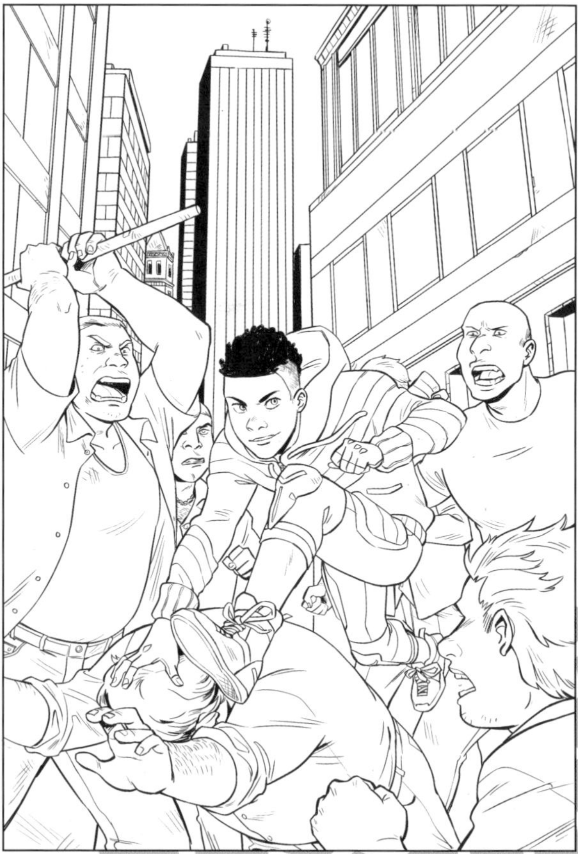